OSS:

OFFICE OF SUPERNATURAL SERVICES

OSS:

OFFICE OF SUPERNATURAL SERVICES

BY SCOTT M. BAKER

ALSO BY SCOTT M. BAKER

A Schattenseite Book

OSS: Office of Supernatural Services
by Scott M. Baker.
Copyright © 2024. All Rights Reserved.
Print Edition
ISBN-13: 979-8-9884973-5-6

Cover Art © Uwe Jarling

To Jeff Thomson
A fellow writer and history buff who left us much too soon.

CHAPTER ONE

Cairo, Egypt
17 May 1941

UNEASE HAD SETTLED over Cairo following the setback of Operation BREVITY at the Halfaya Pass, especially amongst the British. So far, it had manifested itself as an air of concern among high-ranking government officials and military officers, trepidation among British soldiers that they might soon be transferred to the front, and an underlying jitteriness among the rest of the city. At least among those locals who feared a German occupation. Many Muslims supported the Third *Reich* and their antisemitic policies, which generated anxiety among the leadership of a possible insurrection in support of the advancing *Afrika Korps*. Why worry? The fighting took place six hundred and fifty kilometers to the west along the Egyptian-Libyan border, far enough away not to pose an immediate threat. Besides, the British Middle East Command had grown accustomed to glitches in its campaign against the *Afrika Korps*.

This attitude would soon change. What no one in Cairo realized was that the setback at Halfaya Pass had been intentionally orchestrated. When Operation BREVITY collapsed, the situation would devolve into a full-fledged rout and panic would take over Cairo, a panic that would be exploited by German spies to bring about the inevitable British defeat in North Africa.

Agrat was about to initiate that phase of the operation. Once that occurred, her mission would be complete.

She strolled through the *As Sabtiyyah* District, the British government center located along the Nile River between the rail station and The Citadel. She stood slightly less than six feet in height, slender, with long, shapely legs. Blonde hair cut into a bob and emerald-colored eyes accentuated a flawless face. She wore the traditional olive drab skirt and jacket uniform with a tan dress shirt, although she forewent the tie to keep the top three buttons open and opted for high heels over the drab, brown, flat sole lace ups. It was a technique fine-tuned over centuries. With Agrat's ability to mask her allure, she could blend into the background or, if glamouring was necessary, could exploit her sensuality to its utmost.

Entering the Garden City area, Agrat continued to the block of modern flats that had been commandeered by the British and converted into British General Headquarters, then made her way inside. As she approached the main office, a corporal standing sentry duty placed himself in front of the door.

"Sorry, miss. The general asked not to be disturbed."

Agrat stepped to one side to go around him. "He's expecting me."

The corporal blocked her path. "He distinctly said *no* visitors."

Agrat suppressed the urge, however satisfying it might be, to snap this annoyance's neck. Instead, her emerald eyes sparkled. The corporal's demeanor became docile. His gaze focused on the ample cleavage pushing against her tan dress shirt. She allowed him to gawk for a moment, and then placed her forefinger under the corporal's chin and lifted his head so their eyes met.

"Do you really think the general is referring to me when he says no visitors?"

"Of course not." The corporal hurriedly moved aside. "I'm sorry for the inconvenience."

"No apologies necessary." Agrat ran the tips of her fingers along the corporal's neck and down the front of his uniform jacket. Stepping around him, she entered the office.

Agrat closed the door and paused to lean against it, needing a moment to regain her strength. Glamouring men used up considerable amounts of energy, especially when the attention is focused on one individual for an extended period, as she had been doing these past two weeks, so much, in fact, that even a brief allure like she had given the corporal could be exhausting. She would need all her energy to pull off the next phase in her plan.

As Agrat recovered, she looked around the office. In the center of the floor sat a wooden conference table large enough to seat eight people. Bent over the table stood her primary victim, General Archibald Percival Wavell, General Officer Commanding-in-Chief of the Middle East Command.

When Agrat first met him, the general had been a dignified and attractive man in his late fifties, distinguished and professional, the epitome of English grooming and military training. Now, after a fortnight of seduction, he remained a shadow of his former self. His well-groomed greying hair and mustache had become white and unkempt, and his confidence and bearing had been stripped away. The general had become physically weak and emotionally exhausted. Wavell looked and acted more like a strung-out alcoholic than a commanding officer. He glanced up, his tired eyes taking several seconds to focus on her. When they did, a glint of recognition lit up his gaunt face.

"Aggie. Thank God you're here." Wavell lifted a trembling hand and motioned for her to join him. "I need your advice."

"Anything for you," said Agrat in her most sultry voice. As she approached the table, she noticed Wavell studying a campaign map of the BREVITY battlefield. The operation had called for a three-pronged British attack that was launched two days ago with the goal of capturing the Halfaya Pass and the German-Italian encampments beyond, securing the area for Operation BATTLEAXE in June, which would break through into Libya and relieve the British troops surrounded at Tobruk. The initial thrust had been successful until Agrat had convinced Wavell to pull his forces back to the pass. Today, she would ensure total defeat.

Wavell pointed to the map, his index finger tapping the escarpment that Halfaya Pass cut through. "I did as you suggested. I ordered General Gott to fall back and set up his defenses here."

"Very good." Agrat placed her right hand on Wavell's left shoulder and lightly squeezed. The general tilted his head so his cheek rested on her hand and sighed in erotic contentment.

"We should be able to stop Rommel now," he said.

"Don't underestimate him. He can easily outflank us along the coast or through the desert."

"Good thinking." Wavell lifted his head. "He has tricked us like that before. I'll have General Gott reinforce the highway east of Sollum and extend his left flank out into the desert."

"That won't be enough. You can't afford to be surrounded like at Tobruk."

"That's true." Wavell nodded his head. "What do you suggest?"

"You need to abandon Halfaya Pass."

"N-no," Wavell stammered. He stared at Agrat, his eyes filled with uncertainty. "It would be foolish to give up the advantage for no reason."

"It would be foolish to risk losing your entire force."

"But... there's no other defensible position for hundreds of kilometers."

Damn it, the military commander in Wavell struggled to regain control. Agrat turned the general to face her and placed both hands on his cheeks, forcing him to make eye contact. She adopted a façade of affection and understanding as she increased her glamouring, though her eyes and voice took on a firm and commanding quality.

"Listen to me. You cannot attempt to hold Halfaya Pass.

It's too dangerous. Radio General Gott and order him to withdraw his forces. Have him fall back to Alexandria and set up a defensive perimeter there."

"I'm afraid I can't allow that," said an unknown voice from behind Agrat.

She spun around to face a British colonel who stood inside Wavell's office. He reminded her of Wavell in height, stature, and demeanor, only this man had close cropped blonde hair and a neatly-trimmed beard, both of which showed hints of grey. Agrat seethed at the insolence of this mere human who challenged her. With all her energy focused on Wavell, she could not attempt to glamour this intruder, but she certainly could intimidate him.

"You can't allow that?" said Agrat, her tone growing deep and menacing. "You have no way of stopping me."

"Actually, I do." As the intruder spoke, eight soldiers rushed into the room. Each one pushed a wheeled platform. Whatever was mounted to the platforms measured the height and width of a man and were covered with military-issue blankets. The soldiers fanned out around the room and surrounded the conference table, taking up a position five feet from the pair. The general glanced between Agrat and the intruder, panicked and confused.

"What is this?" Agrat snarled.

"Hand over the general and give yourself up, and no one will get hurt."

Agrat laughed. "You'll pay for your insolence with your life."

"Have it your way." The barest hint of a smirk pierced the intruder's lips as he gave a slight nod. The soldiers pulled the blankets off their wheeled mounts, revealing eight full-length mirrors encircling Agrat and pointed directly at her.

"Nooo!!" Agrat shoved Wavell aside. The general hit the conference table and slid to the floor. Agrat did not notice. She jerked from side to side, desperate to find a way to escape but, in every direction, she was greeted by her own reflection. Lowering her head, she stormed the soldier nearest the exit. As one, the soldiers moved with Agrat, keeping her centered in the circle of mirrors. When she glanced up to get her bearings, she caught a glimpse of her reflection in one of them.

Her eyes glazed over, the emerald pupils and white irises darkening into a deep red that shone like embers in a raging fire. A moment later, the pain began deep inside her, an intense burning that seared its way through her body and erupted through her skin. Her body ignited. Agrat shrieked, emitting a blood-curdling cry that sounded like a wounded animal in its painful death throes. The disgusting stench of charred flesh filled the confined space. The flames burned out after a minute and the torment subsided. Agrat lay on the floor, agony wracking her body, physically and emotionally exhausted.

ONE OF THE soldiers bent over and vomited across the surface of the conference table. Three had pissed themselves and, judging by the odor of shit, at least one had fouled his pants. Not that Bellingham could blame them. They were all battle-hardened veterans who had seen more than their fair share of death; however, nothing they had experienced on the battle-field could have prepared them for what they had witnessed. As the flames died out, they had expected to see Agrat's charred corpse. That would have been preferable to what confronted them.

A hand with elongated fingers and five-inch-long talons emerged from the dissipating smoke and dug itself into the top of the conference table. What pulled itself into a sitting position was not the beautiful woman from a moment ago but a monstrosity. Its legs had mutated into a snake-like tail that stretched for five feet, the end wrapping itself around one leg of the table. Scales covered its entire body. Although shaped like a human skull, its head bore the appearance of a reptile, with holes in place of ears and a nose and fangs replacing its cuspids. A pair of wings similar to those of a bat unfolded from its shoulder blades, extending to a width of seven feet. Even this minimal effort strained the demon, and the wings retracted and went limp. The demon stared at Bellingham for a few seconds with its coal-black eyes, trilled once, and collapsed with a meaty thud.

"What the bloody sod is this?" asked one of the soldiers holding a mirror.

"This is classified," answered Bellingham, the question snapping the soldier back into reality. He spoke loudly so the others in the room could hear. "Is that understood?"

Each soldier responded in the affirmative.

Bellingham motioned toward the door. Eight more soldiers entered the room, allowing those with the mirrors to leave. As four of the soldiers applied shackles to the demon, the others stood nearby, their Thompson submachine guns aimed at Agrat. Bellingham stepped over to Wavell and helped the general to his feet.

"Wh-where am I?" asked the general.

"You're in General Headquarters in Cairo," answered Bellingham.

Wavell leaned back against the edge of the conference table to support himself. If he noticed the demon only a few feet away, he did not show it. The general stared at the floor.

"The last two weeks have been a blur. Have I been ill?"

"Yes, sir. You were under someone else's control."

Wavell looked up. "Do you mean I was hypnotized?"

"Something like that, sir. Do you remember anything about the past two weeks?"

The general shook his head. "Just fuzzy memories, like I was feverish. Although I do recall something about issuing military orders to retreat. Did we lose a battle?"

"Everything is now under control."

"Good." Wavell lost his footing and almost slid off the conference table, but Bellingham caught him at the last moment.

"Are you okay, sir?"

"Not really. I'd like to go to the infirmary."

"Of course, sir." Bellingham leaned back and called out. "Captain Taylor."

An officer with red hair rushed into the office and presented himself to Bellingham. "Yes, sir?"

"Escort General Wavell to the infirmary and stay with him until I arrive."

The captain saluted and took the general by the arm, leading him around the shackled demon and toward the exit. As he was about to leave, Bellingham called out, "Captain?"

The officer paused and turned toward Bellingham. "Yes?"

"Contact Lee back in London and tell her it's time to get the Yanks involved."

CHAPTER TWO

Munitions Building, Washington, D.C
29 May 1941

"STOP THAT," KATHLEEN giggled.

"You didn't say that last night." Cody tried to unbutton her blouse.

Kathleen playfully slapped his hand away. "We were at your place, not in the office."

"Prude," Cody joked.

Kathleen leaned back against the desk and wrapped her legs around his hips. "I think I proved last night I'm anything but a prude."

"You sure did." Cody reached up and attempted to unbutton her blouse again.

Kathleen clasped his hands and squeezed. "Not here."

"Are you serious?"

"Yes. You're in the Army. I'm a civilian employee. If we get caught, the worst you'll get is a reprimand. They'll fire my ass."

Cody slid his hands down Kathleen's thighs, cupped her behind through the skirt, and massaged. "If they do, I'll kiss it and make it feel better."

Kathleen wrapped her fingers around his necktie and pulled him in for a kiss. "You're lucky you're so handsome."

That I am, Cody thought as their tongues met. Handsome and lucky. Life had finally gone his way since joining the military.

After running away from home when he was fifteen, Cody

had spent the next three years wandering through the Midwest picking up odd jobs or doing stints as a farm hand to survive. As uncertain as his future had been at the time, now he could only remember it as being fun and adventurous. All that changed for the better on his eighteenth birthday when he enlisted in the Army at a recruiting center in Omaha. He had a stable job, a steady if somewhat limited income, and three hots and a cot, all of which he truly appreciated when the Great Depression swept across America. Plus, Army life offered the fringe benefit of making him a ladies' man. Standing at five feet eleven inches and with a muscular physique, he cut a dashing figure in his sergeant's uniform, none of which was hampered by blonde hair, piercing blue eyes, and stunning good looks. He never wanted for a girlfriend.

Kathleen had started to voluntarily unbutton her blouse when a knock sounded on the door. Cody stepped back several paces as Kathleen moved away from the desk and straightened her skirt.

"Who is it?" Cody asked.

"Corporal Ross."

"Just a minute."

The door to Cody's office opened, and a young man in his early twenties stepped inside. Kathleen spun around so her back faced the corporal as she buttoned her blouse.

"Corporal, didn't you hear me tell you to wait a minute?"

"I did," said Ross, a nervous quiver in his voice. "I'm under orders to get you, and to barge into your office if you didn't immediately invite me in."

"Who gave you those orders?"

"Major Bietz. He wants to see you in his office at once."

"Let's go."

Cody headed for the door, grabbing his cap off the coat rack. Kathleen turned to face him as she brushed her fingers through her hair. Cody mouthed the words "I'll call you" before closing the door.

The major's office was on the third floor of the western-most corridor with a view that overlooked the Lincoln Memorial. Upon being escorted inside, Cody removed his hat and placed it under his arm. Major Bietz sat behind his desk. The two men had not gotten along since Cody had been assigned to his command two years ago. Cody had instantly pegged the major as an unimpressive overachiever whose career enhancement owed more to his obsequiousness to his superiors than to any inherent abilities. For his part, Bietz constantly criticized Cody for his attitude and sought out every opportunity to reprimand him. The smirk on the major's smug face warned Cody this would be one of those times.

Cody did not recognize the figure seated in the chair across from Bietz. He was of average height and build, although twenty or so pounds overweight. Cody guessed him to be in his late fifties because of his greying hair, although he carried himself as a much younger man, especially in the face with its ruddy complexion and deep, intense blue eyes. The man wore an expensive business suit, although his manner was more military than civilian.

"Major Bietz," said Ross. "I brought Sergeant Williams as you requested."

"Thank you. That'll be all, corporal."

Bietz spoke to the civilian as he waved Cody into the room. "This is Sergeant Williams."

As Cody approached, the civilian stood and extended his hand. "I'm William Donovan. It's good to meet you, sergeant."

"Thank you, sir." Cody shook his hand. The civilian's grip was firm.

As the two men sat down, Bietz took over the conversation. "Mr. Donovan has spent much of the last year in England as an informal emissary of President Roosevelt studying their ability to survive the current war with Germany."

"Do you think England will be defeated?" Cody asked.

Donovan shook his head. "As long as Churchill is prime

minister, England will survive whatever the Nazis throw at them. At least, I thought that way until a month ago."

"Is it that serious?" Cody asked.

"It could be a game changer," said Donovan.

"That's where you come in," said Bietz. "I'm reassigning you to serve as a liaison officer with British intelligence in London."

"But I already have an assignment," Cody protested. "I have orders to deploy to Hickam Field at Pearl Harbor next month."

"Those orders have been rescinded."

"I don't understand."

"Only a handful of people outside of Nazi Germany realize it yet, but we've entered a new and dangerous aspect of this war," said Donovan. "Hitler has begun using the occult against England."

"You mean like Middle Earth and the Lost City of Atlantis type of occult?"

"It's much more malevolent than that. I can't go into details here. Suffice it to say, Germany is engaged in an occult war with England, and so far, has achieved some impressive victories. If we don't find a way to defeat them on this front, it's quite possible Britain will lose the war."

"Why am I so vital to this assignment?"

Donovan removed a folder from Bietz' desk and handed it to Cody. "Because you are the only one in the United States military that has any expertise in this matter."

Cody opened the file, and a flood of suppressed emotions flooded into his consciousness. Frustration. Humiliation. Anger. Guilt. Hatred. He thumbed through the pages, scanning the text and attached photographs. It was all there, everything he had run away from. Everything he had spent the last fifteen years trying to bury. His past had been laid out before him, ripped open like a sutured wound. Cody struggled to control the rage welling up inside of him. He took a deep breath and exhaled slowly, then closed the file and tossed it onto Bietz's desk.

"With all due respect, I don't want this assignment."

"Don't be stupid," said Bietz, trying to be reasonable. "This assignment is excellent for your career."

"I don't give a shit about that. If you make me take this assignment, I'll refuse to go."

"Then I'll throw your ass in the brig for insubordination."

Donovan interrupted the argument before it spiraled out of control. "I understand you don't want this assignment. Trust me when I say you are not the person I would have chosen to carry it out."

"How so?"

"You ran away from home to escape an extremely traumatic situation rather than confront and deal with it. Since joining the Army, you've worked hard to achieve mediocrity. Except for when your unit protected American assets from the Japanese occupation in Shanghai in 1932, your military career has been lackluster. You have never volunteered for any assignment, nor have you shown initiative or leadership ability, which is reflected by the fact that you haven't been promoted in seven years. And you're a womanizer. While I won't pass any moral judgment, it's been noted that many of your lovers have been married women, two of which resulted in divorce. At best, your record indicates a man who is unmotivated. At worst, it calls into question your integrity and your loyalty to those closest to you, not the type of person I would hire under normal circumstances."

"I'll say this for you," said Cody, fighting back the urge to clench his fists. "You've done your homework."

"I have." To emphasize his point, Donovan lifted the file folder from the desk and handed it back to Cody. "Which is why, despite any personal flaws in your character which may cause me misgivings, I feel you're the only person in the military qualified to handle this assignment. Trust me on this.

You're not being offered this for career enhancement or to redeem past mistakes. England is in a fight for its survival, and this new phase of the war could end in a German victory. And with England out of the way, it'll only be a matter of time before Hitler sets his sights on us. You're our best hope of averting such a tragedy."

"What do you say?" Bietz asked.

Cody thought for a moment before asking Donovan, "Are you certain this is legitimate? I'm not going to be spending the next couple of years tracking down German archaeologists searching for ancient relics or chasing wild geese?"

Donovan leaned forward and rested his elbows on the arms of his chair. "Do I look like the type of man who enjoys chasing geese?"

"I'm in."

Donovan responded with a nod.

"What do I have to do?"

"All the details of your assignment will be provided once you arrive in London. I'll arrange to have a military flight take you to Port Washington, New York, tomorrow afternoon. Be on the tarmac at National Airport no later than 0500. Your flight to London leaves from Port Washington at 0730. I'll have a seat reserved for you. Your cover story is that you're being assigned as a military attaché to the American Embassy in London. In reality, you'll be working with British intelligence and will be under their authority. Since you'll be collaborating with officers in the British military, I've arranged for you to receive the brevet rank of major, which will give you more clout amongst our allies. All the appropriate paperwork will be completed by tomorrow afternoon."

"Wait a minute," Cody interrupted. "You assumed I'd agree to all of this?"

"I'm used to getting my way. May I continue?"

Cody suppressed a grin. "Go ahead."

"Once you arrive in London, someone from British intelligence will meet you, take you to your housing, and brief you. If you need to talk to anyone in the U.S. government about this assignment, you'll do so with me via the ambassador. Is that clear?"

"Yes, sir."

"Needless to say, the nature of this assignment is Top Secret. You will not discuss this with anyone unless I or my counterpart in London certifies that an individual has been cleared into the program. Failure to comply will result in the strictest measures being taken."

"I don't want to ask what you mean by 'the strictest measures'."

"Trust me, you don't want to know. Do you have any questions for me?"

"Dozens, but I assume I won't get any answers until I arrive in London."

"You catch on quick." Donovan stood, and Bietz did the same. He extended his hand and gave Cody's a single firm pump. "I wish I could say I envied you for this assignment, but I know better. You're about to face the toughest and most dangerous challenge of your life. I hope you're a praying man."

"And if I'm not?"

"Now would be a good time to start. Good day, Sergeant Williams. And good luck."

Once Donovan departed, Cody turned to the major. "Do you have any idea what that was all about?"

"I wish I did, but I'm as much in the dark as you are. I can tell you one thing, though."

"What's that?"

Bietz chuckled. "For as long as I've known you, this is the first time I feel sorry for you."

CHAPTER THREE

Berlin, Germany
29 May 1941

*O*BERGRUPPENFÜHRER WERNER DIETRICH sat in the back of his staff car as it drove beneath the Brandenburg Gate, studying the Berliners through the side window. Not that he showed any interest in the individual citizen. Outside of those in the party, he found Berliners insignificant and pliable. Dietrich was fascinated by the shift in the mass mentality that had taken place in the last two years. In the first six years of Nazi rule, when Hitler's aggressive foreign policy had expanded both the *Reich*'s territory and international prestige, Berliners had adored the *Führer*. They had cheered the reoccupation of the Rhineland, the *Anschluss* of Austria, and the annexation of the German-speaking Sudetenland. You could feel the national pride among Germans, you could see it in the way they bore themselves and gave their support to Hitler and the party.

That euphoria ended following the annexation of the remainder of the Czech Republic and the declaration of war between Germany and Great Britain following Hitler's invasion of Poland. Memories of the Great War still pervaded Berliners' thinking, especially the recollections of the domestic economic and social deprivations as well as the unbearable cost of defeat. The depression only deepened during the Battle of Britain when Churchill retaliated for the Blitz with air attacks on Berlin. Fortunately, the sporadic bombings had let up a month ago and the damage to the city had been minimal, far less than what the *Luftwaffe* had inflicted on London. Yet it did not alter the fact that the past nine months had left Berliners with deep psychological scars. Outside of the *gauleiters* and those within the security services tasked with stopping dissent within Germany, few within the party understood the impact this attitude could have on popular support for the upcoming expansion of the war.

As a German citizen, Dietrich shared their concerns about what would happen to their country if this war dragged on indefinitely. However, as head of *Sonderkommando* H (*Hexen*), Dietrich oversaw the program that would ensure a swift victory for Germany.

Unfortunately, today he had to inform the *Reichsführer* about a temporary setback in their plan.

The staff car stopped in front of 8 *Prinz Albrecht Strasse*, the headquarters of the *Geheime Staats Polizei*, more commonly known as the Gestapo. Climbing out of the back seat, Dietrich entered the main hall. The lobby had been purposefully designed to intimidate those Berliners summoned to appear before the Gestapo for questioning, with a high arched ceiling and an over-sized sloping flight of stairs that led to a spacious and sun-lit main corridor, creating a display of grandeur and power before one passed through the glass door into the restrictive confines of the state police's inner machinery. Dietrich made his way to the *Reichsführer's* suite. As he entered the outer office, the SS aide snapped out of his chair and extended his arm in the Nazi salute.

"*Heil* Hitler."

"*Heil* Hitler." Dietrich returned the gesture with all the vigor deserved by an unimportant subordinate. "I have an appointment with the *Reichsführer.*"

Without sitting back at his desk, the aide lifted the phone. "*Obergruppenführer* Dietrich is here to see you." After a momentary pause, he placed the phone back on its receiver and gestured toward the door. "He's waiting for you."

Dietrich entered the inner office and waited. It always surprised him how one of the most powerful men in Germany possessed an office so modest. A large, simple desk sat against the far wall and contained the barest of necessities—lamp, phone, pen holder, ink well, blotter, and a stack of files. The other furniture in the room consisted solely of two easy chairs in front of the desk and a wooden cabinet in one corner. There were no wall hangings, no ornamentation, not even a framed photograph of his wife and child. The only nod to décor was a bust of Adolf Hitler that stood on top of the cabinet. Not that any of this should have surprised him. Unlike *Reichsmarshall* Goring, the *Reichsführer* shunned ostentation and dedicated all his energies toward the task at hand, which was protecting Germany from its numerous enemies.

Heinrich Himmler sat hunched behind the desk, thumbing through a document he held in his small, manicured hands. In addition to his position as *Reichsführer* of the *Schutzstaffel*, or SS, he also served as Chief of the German Police. In the latter role, Himmler oversaw the most powerful and intrusive security apparatus in history—the *Reichssicherheitshauptamt*, or *Reich* Main Security Office, otherwise known as the RSHA. The RSHA encompassed every security and police organization within Germany except for those belonging to the military, a list that included the Criminal Police; the *Sicherheitsdienst*, or SD, the SS intelligence service; and the infamous and fear-inducing Gestapo. Himmler held the power of life and death over every civilian in Germany.

At first glance, Himmler did not fit the description of what one would expect from the man who oversaw the largest internal security apparatus in history. For all his power and influence, Himmler had a diminutive appearance, possessing none of the Aryan features demanded of his SS officers. He was short in stature, with dark hair, dark eyes that blinked constantly behind a pair of *pince-nez* glasses, and a receding chin. If not for the uniform, Himmler could easily be mistaken for a finicky school master. Until you met the *Reichsführer* face to face, and then it became clear why Europe feared him. Himmler exuded menace. Upon meeting Himmler for the first time, a colleague had warned Dietrich not to be taken aback by the *Reichsführer's* "Mongolian eyes." Only when the two made eye contact did Dietrich understand the term. Himmler's eyes were small and old, and staring into them you could almost sense the void where his soul should be.

Himmler glanced up. Upon seeing Dietrich standing by the door, he placed the papers on his desk and gestured toward one of the easy chairs.

"Please, have a seat," he said in a soft voice.

"Thank you, *Reichsführer.*" Dietrich crossed the office and sat down.

"I hope you have good news about Agrat."

"I have news, but it's not good."

Himmler nodded once, a move barely perceptible. He picked up the phone. "Have Dr. Vonnegut and his *helferinnen* come to my office immediately."

"Yes, sir," the aide responded.

Himmler set down the phone. "We'll wait until the others arrive so you can brief us all at once."

"Of course."

"In the meantime, you might be interested in this." Himmler took the paper he had been reading and passed it to Dietrich.

"What is it?"

"It's the orders outlining what the SS's role will be during Barbarossa. Read it and tell me what you think."

Dietrich thumbed through the order.

The Jews are the sworn enemies of the German people and must be exterminated. All the Jews within our reach must be eradicated during this war, without exception. If we do not succeed in destroying the biological foundation of Jewry now, then one day the Jews will destroy the German people.

Dietrich handed the order back to Himmler. "Do you think it's achievable?"

"It has to be. We have a lot to accomplish to fulfill our part of the bargain and ensure the survival of a Thousand-Year *Reich*. I've discussed this with the *Führer*, and he's in complete agreement with—"

A knock at the door interrupted the conversation, followed a moment later by Dr. Karl Vonnegut, Himmler's chief occultist. Dietrich detested the man on every level. In his mid-fifties, standing only five feet four inches in height, with dark hair and brown eyes, and a well-trimmed mustache that made him look like Mephistopheles, the man would never have been allowed to join the SS, especially if anyone got a look at his personnel file. A proclivity for bisexuality, indications of possible Jewish blood in his ancestry, and a thirty-third degree in Freemasonry were more than enough to confine him to Dachau for the rest of his life. Fortunately for Vonnegut, he happened to be one of the most respectable occultists in Germany, and the only demonologist. Not content with being spared his fate solely because of his usefulness to the *Reich*, Vonnegut flaunted his special standing with the *Reichsführer*. Dietrich could not determine what angered him more—the fact that Vonnegut wore an SS uniform even though he was not officially a member, or that he had created a special SS ring for himself cast in gold and containing the traditional skull and runes of the SS as well as the runes for the occult.

Two tall, beautiful women stood on either side of the doctor. Both wore black skirts and traditional SS tunics, although without rank insignia. To the right was Lilith, the slightly more attractive of the two. She towered a good six inches above Vonnegut, with long, shapely legs. Brunette hair fell down to her shoulders, framing a face that reminded Dietrich of paintings of Nordic goddesses he had seen at university, although made more enticing by a pair of gleaming emerald eyes. The other woman, Malalath, was almost identical to

Lilith in appearance except for auburn hair.

"I assume you have good news from Agrat," Vonnegut asked Dietrich.

"I heard from MARLENE, and it's not good." Dietrich focused his attention on Himmler. "According to MARLENE, General Wavell is no longer under Agrat's influence and, as best as she can tell, is no longer in Cairo."

Lilith rushed forward. "What happened? Is she okay?"

"We don't know for sure. MARLENE is not able to summon up any details. All she can say for certain is that Agrat no longer has any control over Wavell, so that part of the operation has failed."

"Not entirely," Himmler reassured him. "Rommel reported that Wavell did withdraw his forces back to Halfaya Pass, and he's confident that when the *Afrika Korps* launches its attack next week, they'll be able to roll up the British and push them back to the Nile. In theory, Operation *Hexen* is going according to plan. We anticipated some minor setbacks as a result of recent events. I see this more as an adjustment than a failure."

"Thank you, *Reichsführer*."

"Has there been any word from Naamah?" Lilith asked.

"None," said Dietrich. "But that part of the operation doesn't take place for several weeks yet, so it's not unusual that we haven't been in contact."

Himmler turned to Lilith and Malalath. "I'm truly sorry about Agrat. If there's anything I could do to get her back, you know I would."

"There might be a way," offered Dietrich. "With your permission, I'd like to talk with MARLENE. And I want to take Lilith with me. If I'm right, we might be able to contact Agrat."

"Will this pose a danger to MARLENE?" Vonnegut asked.

"Possibly."

Vonnegut shook his head. "Then I can't condone it."

"Thankfully *I* can." Himmler cast the doctor a disapproving look. "*Obergruppenführer*, I'll have a plane ready at Tempelhof tomorrow morning at eight o'clock sharp to take you and Lilith to Wewelsburg. Do what you feel is necessary. I trust your judgement. That is all."

Dietrich and Vonnegut offered a Nazi salute, and then the *obergruppenführer* ushered the others out. As he turned to close the door behind him, he noticed Himmler pick up a pen and sign the order. With the dice having been cast, Dietrich knew the situation in the east was destined to be barbaric.

CHAPTER FOUR

The Stafford Hotel, London, England
1 June 1941

CODY TOSSED HIS duffel bag onto the bed, and then collapsed face first beside it. It felt good to lie down on a comfortable mattress. Not that the flight on Pan Am's *Atlantic Clipper* was bad. The long-range flying boat was designed for luxury air travel, with seats that converted into bunks as well as a lounge and dining area. He definitely had far worse accommodations during his years in the Army. Yet all the luxury Pan Am offered could not change the fact that he had been closed up in the confines of a trans-Atlantic flight for more than twenty-four hours, and that did not include the connecting flight from Washington the day before or the two-hour train ride from Southampton to London. In total, he had been on the road for close to two straight days and wanted nothing more than a hot shower and a long sleep. Thankfully, Donovan had seen fit to book him into The Stafford on St. James Place, right in the center of London and one the nicest hotels in London, so resting would not be a problem.

Cody would have preferred going right to bed but, upon checking in, the concierge had given him a message that Major Lee Harris of the RAF would call on him at six o'clock, less than an hour from now. Pushing himself off of the bed, which required a lot of effort, Cody stripped down and took a long shower. He was dressed and stowing away his gear when someone knocked on the door. He opened it, expecting to greet some dodgy British officer.

Cody was pleasantly surprised to see a woman standing before him. She was of average height and slight build, the latter from restricted rations resulting from the war. The woman had pinned her brunette hair back against her head and hidden most of it under a Greek fisherman's cap. She wore a black skirt and white sweater that, while stylish, had seen better days. Despite the frumpy demeanor, she had attractive features, especially her light green eyes. If she smiled and wore a better wardrobe, she might be attractive.

"Are you Major Williams?" Her voice had a seductive quality to it enhanced by the accent.

"That's me." Cody extended his hand. "Are you here on behalf of Major Harris?"

"I *am* Major Harris," The woman clasped his hand and gave it a firm pump, obviously enjoying his confusion. "Major Ashley Harris, but my friends call me Lee."

"Can I call you Lee?"

"You can if you invite me in so I don't have to stand out in the hall."

"Sorry." Cody stepped to one side and gestured toward the room.

Lee lifted a valise off the rug, brought it into the room, and placed it on the bed. "I wanted to drop by and give you instructions for tomorrow morning."

"I assumed I'd head over to SIS headquarter."

"You wouldn't get in."

"Why?"

"Because you're not working for SIS."

"Then who am I working for?"

"The Special Operations Executive, or the SOE."

Lee opened the valise and withdrew a white letter-sized envelope which she handed to Cody.

"I never heard of it."

"Then we're doing our job." A slight grin pierced her lips. "Officially, we don't exist. SOE was set up last July to take the war back to the Nazis. We mostly run sabotage operations and support resistance movements across Europe. But when the Prime Minister heard about this... incident... he ordered us to take jurisdiction to keep Project Samail as covert as possible."

"What incident are you talking about?"

"You'll find out about that tomorrow." Lee motioned toward the envelope Cody held. "The address and directions are inside. I'll meet you in the lobby at eight o'clock."

"And then you'll introduce me to who's in charge of Project Samail?"

"That would be me," said Lee, unsuccessfully attempting to hide her frustration.

"I'm sorry."

"Just be on time."

"I will."

Lee reached into the valise and pulled out a British army uniform. "This is for you."

"I brought my own uniform."

Lee shook her head. "An American army uniform would draw too much attention here in London, especially among German spies. We don't want any attention drawn to the SOE, and in particular to Project Samail. When at work, wear this one. When on your own time, please wear civilian clothes."

"Roger that."

Lee closed the valise. "I'm sure you want to go to sleep and get adjusted to London time. Do you have any questions for me before I go?"

"I've probably said way too much already."

"Then I should be on my way." Lee offered her hand. "It's good to meet you."

"Same here. See you tomorrow."

Picking up the valise, Lee exited the hotel room. Cody followed her to close the door, noticing she did not look back on her way out.

CHAPTER FIVE

Beria's *dacha*, Moscow, the Soviet Union
1 June 1941

P AVEL LEVOROV STOOD on the sidewalk opposite the *dacha* at 28 *Malaya Nikitskaya* Street, hesitant to go inside and angry for feeling that way. As a senior lieutenant of state security in the People's Commissariat of Internal Affairs, or NKVD, Levorov was fully committed to the Communist Party, the Soviet Union, and, most importantly, to Stalin. He had a service record to prove it, including three years in the Russian Far East fighting White Russians as well as a year in Spain and one in Poland. His character, integrity, and loyalty were beyond reproach. What gave Levorov pause was that the *dacha* across from him belonged to Lavrenti Beria, chief of the NKVD.

Beria's control of the state security apparatus was legendary—or notorious, depending on which side of the interrogation table you sat. A fellow Georgian like Stalin, the control he wielded over the nation was second only to Stalin. He held the rank of Commissar General of State Security, comparable to that of a Marshal of the Soviet Union. That title gave him the authority to conduct purges of undesirable elements, which he recently undertook against the Red Army and the military industrial complex.

Beria's real authority came from heading up the Main Camp Administration that oversaw hundreds of gulags stretching from Ukraine to the eastern portions of Siberia, imprisoning millions of citizens deemed politically unreliable.

Yet Levorov's hesitancy had nothing to do with being intimidated. While everyone in the Soviet Union feared Beria, Levorov knew those who remained loyal had nothing to be concerned about. He held the chief in the highest regard because he realized that only those who can generate terror are worthy of earning respect. Levorov's concern was more personal. Upon meeting Beria, how would he feel if the man did not live up to the expectations Levorov had placed on him?

Stop thinking so bourgeois, Levorov admonished himself.

He crossed the street and approached the guard post by the main gate.

An NKVD senior sergeant blocked his path and held up his hand. "State your business."

"I have an appointment with the chief."

"Show me your papers."

Levorov reached into his inner jacket and withdrew his ID and a letter from the NKVD main office ordering him to report to the *dacha*. The senior sergeant checked them carefully, examining each one three times and carefully studying Levorov's face. He did not blame the senior sergeant for being overcautious because of his appearance. He had always been unattractive, even as a child, with unkempt blonde hair and cruel eyes. Nor did it help that a three-inch scar cut across his left cheek, the result of a bullet wound received while battling Alexander Kolchak's White Russian counterrevolutionaries outside of Irkutsk in 1919.

After several seconds, the senior sergeant took the paperwork inside the guard shack. He picked up a phone, talked for several minutes with another party, and exited the guard shack.

"Comrade Yurchenko is expecting you," said the senior sergeant as he handed back the documents. "He'll meet you in the lobby."

Levorov took the papers, slid them inside his jacket, and crossed the courtyard to the *dacha*. Inside the lobby, a middle-aged man in a business suit stood by a table at the bottom of an elegant flight of stairs. A bouquet of flowers sat on its surface. As Levorov entered, the man motioned to join him.

"I'm Vladimir Yurchenko," he said without offering his hand. "I'm Beria's personal assistant. You must be Senior Lieutenant Levorov."

"I am."

"Excellent. Beria is anxious to meet you. He should be down in a—"

From somewhere upstairs, a door opened and then slammed shut. A young woman rushed down the hall and descended the steps. She was in her early to mid-teens. Her blonde hair was tussled, and the front of her blouse had been torn open, the tails dangling on either side of her skirt. Her left cheek sported a red welt. She was sobbing. On seeing the two men in the lobby, the young woman sniffed back her tears, grabbed the loose plackets in each hand, and clutched the blouse across her chest.

Yurchenko picked up the bouquet and extended it toward the young woman. His pleasantries were so forced as to be obvious.

"Miss Anastasia, please accept these as a token of gratitude from Beria."

The young woman moved as far away from them as possible, sliding along the wall as she passed. She lowered her head, all the while keeping her eyes fixed on Yurchenko. Once beyond the two men, she ran for the exit, racing outside and leaving the door open behind her. Yurchenko showed no emotion. Placing the bouquet back on the table, he crossed the lobby and closed the door. Returning to the bottom of the stairs, he picked up the phone and made a call.

Another noise from the top of the stairs attracted Levorov's attention. This time a man descended. Stocky and below average height, he did not present an imposing figure. Nor did he present an attractive one with his round head, prominent nose, receding dark hairline, and the *pince-nez* glasses he always wore. It was only when you met his gaze that one could get an accurate measure of the man, for the protruding and cold blue eyes mirrored not only his supreme confidence but the brutality and lack of humanity that tarnished his inner soul.

Levorov immediately recognized Beria.

When Beria reached the lobby, he paused and stared at the bouquet on top of the table. "I assume she refused the flowers?"

"She ran out of here all upset. The poor thing didn't even have the courtesy to close the door behind her."

Beria sighed. "What a shame. I enjoyed that one. You know what to do."

"I've already called the main gate. They're on it." Yurchenko moved to one side. "Senior Lieutenant Pavlov Levorov is here."

Levorov stepped forward and stood at attention. "It's an honor to meet you, sir."

"The honor is mine. You have quite an impressive service record. You were in Omsk when that traitorous bastard Kolchak turned his back on the revolution. You tried to assassinate him before escaping and joining the Red Army forces near Ufa."

"I didn't succeed in killing Kolchak."

"But you tried, which is even more impressive considering you were only eighteen at the time. If I remember, you also fought with distinction at Chita, Transbaikalia, and Vladivostok. After the civil war, you stayed with the Red Army for another ten years before transferring to the NKVD in 1932. You served a year in Spain during their civil war helping the Republican Government set up secret prisons around Madrid, and then returned to Moscow to take part in the operation against Polish spies operating in Russia. Didn't your commanding officer write you a commendation for your zealotry and devotion to duty in rooting out and eliminating Polish spies?"

"He did, sir."

Beria nodded. "Very impressive."

"Thank you, sir."

"Stop with the formalities. Where you're being assigned, such niceties will only get in the way."

"That was going to be my next question. What exactly is my assignment? I was told to be here this morning and everything would be explained."

"Walk with me," said Beria as he headed for the exit. Levorov fell in behind him. "You understand that some things must be kept secret for security purposes. The reason I called you here today is because you've been selected to be Stalin's personal bodyguard."

Levorov stopped walking, taken aback by the news. Beria continued for a few feet before glancing over his shoulder. The twisted smile on his face showed he took great delight in shocking his subordinate.

"You mean I'll be working in Stalin's office in the Kremlin?"

"No. I mean you will be Stalin's personal bodyguard. Is there a problem?"

"Not at all, sir."

"Then keep up."

Levorov caught up with Beria in the driveway. A staff car was parked near the *dacha*. "May I ask what happened to the previous bodyguard?"

"For some reason he fell out of favor. A week ago, Stalin requested I find a new bodyguard. You were the best candidate for the position, so I chose you."

"Thank you. It's an honor."

"It's more than that. It's a major responsibility."

"How so?"

Beria stopped a few feet from his staff car and scanned the area to make certain no one was in earshot. "Stalin has been distracted lately. He's made several rash decisions, like changing his personal bodyguard. Some of those he has not explained to the rest of us."

"Do you know why?"

Beria shook his head. "I'm hoping it's just the effects of stress, and that with a little rest he'll be fine. Yet I can't rule out the possibility that it could be something more serious. That's why I chose you. Your loyalty is unquestioned. I need you to report back to me anything out of the ordinary that you see."

"You want me to spy on Stalin?"

"I want you to assess the situation. Look for any signs that he might have suffered a stroke or a breakdown. Try to determine from his conversations if there's anything bothering him. Stalin bears the weight of the Soviet Union on his shoulders. It's my responsibility to ensure those shoulders are capable of bearing that weight." The glint in Beria's eyes left no doubt as to how sensitive this conversation had become. "You do understand what I'm telling you?"

"Of course. My duty is to what's best for the country."

"Excellent." Beria smiled and slapped Levorov on the side of the arm. "I knew I made a wise choice. Now get in and we'll meet your new boss."

THIRTY MINUTES LATER, Levorov and Beria stood in the reception area outside of Stalin's office in the Senate Building, with the latter briefing the new bodyguard on his responsibilities. The two had been chatting less than twenty minutes when laughter filtered through the door. Stalin stepped out, accompanied by Foreign Minister Vyacheslav Molotov and Anastas Mikoyan, the deputy chairman of the Council of People's Commissars and Stalin's go-to man when special tasks out of the ordinary needed to be done. He placed his hands on their shoulders and the two men leaned in close. Stalin bowed his head and whispered, and all three again broke into laughter.

When Stalin raised his head, he noticed Levorov and Beria waiting for them. He broke into a huge smile and, with arms outstretched, crossed over to them. "Lavrenti, sorry to keep you waiting."

"It's not a problem."

Stalin turned to Levorov. "You must be my new body-guard."

"This is Senior Lieutenant Levorov," said Beria.

Levorov snapped to attention. "It's an honor."

"Stop with the formalities. You're among the inner circle now." Stalin placed a hand on Levorov's shoulder and ushered him to the others. "You know Foreign Minister Molotov and Deputy Chairman Mikoyan."

"I've never met them, but I know them by their reputation."

After pleasantries were exchanged, Stalin asked, "When do you start?"

"He can start right now," Beria answered.

"Excellent." Stalin moved closer. He flashed a grin both humorous and ominous as he spoke just loud enough for the others to hear. "I never know when someone around here is going to try and get rid of me."

Levorov had no idea how to respond. Thankfully, a female voice from inside the office saved him. "Iosif, where are you?"

Stalin instantly lost his bravado. "Out here, Naamah."

A young woman exited the office, moving up beside Stalin and resting one hand on his shoulder. She was the most beautiful woman Levorov had ever seen, from the long blonde hair flowing down her chest to the long, seemingly endless legs. Two attributes caught his attention most—her Georgian accent, which added an enticing quality to an already sensual voice, and her captivating emerald eyes. Even the other men seemed enthralled with her.

"I hope I'm not disturbing anything?" she purred.

"Beria was introducing me to Senior Lieutenant Levorov, my new personal bodyguard."

"Oh." While her outward demeanor remained social and

pleasant, her gaze bore into Levorov as if trying to examine his soul. For a split second, the emerald eyes seemed to glow. When that illusion faded, so did his infatuation with her. Naamah must have sensed the break, for she looked away and focused her attention on Stalin.

"Are we still going to have lunch together?" she asked.

"Of course."

Levorov stepped forward. "Would you like me to accompany you?"

"What?" Stalin answered uncertainly.

"You said a moment ago that you wanted me to begin immediately as your bodyguard."

Naamah gave Stalin a barely perceptible squeeze on the shoulder.

"That's quite all right, Comrade Levorov. I'll be fine. Make yourself at home and get acquainted with the Kremlin. I'll call you when I need you."

Without waiting for a response, Stalin and Naamah disappeared back into his office. Molotov and Mikoyan departed without saying a word. Only Beria spoke.

"It looks as though Stalin has found a distraction for the rest of the day."

Stalin has found something much more dangerous than a distraction, thought Levorov.

CHAPTER SIX

SOE Headquarters, London, England
2 June 1941

C ODY ARRIVED AT his destination a few minutes before eight—64 Baker Street. He had walked because the instructions Lee had provided ordered that he not take a taxi, which might bring unwanted attention to the location. Fortunately, it was less than two miles from his hotel. Given the importance Lee placed on this organization, Cody had expected to navigate his way through security checkpoints to get here. That had not been the case.

Baker Street looked like a thousand other residential and commercial streets in London. In fact, he had missed the address his first time and had to go back to find it. As he stood in front of SOE Headquarters—a cream-colored, six-story stone building—for a moment he wondered if he had found the right place. Either their security was far better than anything he had experienced in the U.S. Army, or Lee had grossly overstated SOE's significance. There was only one way to find out.

Cody entered the lobby.

Lee stood by a security station chatting with a British police officer. For a moment, he was taken aback by the change in her appearance. The frumpy clothes she had worn last night had been replaced by her WAAF uniform, which looked stylish on her. She had let her hair down into its natural bob. Lee looked more commanding than she had on their previous engagement.

Don't make an ass out of yourself this time, Cody admonished himself as he stepped across the lobby.

Lee turned to greet him as he approached. She seemed to be in a better mood than last night. "Mr. Williams, it's a pleasure to see you again."

"Good morning, Major Harris."

Lee's expression went stern. "We don't use ranks in the lobby. It could draw attention to us."

"Sorry."

Lee ushered Cody over to the police officer. "Mr. Williams is working with me. His pass should be ready in the next day or so. In the meantime, please grant him access to the building."

"Anything for you." The officer reached under the platform and pressed a button. The door behind his station clicked and buzzed until Lee stepped over and opened it. As Cody walked by, the officer said, "Welcome aboard, mate."

"Thanks."

As they made their way to the bank of elevators, Cody chuckled.

"What's so funny?" Lee asked.

"For all the security you tout about this place, I was surprised to see a single cop guarding it."

"That cop, as you call him, is Lieutenant Jonathon Martin of the Strategic Air Service and served with the Long-Range Desert Group in North Africa. He was wounded in the leg at Kufra while pushing the Italians out of Egypt, and is no longer fit for front line service, so he works here as one of our guards." Lee pressed the UP button. "Don't let his wounds fool you. He's still one of the toughest people in this building. If you had tried to push past him, he could have killed or incapacitated you in seconds."

"I had no idea."

"No one is supposed to." The elevator announced its arrival on the first floor with a ping, and Lee stepped inside. "If you'll follow me, I'll introduce you to the boss."

"I thought you were the boss."

"I'm in charge of Project Samail. Group Captain Bellingham is in charge of the overall operation."

The elevator stopped on the sixth floor. As they exited, Cody said, "I want to apologize for last night. I acted...."

"Insensitive?"

"I was going to say, like an ass."

Lee snickered. "You were rather boorish. I tried not to take offense at it. You Yanks aren't used to having women in influential positions yet. With all the men off fighting, women are taking their place on the home front."

"Thanks."

"To be honest, I thought that if you apologized at all, you'd blame it on the long flight and lack of sleep."

"I may be an ass, but at least I'll admit to it."

"I like a man who has integrity." Lee looked at Cody, her eyes showing respect. "You'll need it, and a whole lot more, for what you're about to face."

Lee stopped in front of a door at the end of the hall facing the front of the building and knocked. A voice on the other side told them to come in. Lee opened the door and ushered Cody inside.

The office was spacious but sparsely furnished. A large wooden desk sat in front of the window overlooking Baker Street. In front of it, two sofas and two easy chairs were arrayed around a coffee table, with a tea table positioned by the head chair. A row of clocks on the wall to the right of the desk gave the times in London, Washington, Berlin, and Cairo.

As Cody and Lee entered, the man from behind the desk rose to greet them. He cut an impressive figure, standing an inch shy of six feet in height with a lean figure and angular face. He wore his blonde hair close cropped and sported a neatly trimmed beard, both streaked with grey. Cody assessed him as being in his early sixties, although it was difficult to tell. The man presented a calm and proper demeanor. When he spoke, his voice was commanding but quiet.

"You must be Major Williams."

"I am."

"I'm Group Captain Cedric Bellingham. I'm in charge of Operation CROWLEY." Bellingham took Cody's hand and shook it. "And of course, you've had the privilege of meeting Major Harris."

"I have."

"Excellent. Have a seat, please. Can I get you some tea?"

Cody sat down on the sofa to the right of the head chair. "No, thank you."

"How about some coffee?"

"I'm fine."

"Good." Bellingham sat in the head chair. Lee took the sofa across from Cody. "Let's get right to it. We don't have time to waste, and I'm certain you have a thousand questions you want answered."

"To be honest, I have no idea what's going on."

"You'll understand soon enough why it had to be that way." Bellingham placed his fingertips together and held his hands in a pyramid in front of his chest. "You were selected for this assignment because you have an experience very rare among those in either the British or American governments, but one that is vital to our mission."

"What's that?"

Bellingham locked his gaze on Cody. "You have a predisposition toward accepting the occult and the paranormal."

Cody bristled. He hoped the others didn't notice. "I have no idea what you're talking about."

"I've read your file. I know that your mother possessed psychic abilities."

"No, she didn't."

"Your mother was able to communicate with the dead, to talk to those in the afterlife."

"My mother was a sideshow freak," Cody barked.

"No, she wasn't." Bellingham kept his tone sympathetic and firm. "That's what others made of her. Your mother had a rare ability that, for a while, she used to help people. The fact that others exploited her gift shouldn't be held against her."

"I don't want to talk about this."

Lee sat forward on the sofa. "It's okay. It's nothing to be ashamed about. I have the same ability your mother had."

Cody felt some of the anger drain away. "You can talk to the dead?"

"Not as well as your mother did. She could summon individuals from the afterlife. I can only talk to those who seek me out. I know what your mother went through. I know the range of emotions she endured and how badly friends and family can treat you when they find out.

"It's why we brought Major Harris into the program," added Bellingham.

Cody looked between Lee and Bellingham for a moment, and then stared at the floor. Damn both of them for making him dredge up those memories. Part of him despised them for it. The other part realized they wouldn't have brought him all the way to London just to tear at his soul unless they had a good reason for it.

"Are you okay?" asked Lee.

"No." Cody raised his head. "I think it's time you tell me what Operation CROWLEY is about."

"You're absolutely right." Bellingham stood up. "You know why we selected you. Now you need to know the reason you're here. Follow me."

FIVE MINUTES LATER, the three stood in front of a heavy steel door located in the basement. It stood five feet wide and nine feet in height.

"Why are you taking me to the bomb shelter?" Cody asked.

"It's not a bomb shelter." Bellingham lifted a phone off its receiver located to the right of the door. "This is Group

Captain Bellingham. Buckingham Alpha Waterloo Six Three Three."

"What's that?" Cody asked.

"The access code," replied Bellingham as he replaced the phone. "It changes daily. Not even Churchill himself can get in here without it."

A loud metallic hum preceded a click and the steel door popped open. A British soldier holding a Thompson submachine gun stepped through the opening, his weapon ready for quick fire. Upon seeing Cody, he raised the barrel and aimed. "Who's this?"

"This is Major Williams."

"Sorry, guvnor." The soldier lowered his Thompson. "Can't be too careful with that thing in there."

Bellingham led the way inside, with Cody and Lee behind him. The soldier closed and secured the door behind him, and then took his position beside the jamb. His mate stood guard on the opposite side. Both men faced into the room. Cody could not see well because only a few small ceiling lamps lit the area. A large cage dominated the center of the basement, twenty feet square and stretching from floor to ceiling.

Something large moved in the shadows. It beckoned to him, mentally calling him to come closer. Cody approached the cage, moving slowly and straining to see what had been contained. The prospect enticed him. He stepped up to the bars and peered through. For a split second, his heart leapt with joy as he thought he saw his mother curled up in the corner.

Then, as suddenly as it began, the euphoria passed. The thing in the corner morphed from being his mother into something hideous. At first, Cody thought it was a giant snake, maybe an anaconda, until he realized that the top portion was human-like. Shifting itself onto its tail, the demon slithered across the cage toward him, though not in a threatening manner. Even so, Cody stepped back. Its hands grasped the bars to pull its body closer, the taloned fingers wrapping around the steel supports. The reptilian head tilted to one side, and the black eyes focused on him. When the demon shifted position to study Bellingham, Cody noticed a pair of circular stumps on its shoulder blades.

It suddenly swung its head back to Cody, pressing its nose against the bars. Its nostrils flared.

"I've not met this one before," the demon hissed.

Cody shuddered. Its voice was cold and emotionless.

"Oh, do I frighten the man?" The demon closed its eyes. "You saw me as your mother. What a dirty little boy."

The demon laughed, a horrifying sound like a hiss, and then slunk back into the far corner. Cody walked back several feet from the cage.

"What was that?" he asked, a quiver in his voice.

"As best we can tell, it's a succubus," someone said from behind him. A gentleman in a wheelchair rolled up beside Cody and spun to his left to face him. He had a long and full face, buzz cut blonde hair, full beard, and brown eyes. Cody assumed him to be non-military because of his civilian clothes.

The man smiled. "You must be Major Williams?"

"I am."

"I'm Dr. Brown. You can call me Curtis."

"Thanks." Cody had no idea what to say.

"Don't worry about being tongue tied." Curtis spun his chair around and rolled toward the cage. "Everyone has the same reaction when they first meet our exhibit."

From across the cage, Agrat bared her fangs and snarled at Curtis. He blew her a kiss.

Cody had regained his composure. "Aren't you worried about having it locked up down here?"

"She's been pretty docile since we changed her out of her human form and cut off her wings."

"What if it breaks out of that cage?"

"It's not likely. The cage is made of steel, with a similar

40

covering imbedded in the floor and ceiling." Curtis gestured to the two soldiers guarding the door. "If she acts up, they have orders to shoot her."

"And what happens if it does break out of that cage?"

"Not to worry. The walls and ceiling are covered with two feet of brick, a thick layer of asbestos coating, and another three feet of brick. See that red button by my office door? There are a dozen of them scattered around the basement. Press those, and this room becomes a giant incinerator that will burn at close to a thousand degrees for sixty seconds."

"That sounds kind of extreme," said Cody.

"Believe me, it's not. You wouldn't want to be in the same room with her if she's loose and angry."

"Which brings me back to my original question. You said it's a succubus. You mean like a siren?"

Curtis shook his head. "Sirens are legend. Succubi are reality."

"Wait a minute." Cody did not attempt to hide his confusion. "You said succubi. You mean there's more than one?"

"I think so." Curtis headed for a door off to the right of the cage. "Let's go into my office and talk. It'll be more comfortable."

As the others grabbed seats around the room, Curtis wheeled his chair behind his desk.

"Every culture around the world has legends about sex goddesses who seduce men and suck the life out of them. The difference here is, as you can see, that demon in there is a reality and not a myth."

"We captured her in Egypt about a week ago," said Bellingham. "She had General Wavell under her spell and had convinced him to fall back to Alexandria before we stopped her. If she had been successful, we might well have lost all of North Africa to Rommel."

"But you captured it," said Cody. "It's over."

"We can't be certain of that," Curtis replied. "That thing

out there is identical to the succubus described in the Talmud. Assuming that the Talmud is the most accurate documentation for this demon, then there are three more succubi we need to worry about."

"Shit," said Cody under his breath.

"A bit understated, but the sentiment is correct."

"Now you see the importance of Project Samail," said Lee. "If there are three other succubi out there, who knows where they are and what damage they can cause. This one came close to having us driven out of Egypt. Can you imagine what would happen if one of them gets close enough to influence one of our senior military commanders, a cabinet minister, or the prime minister?"

"Or even President Roosevelt," Bellingham added.

"The repercussions of losing this war to Nazi Germany are much greater than you can imagine."

"How so?" asked Cody.

"There's one more person you need to meet this afternoon. He can explain it better than Major Harris or I can."

"Why didn't you take me to meet him first?" Cody asked.

"If you were not able to accept what you witnessed here, you would never be able to accept what this person will tell you."

CHAPTER SEVEN

London, England
2 June 1941

A STAFF CAR waited for them when they exited SOE Headquarters. In truth, it was Bellingham's personal vehicle which he opted to use so as not to draw attention to them. Cody sat in back with Lee as Bellingham navigated through the London streets. Cody stared out the side window though not actuality focusing on anything. His thoughts jumbled together. Because of his mother, he had always believed in psychic abilities, spirits, and the supernatural. Never in his wildest imaginations could he conceive of something so bizarre as a succubus… no, *one* of possibly *four* succubi waging war against England on behalf on the Nazis.

As Bellingham turned onto the road paralleling the Thames, Lee reached out and touched Cody's upper arm.

"Are you okay? You've been quiet."

"I'm trying to wrap my head around what you showed me."

"It's not easy," Lee replied. "When they first approached me, I told them to sod off. I thought it was some of my work mates making fun of my abilities. It was only after the group captain called me into his office was I convinced this was legitimate."

"If it's any consolation," said Bellingham from the front seat, "I was also skeptical when the prime minister asked me to set up Operation CROWLEY. I went to Cairo convinced I would make a fool of myself and end my career. Knowing what

I do now, I wish this had all been a farce."

Cody thought for a moment, wanting to make sure he phrased his next question so that it sounded the least offensive as possible. "I'm not denying that what I saw back there was a succubus. What about Dr. Brown's assumption that there are three more out there? Does he.... I mean...."

"You want to know what his qualifications are?" Lee asked.

"Yes."

"Dr. Brown is England's leading demonologist. His doctorate is in Ancient History from Cambridge University, but that's only because it's the closest program to his official interest. He's so well respected in his field that he has collaborated with the Catholic Church on numerous cases. Ten years ago, the Vatican bestowed on him the title Religious Demonologist, which is usually reserved for members of the clergy who have specialized in this area."

"It's hard to fathom."

"It is, and it'll take a while for you to get your head around this. Keep in mind one thing. Dr. Brown's been studying demon myths and legends his entire adult life and has forgotten more about them than the three of us will ever know. If he says there's something to be concerned about, we take it seriously. And he's worried about the existence of the other succubi."

Cody spent the rest of the trip trying to figure out what nightmare he had gotten himself involved in.

After a few minutes, Bellingham pulled off the main road into a parking lot adjacent to a castle. Cody remembered seeing photographs of it as a kid.

"Is that the Tower of London?" he asked.

Lee nodded.

"Why are we here?"

She admonished him with her stare to stop asking questions.

Bellingham drove through the Middle Tower Gate and crossed the moat via the drawbridge. Once he had entered the outer ward between the interior and exterior walls, he pulled off to the side and parked beneath Bell Tower. Exiting the car, Bellingham led the group through Bloody Tower and into the innermost ward. A flight lieutenant from the RAF stood by the entrance. As they approached, the flight lieutenant stiffly saluted.

Bellingham returned the salute. "Is everything prepared for our visit?"

"Yes, sir."

"Then you may proceed."

The officer saluted again, spun around, and marched off across the compound. They followed him to the early 16th Century half-timbered row of buildings along the southwest corner of the inner wall in front of Tower Green where Anne Boleyn was beheaded. A sign out front read Queen's House. Upon entering the building, the officer led them upstairs to the second-floor landing. Two British soldiers carrying Enfield rifles snapped to attention. The officer saluted, and the two soldiers stepped aside. Taking a set of keys from his pocket, the officer unlocked the door and swung it aside. Bellingham and Lee entered first.

Cody stepped into the room and stopped short.

The figure who sat in the chair across from him had one of the most recognizable faces in the world with his blue eyes, thick black eyebrows over a bony face, and protruding forehead. The only thing Cody could think to say was, "Jesus Christ."

The figure laughed and rose from his chair. "You flatter me."

"This is Major Williams," said Bellingham. "He's going to help us stop Himmler."

"Then it's truly a pleasure to meet you." The figure held out his hand and gave Cody's a strong, firm pump.

Bellingham continued. "Major Williams, I'd like you to meet Deputy *Führer* Rudolf Hess."

CHAPTER EIGHT

Tower of London, London, England
2 June 1941

C ODY COULD ONLY stare in stunned silence. After several
seconds, he finally said, "The news reported that you flew
to England to enter into peace negotiations with those sympathetic to Germany."

Hess laughed again. "You can thank the group captain for
that. He came up with that deception campaign to conceal my
real purpose for coming."

"So, you're connected to the Nazi occult dealings?" Cody
asked.

"More so than I care to admit." Hess' good humor drained
away. He motioned for the others to have a seat before taking
one himself. "Can I get you some tea?"

"We're fine," said Bellingham. "Major Williams is from the
United Sates. He joined our effort this morning."

"Good," Hess nodded. "You were able to convince Washington of the necessity of action."

"It was easy after you gave us the information that allowed
us to capture the succubus glamouring Wavell."

"Are you a prisoner or a defector?" Cody asked.

Hess stiffened at the last word. When he answered, his tone
was both proud and arrogant. "Major, you must understand
that I am not a defector. I have been, and always will be,
fiercely loyal to my country, my party, and my *Führer*. Someday
the world will recognize that we were right about the communists and will thank us."

"So why are you here?"

"Because Himmler is a madman," Hess yelled. "He will stop at nothing to ensure Germany's success. And in the process, he's convinced Hitler to sell Germany's soul, as well as those of millions of other people."

An awkward silence fell over the room. Hess took a deep breath and held it for several seconds before exhaling slowly.

"Forgive my outburst. I meant what I said a moment ago about loving Germany, the party, and Hitler. What Himmler is doing will destroy the things I love. More than destroy them, he'll turn them into something so disgusting that history will revile us forever. I love them too much for that to happen. I'd rather see Hitler defeated and Germany and the party destroyed than become demonized for all eternity."

"I don't understand," said Cody. He glanced over at Lee, confused and scared.

"*Herr* Hess," said Bellingham. "Please relate to Major Williams the story you told us when you first arrived in England."

Hess leaned back into his chair.

CHAPTER NINE

Berghof, Obersalzburg, Germany
10 October 1940

HESS CHECKED HIS watch. Karl Vonnegut and his guest should be here in a few moments. He straightened his tunic jacket, a nervous gesture.

Hess stood on the top of the grand staircase outside the Berghof, ready to descend to the driveway on their guests' arrival to extend the typical, stage-managed welcome. The Berghof, located on the mountain slopes above Berchtesgarden, one hundred and fifty kilometers southeast of Munich, had become much more than Adolf Hitler's Alpine residence. Ever since Hitler had become *Führer*, he had been using the Berghof as an instrument of foreign policy, especially the extensive bay window in the Great Hall overlooking the Unterberg Mountain. The view was majestic and symbolic, purposefully designed to leave visitors with the impression of both the majesty of the Third *Reich* and its power and inevitable longevity. Hitler had used its grandeur to impress allies such as Benito Mussolini and the Duke and Duchess of Windsor as well as to intimidate opponents, most notably Austrian Chancellor Kurt von Schuschnigg prior to the *Anschluss* and British Prime Minister Neville Chamberlain during the Sudetenland crisis.

Hess felt the dignity of the Berghof would be lost on their guest. The individual they were meeting with this afternoon would likely scoff at the pomp that was soon to be played out. From what he had been able to infer from Dr. Vonnegut's conversations with the *Führer*, this individual was all business and saw the coming encounter not as a transaction among equals, but as a business arrangement with Hitler in the subordinate position.

Even the *Führer* realized the intensity of the upcoming meeting. Hess had known him since 1920, and never had he seen his friend so agitated. Hitler usually waited for such meetings with a child-like anticipation, laughing with his entourage and fostering a jaunty atmosphere. Even when the meeting involved an international crisis, the *Führer* maintained his composure, sharp as a tack and politically in tune. This time, he seemed like a chastised schoolboy in front of the principal's office waiting to hear his punishment. He paced back and forth along the top of the staircase, every few seconds checking the driveway for the car, and rubbed the palm of his left hand with the knuckles of his right.

Himmler, on the other hand, could barely contain his enthusiasm. He grinned like a Cheshire cat and rocked back and forth on the heels of his boots.

Hess wondered what the rest of the party leadership would think, and even the average German, if they knew that the individual being entertained was Satan's representative.

What had happened to their aspirations? Hess had joined with Hitler because he believed his friend was the only person who could lift up Germany from the depths of despair back to the greatness it once had commanded on the European stage. Hitler and the Nazi party had accomplished that and so much more. Now fear and stupidity threatened to drag the nation back down again, all because of the insanity of one man who had lost touch with reality and the ambition of another. Following the cancellation of the planned invasion of England, Dr. Vonnegut, on his own initiative, used his knowledge of the occult to summon the underworld in the hopes of arranging protection for Germany. Hess had been present when Vonnegut burst into the meeting with Hitler and Himmler to share the news that Satan was willing to send a representative to form an alliance with Germany. At first, Hitler had been outraged that Vonnegut would take such a unilateral action and threatened to have him sent off to Dachau, until Himmler intervened. The *Reichsführer* had suggested to Hitler that it might be worth listening to what the representative had to offer. Much to Hess' shock, the *Führer* agreed. Now they stood in front of the Berghof waiting to discuss an alliance between Nazi Germany and the underworld.

The sound of a running motor caught their attention. All three men saw a Mercedes swing off the road, proceed up the driveway, and stop at the foot of the stairs. Because of the secretive nature of their guest and the purpose of his visit, the *Führer* had opted to forego the SS Honor Guard and driver. Instead, Dr. Vonnegut jumped out of the driver's seat and headed around to the passenger door. Hitler tugged once on the bottom of his tunic, and then headed down the staircase. Himmler hurried along on his left, eager to keep up. Hess lingered behind a few steps on the right, wanting to delay this as long as possible. He felt uncomfortable about this meeting.

As they drew near, the passenger door of the Mercedes swung open. A man stepped out and faced them. The man presented the ideal image of an Aryan—tall, muscular, angular face, blonde hair, blue eyes. Adorned in the uniform of an SS *Obergruppenführer*, this individual could have been the poster child for the Master Race. Even from this distance, he exuded an air of confidence and power that competed with that of the three most powerful men in the *Reich*. Hess was both impressed and intimidated. The man allowed Vonnegut to escort him around the rear of the car.

"*Mein Führer*," said Vonnegut. "Allow me to introduce Jo-chen Steiner. This is the gentleman I told you about who can help us with our problem."

Steiner grinned and nodded. "Actually, my boss is the one who can help you with your problem. I merely represent his business interests."

"Welcome to the Berghof," said Hitler.

"It's a pleasure to be here."

"Shall we go inside?" Hitler ushered Steiner up the grand staircase and into the Berghof, engaging in exuberant small talk with their visitor. The latter smiled and said nothing.

When they entered the Great Hall, Hitler led Steiner across the room to the bay window, hoping to impress him with the panoramic view. Steiner remained polite and professional but was clearly unimpressed with the display of grandiosity. When the party took their seats in the comfortable chairs around the circular conference table in front of the window, Hess noted that Steiner purposefully selected the chair that faced away from it. After everyone had taken a seat, Hitler asked, "Would you like something to drink, *Herr* Steiner?"

"I'd like to get down to business. While I appreciate your hospitality, my boss and I are incredibly busy."

"I understand." Hitler bristled at being dressed down in such a manner but allowed the insult to pass. "I take it you know why you're here?"

"When Dr. Vonnegut summoned me, he explained to me that the *Reich* has experienced some military setbacks, and that you want my boss' assistance in ensuring your eventual victory. Is that correct?"

"It is," said Hitler.

"We had hoped to defeat England quickly and sign a peace treaty with London," added Himmler. "Unfortunately, Churchill is too stubborn for his own good. He knows he can't win against us, yet he refuses a negotiated settlement."

"Why should he settle?" Steiner asked coldly. "You have not been able to bring him to his knees."

"We could have," replied Himmler, his voice dripping with contempt. "But that fat excuse of a *Reichsmarshall*—"

Hitler raised his hand, cutting off the diatribe. "*Herr* Steiner, my focus has always been to the east where the real enemies are located—the Jews and the Bolsheviks. We need to eliminate that threat to guarantee the continued existence of the German people. A two-front war could be disastrous for Germany. I need your help if we're going to win this war."

"What about your Axis partners?"

Hitler dismissed them with a wave of his hand. "They're useful idiots, at best. Mussolini has caused me more problems in North Africa then he's worth. I need someone I can rely on."

"And you feel there is no one more reliable than my boss?"

"Yes."

Steiner sat back in his seat and casually placed his arms on the armrest, contemplating his answer. "It can be done."

Hitler and Himmler bristled with excitement.

"But there will be a price," added Steiner.

"Our immortal souls?" Himmler chuckled.

"Not quite." A sardonic grin pierced Steiner's mouth. "The number I had in mind was twenty-five million."

Silence fell across the table.

"Twenty-five million?" Hitler asked.

"That's only twenty-five thousand souls for every year of your Thousand-Year *Reich*. It's quite a bargain if you ask me."

"You can't be serious," said Hess.

"Did you think this would be easy?" Steiner's pleasant demeanor hardened. "Did you think that my boss would grant you so much power, and all you'd have to do is sacrifice a few virgins? If that's the case, *Herr* Hitler, you are way out of your element."

Himmler bristled. "You will address him as *Mein Führer*."

Steiner cast the *Reichsführer* a glance that sent a cold chill down the man's spine. "I already have a *führer*, *Herr* Himmler. Neither he nor I are intimidated by the likes of you."

Himmler leaned back in his seat, fighting back the urge to cower.

"You're not the first person who has asked my boss for help," Steiner continued. "But you are the first whose goals are so grandiose. You want to rule Europe for a millennium and have the rest of the world pay homage to you as vassals. Fair enough. But such ambition comes with a price."

Hitler shook his head. "You realize it will be next to impossible to find twenty-five million people who are already condemned to Hell?"

"That's the beauty of this arrangement. Once you enter into an agreement with my boss, then anybody who dies at the hands of the regime, their soul will be forfeited. Infant and elderly. Military and civilian. Aryan and non-Aryan. Every life taken will count toward the twenty-five million."

"That number is daunting," said Hitler, doubt tinging his voice.

"It is," agreed Steiner. "My boss has been watching you carefully these past seven years, and he thinks you're up to the challenge."

Hitler looked to Himmler for guidance. The *Reichsführer* offered a slight nod of assent that such a goal was achievable.

Hitler stood and maneuvered behind his chair, his left arm draped across his chest, his right propped on it and supporting his chin. He paced in a circle for several seconds, contemplating the proposal.

"By entering into this arrangement, your boss guarantees we'll be victorious?"

"Not immediately. This is a business arrangement. Once the twenty-five million souls have been accounted for, then your Thousand-Year *Reich* will be guaranteed."

Hess desperately tried to inject rationality into the discussion. "Until we reach that number, Germany could still be defeated?"

"Yes. Your actions and decisions will still influence how events play out until that number is reached."

"This is risky, *Mein Führer*," Hess pleaded. "We're not prepared for a two-front war. If we even reach this goal, there might not be much of the *Reich* left to rule for a Thousand-Years."

"That's irrelevant," Steiner replied. "What my boss offers at the fulfillment of your side of the agreement will make Germany invincible. Even if your enemies are rampaging through the streets of Berlin, they will be helpless against you."

Hess shook his head. "It's too risky."

"It's not risky," countered Vonnegut. "It's daring. It's bold."

Hitler stopped and pointed repeatedly toward Vonnegut. "It is bold. Politics always favors the bold. You should know that better than anyone, Hess."

"But if we fail—"

Hitler cut off his deputy with a wave of his hand. "Failure is merely the bastard child of a love affair with the bold. We failed in Munich in 1923 and look at us now. We can do this."

Himmler's head bobbed up and down like a children's nodding donkey toy. "This proves providence chose you to be *Führer*."

"Yes!" Hitler crossed over to the bay window and stared out, impressing himself with the view. "We'll just need to keep those cowardly, narrow-minded generals in line to make certain their defeatism doesn't cause us to lose on both fronts."

"My boss may be able to help you with that," said Steiner. His tone dripped with confidence, a seasoned salesman closing the deal. "There are ways we can assist you in dealing with your British problem."

Hitler turned from the window. "What will it cost me?"

"Nothing. My boss has been impressed with your work so far and wants to offer these 'services' as a show of admiration."

Hitler bowed slightly. "Your boss has my gratitude."

"All we need to do now is work out the details," said Vonnegut.

Himmler glared at the doctor. "What details?"

"Nothing major," said Steiner. "Once twenty-five million have been provided, a certain ritual needs to be performed to grant the permanence of a Thousand-Year *Reich*. Even Hell has bureaucracy."

Hitler chuckled. "It figures the bureaucrats would all be in Hell."

Even Steiner laughed. The only one who found no humor in this situation was Hess. He still tried to get his head around the infamous decision his friend, his leader, his mentor had just made, and the nightmare it would generate not only for Germany but also the world.

As the humor died down, Hitler returned to the table. "Hess, you may leave us now."

"I don't understand."

"You're a good man and a good friend. I may need you in the future to counsel me, and you can't do that if you're intimately involved in the details."

Hess wanted to argue but did not. He knew it would be futile. Maybe in the future he could serve as a voice of reason within the regime and steer his friend away from the excesses that were bound to result from this Faustian bargain. He would not be able to do that if he burned all his bridges now.

Bowing to the inevitable, Hess replied, "As you wish, *Mein Führer.*"

"Thank you."

Hess crossed the room and exited. As he closed the door behind him, he watched the others hunch over the table. He knew that this moment would seal Germany's fate. What that fate would be, he had no idea.

CHAPTER TEN

Tower of London, London, England
2 June 1941

C ODY HAD NO idea what to say. If he had not seen the succubus earlier that morning, he would have dismissed Hess' story as the educated ravings of a madman, and Bellingham and Lee as gullible fools. He wished he could rule this out as a bout of insanity but knew better.

"I felt the same way when I first heard Steiner's proposition," said Hess.

"Did you ever find out the details about the ritual and how Hitler intends to offer up twenty-five million souls?" Cody asked.

"Not about the ritual. Among the top leadership, only Hitler and Himmler are privy to all the details, as well as a few in the lower echelons. Everyone else who's involved knows only what they need to in order to complete their job. As for how Hitler intends to offer up so many souls…." Hess took a deep breath. "Hitler is talking about switching the policy toward the Jews from expulsion and deportation to extermination."

"You mean genocide?"

Hess closed his eyes and sighed. "Yes."

"How many Jews are there in Europe?"

"Approximately eight million west of the Urals," Bellingham answered.

"Then Germany will fail," said Cody. "He doesn't have the numbers."

"Hitler won't fail," said Hess. "He's planning to wage a war of extermination in the east. Jews, Slavs, and Russians are going to be slaughtered *en masse* to create *Lebensraum* for the German people. If he succeeds in establishing a Thousand-Year *Reich*, nothing will stop him."

Cody glanced over at Bellingham and Lee, hoping they would offer some solace. The expression on their faces indicated they agreed with Hess.

"What are his plans for England?"

"The *Führer* has an affinity for the Brits, so he doesn't want to release his full fury on England. I know he has plans to use the occult to force England out of the war early, or at the very least to counter your efforts so he doesn't have to fight a second front. I asked around trying to find out what Himmler had planned, but never could get an answer. Sorry."

"No need to apologize," said Bellingham as he pushed himself out of the chair. "Thank you for your time."

The three officers headed for the door. Hess rushed forward, wrapping his palm around Cody's upper arm to hold him back. "Please understand, despite what you might hear in the news, the reason I flew to England was to warn the British about what was going to take place so they could stop it."

"I understand. I mean it."

"I know you do." Hess released his grip and returned to his chair. "Good luck."

NO ONE SPOKE until they were back in the innermost ward. Bellingham and Lee stood by Tower Green, allowing Cody time to process what he had heard. Good luck with that. He paced back and forth, trying to get his mind around everything he had witnessed this morning. This was like waking up from a bad dream only to discover that reality was an even worse nightmare. After a few minutes, he stopped pacing and faced his counterparts.

"What have you tried to do to stop this?"

"There's not much we can do at the moment," admitted Bellingham. "We only acquired Hess' information two weeks ago. In that time, I've set up Operation CROWLEY, recruited a handful of operatives, and captured the succubus in North Africa. Beyond that, we're still getting our feet wet."

"We've also contacted Moscow to warn them about the impending invasion," added Lee.

"Did you inform them of the occult storm about to be unleashed on Russia?"

"No," said Bellingham. "The prime minister wants to hold some of his cards close to his chest. Not that it matters. The Soviet Foreign Ministry dismissed the whole thing. They responded two nights ago to our warning of a Nazi invasion with a telegram that said in essence 'thank you, we'll take it under advisement, please don't bother us again'."

"What about Washington?"

"The only ones who know about this are President Roosevelt and that gentleman Donovan."

"And you, of course," added Lee.

"What do we do now?" Cody asked.

"We go back to Baker Street and figure out a way to find those other succubi."

CHAPTER ELEVEN

Wewelsburg, Germany
2 June 1941

DIETRICH WATCHED THE Westphalian countryside pass by as the SS staff car took him, Lilith, and Malalath to their destination. He loved the rural setting, especially the small German towns and vast tracks of farmland. This environment was so much more relaxing than the bustle of large cities like Berlin and Munich. It reminded him of his childhood growing up in Bavaria and of a much simpler time when the world and his life wasn't in such turmoil. Times change, and the good inevitably gives way to the challenging. Life is what it is. Both he and Germany had difficult jobs ahead of them. Once they were accomplished and this war ended, then things could return to this more leisurely way of life.

"There it is," said Lilith.

Dietrich leaned forward to look out the side window. Atop the valley heights overlooking the town of Buren sat Wewelsburg Castle, the Renaissance-era structure that at one time had been the residence of the liege lords appointed by the Paderborn prince-bishops or the local bursary officers. The castle had its own dark side before the advent of National Socialism, from it hosting the witchcraft trials of 1631 to the legends that this will be the location where the armies of the east and west will battle.

Since 1934, the castle had become the headquarters of the SS Leadership School to train SS officers in numerous ideological fields. No renovations were ever made to accommodate large classes, with the architects turning the existing rooms into private study halls. Over time, the broad educational overview became more focused, concentrating on archaeological excavations and more mystical subjects such as Germanic mysticism, cult ancestry, and rune worship. Himmler wanted Wewelsburg to become a Grail castle to accommodate an SS variation of the Knights of the Round Table. Because of this, Wewelsburg had developed a reputation as a Black Camelot.

Only a handful of people understood how evil this particular Camelot would be.

The staff car ascended the hill, entered Wewelsburg via the access bridge located in the eastern wing of the building, and parked in the center of the inner courtyard. Wewelsburg was constructed in a triangular configuration with the apex centered on the North Tower, the dark heart of Himmler's occult activities. The other walls formed the rest of the triangle.

As Dietrich and the succubi climbed out of the car, SS *Brigadeführer* Siegried Taubert, the *Burghauptman* of Wewelsburg, entered the courtyard to greet them.

"*Obergruppenführer*, ladies. It's good to see you again. It's been a long time."

"Too long," said Dietrich. "Thank you for hosting us on such short notice."

"My pleasure. I wish I knew what the purpose of your visit was so I could have prepared for you."

"We didn't want to put the purpose in cable traffic for security reasons. We're here to see MARLENE."

Taubert nodded. "I understand. She's in the King Arthur Study Hall. Do you want me to take you there?"

"We can find our own way."

Entering the castle, Dietrich led the way to the hall. A young woman sat at a table, her eyes closed and her hands resting on top with the palms up. She was in her early twenties, a petite girl with a short-cut blonde bob and oversized glasses.

Her attire resembled that of a schoolgirl—long plaid skirt, white shirt buttoned up to the neck, and a blue V-neck sweater—giving her a mousy appearance. Dietrich had never met the girl personally, knowing her solely by her personnel file and her reputation. He stood in the presence of Winifred Voss, Himmler's private psychic. Her abilities were so finely tuned and of such a great asset to the *Reich* that her very existence had been classified. Except for a select few officers within the SS, most people knew of Winifred Voss by her codename MAR-LENE.

Dietrich knocked on the door jamb. The interruption surprised Winifred, who jumped in her seat and let out a soft squeal.

"I'm sorry, *Fraulein* Voss," said Dietrich. "I didn't mean to startle you."

"That's okay," she replied in a voice so soft he could barely hear her. "And please, call me Winnie."

"Is this a good time to talk to you?" he asked, not caring how she responded.

"Yes," she whispered. "I was reaching out into the spiritual world trying to contact Agrat."

"Did you have any success?" asked Lilith as she stepped past Dietrich.

Winnie averted her gaze and shook her head.

"May I sit down?"

Winnie nodded.

Dietrich took the chair opposite Winnie, spun it around so the back faced her, and then sat down, resting his arms on the back edge. Lilith and Malalath stood behind him and to the sides.

"I want you to explain your psychic ability to me, and how you lost contact with General Wavell."

"I never lost my spiritual contact with the general," said Winnie, mumbling the sentence so softly that Dietrich struggled to hear her.

"Speak up."

"I never lost my spiritual contact with the general. But I'm not able to use him to locate Agrat."

"I don't understand," said Malalath. "I thought necromancers could psychically talk to anyone they wanted."

"I'm a psychic, not a necromancer. I can only make spiritual connections with the living. I can sense their presence, see what they see, feel what they feel, but unless they detect the connection and let me into their minds of their own free will, I can't read their thoughts."

"How did you make such a strong connection with General Wavell?"

"That was an unusual situation. His mind was more susceptible, more open to me, because Agrat had him under her influence. Once that connection between Agrat and the general was broken, I lost that link. Now all I can sense from him is confusion."

"Do you know what happened to Agrat?" Lilith asked.

Winnie bowed her head and mumbled, "For several days after the connection was broken, the general was in a state of disorientation. He has no idea what happened that night, and no one has told him." Winnie glanced up at Lilith. "I'm sorry I can't give you any more information about your sister."

"How did you know we're succubi?" Malalath asked.

"I can sense your auras. They're much darker and ominous than the *obergruppenführer*'s." Realizing what she had said, Winnie quickly lowered her head again. "I didn't mean that the way it sounded."

Dietrich ignored her pathetic apology. "Can you focus in on Agrat's aura like you did with General Wavell and determine where she is?"

"No. I can do it with humans because I have a frame of reference."

"What if you had a frame of reference?"

Winnie looked up, confused. "What do you mean?"

"If you channeled through Lilith, do you think you could contact Agrat?"

"I... I guess it's possible."

"Then let's try. How do you want to do this?"

"I would need to be in physical contact with her."

Dietrich stood from his chair, picked it up, and placed it beside Winnie. Lilith strolled over and sat down facing the psychic. Winnie looked between Dietrich and Lilith, obviously apprehensive about attempting such a procedure, yet far too scared to resist. She slid her chair across the floor to face the succubus and held out her hands, palm up.

"Give me your hands."

Lilith obliged. Winnie took a deep breath and held it. She closed her eyes, clasped Lilith's hands tightly, and exhaled.

Nothing happened at first.

Five minutes passed, then ten.

As they approached the fifteen-minute mark, Dietrich was about to end this futility when Lilith twisted her head from side to side and moaned, but not from lust. It sounded more like a moan of pain. A moment later, Winnie tightened her grip on Lilith's hands. Her body arched back and she cried out. Malalath rushed over to help.

Dietrich interceded. "Don't touch them."

"She's in pain."

"You'll break the spell."

Winnie lifted her head and glanced around the room. "Malalath? Is that you?"

"Yes, it is," responded Malalath. "Is this Agrat?"

"Yes."

"Where are you?"

"I'm in such pain," Winnie grunted. "They cut off my wings so I couldn't escape."

"Who cut off your wings? I'll make them—"

Dietrich interrupted Malalath so he could focus the conversation. "Agrat, this is *Obergruppenführer* Dietrich. Can you hear me?"

"Yes."

"What happened?"

"They cut off my wings."

"How did the British capture you?"

Winnie groaned. "It hurts so much."

"You have to tell me what happened."

"Will you come and get me?"

"Yes," Dietrich lied. "But you have to tell me what happened."

"They ambushed me. They surrounded me with mirrors, forced me to face my own image. I turned in front of them. They cut off my wings."

"Where are you now?'

"In a cage."

"Where?"

"In a basement."

"You need to concentrate," said Dietrich. "After the British captured you, where did they take you? Are you still in Cairo?"

"No. They put me on a plane and flew me somewhere."

"To London?"

"I don't know. They kept me blindfolded the whole time."

"Is there anyone there with you?"

"Some doctor in a wheelchair. He knows about us."

"Knows what?" asked Dietrich.

"He knows there are four of us. They're looking for you."

"Who are 'they'?"

"An American officer and a British woman." Winnie paused. "When are you coming to get me?"

"You have to listen to me carefully. I need you to find out everything you can about these two. Especially what they know and what they're planning. Do you understand?"

"When are you coming to get me?"

"Agrat, do you understand me?"

Winnie lowered her head and sniffed. "Yes."

"Good." Dietrich grabbed Winnie's hands and lifted them off of Lilith's. Both women came out of their trance with a gasp. Winnie slumped forward onto the table. Lilith jumped up and backed against the wall, clutching her arms across her chest.

"I can't believe they did that to Agrat. It's barbaric."

Dietrich motioned for Malalath to take Lilith outside. Once the two exited the study hall, Dietrich sat down in the chair opposite Winnie. When he touched her, she recoiled back until she realized it was only him.

"Are you okay?"

"Yes." The shudder that ran through Winnie's body belied that. "That was more intense than I could have imagined."

"With Lilith's help, do you think you'll be able to reach Agrat again?"

"I won't need her help. Once the connection has been made, I can call it up again at will."

"Excellent. Check in with Agrat frequently and see what information she can get on the Brits and that American."

Winnie sighed.

"What's wrong?" Dietrich asked.

"The link takes a lot out of me," she whispered. "Let me rest up a bit first."

"Take your time." Dietrich patted her on the shoulder and headed out. He paused by the door. "Winnie, you did good today. Thank you."

The young woman smiled without looking up.

Once in the corridor, Dietrich walked toward the far end. Lilith leaned against the wall, shaking with anger. Malalath stood behind her, a hand reassuringly placed on her sister's shoulder.

"How is she?"

"She'll be fine," said Malalath.

Lilith spun around and slapped Malalath's hand away. "I'm far from fine. Those bastards tortured Agrat, and I won't be fine until I can make them suffer as much as she has."

"Have patience—"

"Don't tell me what to do."

"I will tell you what to do because I give the orders around here," Dietrich said with enough malevolence in his voice to cause Lilith to back down. "If you have an issue with that, we can discuss this with Steiner."

"There's no need for that," said Lilith.

"I thought so." Dietrich's tone softened. "Whoever hurt Agrat will pay for what they did to her, but all in good time. Understood?"

"Yes." Lilith sighed.

Dietrich turned to Malalath. "I want you to stay here. Make sure you're with Winnie every time she tries to reach Agrat. If she makes contact, find out everything you can about where Agrat is and what the British are planning. Call me the moment you get anything."

"Gladly."

Without saying another word, Dietrich headed for the courtyard. Lilith fell in behind him.

Despite the capture of Agrat, he still felt confident about their chances of success. In fact, this setback could be utilized to his advantage if he could use Winnie to channel Agrat and figure out in advance what the British planned on doing to counter him. Such a method of gathering intelligence wouldn't be easy and could kill Winnie in the long run. That was a risk he was willing to take.

CHAPTER TWELVE

SOE Headquarter, London, England
4 June 1941

"THIS IS GETTING us nowhere." Cody slammed shut the book he had been reading and tossed it onto the desk. "We've been at this for two days and we still have nothing."

"I know," said Lee soothingly. "But we can't give up."

"I'm not giving up. We just need to change our tactics." He gestured to the stack of dusty, old books piled on top of the desk. "We've been reading through these demonology texts Curtis gave us and studying succubi, and we still aren't any closer to figuring this out."

"It has to be in there somewhere."

"I doubt it. Curtis has been studying these things all his life, and even he doesn't have all the answers."

Lee closed her book and laid it in her lap. "What are you suggesting?"

"That the answer is somewhere else. We need to figure out where." Cody spun sideways in his chair to face Lee. "Is there anyone else in the government with abilities like yours we can recruit for this job?"

"I'm the only one working for the government that we know of. If there are others, they've kept it well hidden because of the social stigma attached. Scotland Yard and MI5 are combing their files to see if they have records of anyone in the private sector, but so far, they've come up with nothing."

"Shit."

Lee glanced at her watch. "It's after eight. Let's call it quits for the day."

"I'm fine."

"You're not. You're tired and frustrated, which means even if you stumble across the answer, you're liable to overlook it."

"You're right."

"Come on," said Lee as she placed the book on the desk and stood up. "I'll buy you a drink."

"Can I take a rain check on that? I want to drop by the basement and check out our visitor. Maybe spending a few minutes with that thing will give me some ideas."

"Suit yourself. Just to let you know," Lee joked, "I'm much better company than our visitor downstairs. Good night."

After Lee left, Cody headed into the basement. Five minutes later, he stood twenty feet from the succubus' cage, studying it. The demon was coiled up in the far corner, presumably asleep since he could not detect it trying to influence his thoughts.

Curtis rolled up beside him. "She's addictive, isn't she?"

"She's frightening."

"Even fear can be addictive." Curtis spun around and headed back to his office. "Come on. I have the perfect cure for that."

"What?"

"Replace it with another addiction."

As Cody entered the office, Curtis wheeled over to a tea caddy positioned beside his desk. Opening a humidor, he prepared two cigars and two tumblers, one set of which he placed on the corner of his desk. "Those are for you."

"I don't smoke. Those things are bad for your health."

"We're in the middle of a world war and are battling demons from Hell. Cigars are the least of my worries."

"Fair enough." Cody took the seat opposite Curtis' desk and lit his cigar. He found the first few puffs disgusting but, by the third, the taste had become pleasant. Cody held up the tumbler. "What's this?"

"Twenty-year-old scotch." Curtis raised his tumbler. "Here's to defeating these Nazi bastards and sending them back to Hell along with their succubi."

"I'll drink to that." Cody clinked his tumbler against Curtis' and swigged a mouthful. The scotch burned on its way down his throat, but did it ever taste good. Cody followed up the drink with a puff on his cigar.

After a few minutes of silence, Curtis finally asked, "Admit it, when you first met her, she glamoured you for a few seconds."

"The fact that it could scares me."

"It should. Even though they attach themselves to one person and manipulate them, they can temporarily glamour others. It's part of their defense mechanism. Somehow, they can read our minds and present themselves in the image of the type of woman their target is most attracted to. If she had not been exposed in Cairo and prevented from glamouring again, she might very well have gotten you under her influence."

"Why doesn't it glamour you to let it go?"

"I'm completely paralyzed from the waist down and don't have the same sexual urges as other men. She would have to work harder than usual to glamour me, and in her condition, that's impossible." Curtis drank some scotch. "By the way, *her* name is Agrat."

"I'm sorry?"

"You keep referring to her as 'it'."

"It's not human."

"True. But it is the female of its species."

Cody let the comment slide. "How do you know it's named Agrat?"

"She told me."

"You interrogated her?"

"I chatted with her. I didn't learn anything other than her name, and that she wants to drag us all back to Hell and tear our souls apart."

Cody chuckled, although he was not sure why he found that humorous.

"What little she did tell me was significant."

"How so?"

"By admitting her name was Agrat she confirmed that there are three other succubi out there we have to worry about, assuming that the legends are accurate. So far, they've followed the Talmudic tradition."

"Have you asked about her sisters?"

"I did, but she refuses to talk. She let slip that there are others, although she refused to admit how many. Of course, she won't tell me where they are, who they're glamouring, or why the Germans are doing this." Curtis thought for a moment. "I do think they're trying to contact her."

"Why do you say that?"

"Two afternoons ago, I heard a noise coming from Agrat's cage. When I came in to check on her, I found her curled up in the corner rocking back and forth and mumbling. She seemed to be in a trance. I've asked Bellingham to install a microphone in her cell so we can record what she says and scan it for intelligence."

"Good idea." Cody sipped some scotch. "Has Lee tried to communicate with her?"

"It didn't work. Succubi view women as beneath them. Agrat only talks to me because I'm male and she's hoping to take advantage of me. Besides, Lee can only communicate with the dead."

Cody took a puff on his cigar and held the smoke in his mouth as he contemplated whether to bring up the next topic.

"Have you considered killing Agrat and then talking to her?"

"That was the first thing Bellingham thought of when Agrat refused to cooperate. We convinced him it wouldn't work. Lee can only communicate with the dead who initiate contact with her and can receive information the dead are willing to give up, neither of which would work in Agrat's case. Right now, she's more valuable to us alive."

"What about General Wavell? Has anyone talked to him to see if he has any residual blowback from her memories?"

"The general can only recall being glamoured but is blurry about the details of what he did while under Agrat's control. He never got inside her mind." Curtis took a swig of scotch. "You're good at this."

"Not good enough. We still have no clue where the other three succubi are or what they're planning."

"The answers are out there. We need to figure out how to find them. That's not what bothers me."

"What does?"

Curtis puffed on his cigar and blew the smoke toward the ceiling. "The fact that we have no idea what other demons Himmler may have summoned to pit against us."

CHAPTER THIRTEEN

Stalin's office, the Kremlin, Moscow
5 June 1941

"I WILL NOT listen to this any longer." Stalin waved his hand above his head in a dismissive gesture. "We have nothing to fear from Hitler."

"The evidence is overwhelming. I've talked to the British prime minister," pleaded Molotov. "He stressed to me that Rudolf Hess warned Churchill that Hitler intends to launch an invasion of the Soviet Union with the goal of eradicating the civilian population and use the land for his *Lebensraum* policy."

"Our contact inside the British government confirms this," added Beria.

"Marshal Stalin," said Mikoyan. "Please listen to reason—"

"Enough!" Stalin slammed his hand on top of his desk with enough ferocity to cause Beria, Molotov, and Mikoyan to step back a few paces. The gesture even startled Levorov, although he remained stoic in the corner behind his boss. "Are you saying I'm unreasonable, Mikoyan?"

To his credit, Mikoyan stood his ground. "No. But I am concerned that you may be placing too much trust in this non-aggression pact with Hitler."

"I've met with him and Ribbentrop," said Molotov. "I don't trust them. Hitler didn't agree with it because he wanted peace with the Soviet Union. He did it to buy time so he could concentrate on taking west Europe."

"Which is why I'm not worried about an invasion." Stalin softened his tone. "Hitler is unreliable and untrustworthy, but he's not stupid. He hasn't defeated the British or forced them to accept an armistice. As long as Germany is fighting the British, Hitler would never open a second front."

"What about the warnings from Hess?" Molotov asked.

"Has anyone from our embassy in London talked to Hess personally?"

"No."

"Don't you see what's happening, Vyacheslav? The war in the west has reached a stalemate. Churchill can't win without help. The Americans refuse to get involved in European affairs, so he's trying to convince us that Germany plans to invade so we'll strike first."

"All of our sources in Germany report that a German invasion is imminent," said Beria.

"Are these the same sources that reported the German invasion would begin on 22 May?" Stalin asked. "That was a week ago. Unless you're keeping something from me Comrade Beria, I'm not aware of any Nazi hordes crossing the border."

No one spoke.

"I'm not blind to what Hitler is and what he intends," said Stalin, his tone more conciliatory. "I know in time he'll turn his attentions toward the Soviet Union. That's why I agreed to the non-aggression pact, to give us more time to prepare. We're not ready for war right now."

Levorov noticed the others back down. None of the ministers dared respond that the Soviet Union was unprepared for war because the last round of purges had eliminated fifty percent of the Red Army's officer corps, least of all Beria who had orchestrated the purge.

Naamah entered the outer office, sauntered over to the door, and leaned against the jamb. She ran the tip of her tongue across her upper lip.

Stalin spotted her and stood. "This conversation is at an end. I have other matters to attend to."

Mikoyan left first, followed by Beria and Molotov. The

three men passed by Naamah, who smirked as she stepped out of their way. Once they had left, she glided into the office.

"What was that all about?" she asked.

"They were trying to convince me that Hitler was planning an attack on us."

Naamah's demeanor lost some of its seductiveness. "You don't believe them, do you?"

Stalin contemplated his answer. "Some of what they said made sense. Maybe I should—"

Naamah sat in Stalin's lap, cupped his cheeks in her hands, and kissed him for several seconds. When she finished, she asked, "You don't believe them, do you?"

"Not at all. They're scared and weak."

"Maybe it's time you replace them."

"Do you really think so?" Stalin seemed uncertain.

"Yes, if they're giving you bad advice."

"Maybe you're right."

"Of course, I am." Naamah noticed Levorov standing in the corner. She glanced down at Stalin and nodded in his direction.

"You're dismissed, Comrade Levorov."

"Are you sure?"

"Yes. Now go."

Levorov crossed the office and closed the door behind him, taking a last quick look as he did. This was not the same Stalin who saved the revolution and made the Soviet Union a power to be reckoned with. This man was argumentative, indecisive, and weak. If Beria and the others were right and the Nazis did intend to attack, this Stalin would get them all killed. It all stemmed from Naamah.

Clearly, this woman had an undue influence on him. Unnatural would be a better word. It was as if she had him under a spell. Whatever the answer, he knew Stalin would not listen to anyone else so long as Naamah remained in the picture, and the likelihood of him or the others convincing Stalin to get rid of her was nil. Without further evidence, he would not be able to convince Beria and the others to force the woman out of the picture. They viewed her as a mistress. Levorov knew better. His own experiences warned him that Naamah was much more dangerous than a sexual distraction and would have to be stopped before the entire Soviet Union came crashing down around them.

As Levorov made his way back to his quarters, he decided to find out exactly who—or what—Naamah really was.

CHAPTER FOURTEEN

***Reichskanzlei*, Berlin, Germany,
6 June 1941**

THOSE RESPONSIBLE FOR running Nazi Germany's occult war stood in Hitler's study inside the New *Reich* Chancellery, at the moment feeling overwhelmed. The architectural design added to this feeling of inadequacy. The study was immense, four hundred square meters in size, with expensive red marble adorning the walls. It was designed purposefully to intimidate those whom the *Führer* felt the need to apply pressure on. At the moment, it was having the desired effect on those present as Hitler strolled through the room, berating his occult warriors about the defection of Rudolf Hess.

Nor did it help that several feet behind Hitler stood *Reichsleiter* Martin Bormann, the leader of the Nazi Party and Hess' personal secretary until the latter's flight to England. Physically there was nothing remarkable about the man, and he could easily blend in amongst a crowd. Yet what he lacked in looks he more than made up for in political acumen. As the *Reichsleiter*, Bormann used his control of access to Hitler, isolating lesser functionaries and political opponents. He also exploited Hitler's weaknesses to solidify his position, in the process becoming increasingly important to the *Führer*. Even the top leadership had avoided antagonizing Bormann, afraid of what he might say about them in private conversations with Hitler. Bormann had benefited most from Hess' departure, becoming Hitler's *de facto* deputy *führer* in everything but title. He was a petty and ambitious man who would not fail to use his new opportunity to advance his career and settle old scores.

As befitting his rank, Dietrich stood a meter behind Himmler and Vonnegut. Hitler paced in front of them, like a tiger sizing up its prey, as they bore the brunt of the *Führer*'s tirade. Himmler was clearly ill at ease, sweat forming on his brow and a barely detectable quiver in his hands, concerned this incident might cause him to lose favor with the *Führer*. Vonnegut seemed not to be bothered by the dressing down, his expression one of boredom waiting for the theatrics to be over. Lilith and Malalath stood to Dietrich's right, unmoved by what transpired because they knew that no matter the outcome, the impact on them would be negligible. Dietrich wished he could have felt the same way, but he knew that whatever happened to the *Reichsführer* would more than likely be visited upon him.

"Hess flew to England almost a month ago," said Hitler. "And yet we still know nothing as to what he told the British about Operation STEINER."

"You're in charge of intelligence, Heinrich," said Bormann. "Can you explain why we're still in the dark?"

To his credit, Himmler maintained his composure. "We're far from in the dark. We know he's being kept in the Tower of London and, based on what MARLENE has told us, we can assume he's been interrogated by this newly-established covert action group."

"That's not much," said Hitler.

"It's quite a lot considering that Hess is not an ordinary prisoner of war. He's the second highest ranking officer in Germany."

"*Was*," sneered Bormann.

Himmler ignored the taunt. "Once the English realized who they had captured, Hess was isolated and contact with him kept to a minimum. Few people know what's going on with regard to Hess, and I would venture that only a handful of them are fully aware of the reason for his defection. The British are taking full advantage of the situation, issuing press reports that Hess was seeking peace with England because Germany can't win the war, and implying through other channels that he's mentally unstable, which will hopefully have a propaganda backlash against the *Reich*."

"I don't give a shit about what type of propaganda war the British wage," snapped Hitler. "Germany can survive propaganda. What we can't survive is if Hess betrays Operation STEINER."

"Hess doesn't know anything about the details of Operation STEINER," said Himmler. "You kept him out of the loop on that so he could be impartial."

"A lot of good that did us. Somehow Hess still found out about Agrat."

Vonnegut cleared his throat. "He knew about Agrat because of me."

Everyone in the office stared at the doctor. Finally, Hitler asked, "Why did you tell him anything? My orders were to keep him uninvolved."

"I didn't tell him willingly."

"You mean he forced you?" snorted Bormann.

"Let me explain," said Vonnegut. "Two months ago, Hess came to me saying you had asked him to help arrange Agrat's mission overseas, and he asked for details of her assignment. I told him what I knew. It didn't dawn on me what Hess was up to until after I heard he had flown to England. I wasn't thinking. I'm an occultist, not an intelligence officer."

"And you didn't think to mention this after Hess defected?" asked Bormann.

"By then the damage was done."

"So, Agrat is dead because of you," Lilith hissed.

Vonnegut glanced over his shoulder at the succubus. "Agrat is not dead. You know that."

"She's maimed in captivity because of you. She might as well be dead."

"Enough!" yelled Hitler, jerking his head with such force

that several strands of hair fell across his forehead. He used his right hand to brush them back into place. "We're about to launch BARBAROSSA in a few days, and I have no idea whether Naamah's mission has been successful or not."

"I don't think we have to be concerned about Naamah," said Himmler.

"Why's that?"

"Our operatives in Moscow report there are no signs Russia is preparing for war. I talked this morning to Field Marshal Keitel and General Jodl who both assured me that military intelligence confirms there is no build-up of positions or changes in Russia's defensive posture along the front. All intelligence indicates Russia is completely unaware of the impending invasion. So even if we assume that Hess knew about Naamah's mission and informed the British, and the British passed that information along to Moscow, everything indicates she is doing her job."

"Besides," added Vonnegut. "If something bad had happened to Naamah, either her sisters or MARLENE would have picked up on it, which they haven't."

"That's true," said Lilith. Malalath nodded in agreement.

Hitler calmed down and paused, mulling over what he had heard.

"May I add something?" Dietrich asked.

"Go ahead," said Hitler.

Dietrich moved up between Himmler and Vonnegut, ignoring the menacing glare he received from his boss. "The *Reichsführer* is correct. As horrible as Agrat's fate was, she achieved her mission. She got General Wavell to pull back to Halfaya Pass, and now the British are in a full-scale retreat back to Egypt. Even if Hess did betray Naamah, which is unlikely, it'll have little impact. BARBAROSSA is not dependent on her. Once our army groups cross the border into Russia, it'll be our fighting skill and technological superiority that'll win the war."

Hitler nodded as he processed what Dietrich had said. "What about the pact I made with Satan?"

"So what if the British know about it? What can they do? Churchill might know Satan guaranteed you a Thousand-Year *Reich* in exchange for twenty-five million souls, but he has no clue about the details and the ritual that must be followed to enforce it. Even if he did, he can't stop you. Britain is barely hanging on as it is. Russia will be knocked out of the war in a few weeks. Once Moscow has fallen, then we have a free hand to finish the task and give Steiner the body count he requested. You have nothing to worry about, my *Führer*."

Hitler stared at Dietrich for a few tense moments, and then his face beamed with optimism. "You're right, of course."

Dietrich tried not to outwardly breathe a sigh of relief.

Hitler walked over to Himmler and placed a trembling hand on the *Reichsführer*'s shoulder. "I'm sorry I doubted you, Heinrich. I should have realized you have everything under control."

"Thank you, my *Führer*."

"Will you be staying in Berlin long?" Hitler asked. "I'd like you and Dr. Vonnegut to have dinner with me tonight."

"I'd love to," said Himmler.

"It'd be my honor," added Vonnegut.

"Excellent. See you both at nine."

As Hitler made his way back to his desk, Bormann escorted the others out. Dietrich could not help but notice the icy glare he got from the *Reichsleiter*. Once they were outside in the courtyard, Himmler motioned for Dietrich to stay back with him as the others continued on ahead.

"It looks like I chose the best man to head up Operation STEINER," said the *Reichsführer*. "Thank you."

"It's part of my job."

"Maybe so, but you made a very powerful enemy today."

"You mean Bormann," said Dietrich.

"Exactly. By protecting me, you placed yourself in his

crosshairs."

"Once we've completed this operation, we'll never have to worry about men like him again, will we?"

"No," Himmler chuckled.

"Then what better motivation is there to be successful?"

CHAPTER FIFTEEN

SOE Headquarters, London, England
7 June 1941

LEE WAVED HER hand in front of her face to dissipate the cloud of cigar smoke that had formed around Curtis' desk. She and Cody had come down here thirty minutes ago to consult with the doctor about Agrat, their own research having reached numerous dead ends. To her chagrin, a few minutes ago Curtis had produced a pair of cigars that he and Cody lit up. As Curtis blew out a mouthful of smoke, the wisps billowed in her direction. Lee leaned aside and coughed.

"Are you alright?" Cody asked.

Lee motioned toward the cage in the main basement. "If you want to get her to talk, smoke those things in there and tell her you'll put them out only if she tells you what you want to know."

"Come on," said Cody. "They're not that bad."

"They'll kill you."

"We're in the middle of a war with Nazi Germany and battling demons summoned from Hell. These are the least of my worries."

Curtis smiled and nodded in agreement.

Lee sighed in mock frustration. "Why is it that men always pick up each other's worst habits?"

"My ex-wife used to say it's because men are like dogs," said Curtis. "The only difference is you can train a dog."

"I can see why you divorced her," said Cody.

"I didn't. She died eight months ago during the Blitz."

"Sorry. I didn't mean to be—"

"Don't apologize. It's war. We've all lost someone close to us. It's why I keep on going, to end this thing as soon as possible to stop the killing." Curtis pointed his cigar toward the cage. "And she may be the key to that."

Lee shook her head. "Well, if she's the key, we haven't figured out which door she unlocks."

"It's frustrating," said Cody. "I've read more this week then I have since high school."

"At least now you're an expert on succubi," teased Curtis.

"Not that it's helping me any."

Curtis nodded in frustration. "I know. Even though she's caged and incapacitated, she still has the advantage. We can't compel her to tell us what she knows, and she realizes that. All we can do is sit back, let her taunt us, and hope she makes a mistake that gives away something we can use."

"That's not going to win the war for us," said Lee.

Curtis placed the cigar between his lips. "I would love to dissect her and figure out what makes her tick."

"So would I," added Cody.

"Really?"

"Well, the dissection part," said Cody.

Both men chuckled and blew cigar smoke into the air. Lee stood and left, preferring the company of Agrat over the noxious cloud forming in Curtis' office. She also did not want them to see her own frustration over their lack of progress. Because of her abilities, Bellingham felt she would have an advantage in handling succubi and had entrusted her with Project Samail. Lee had repaid his confidence with failure. Three other succubi were still out there, and her team had not been able to get any information out of Agrat about where they were or what they were up to. If Agrat had been able to cause so much trouble in North Africa, Lee could not begin to fathom the impact the others might have on the future course of the war. Or even what had occurred previously.

The thought had come to her the other night that what if the other succubi had already played their part in Germany's master plan. What if the Battle of France, the Battle of Britain, or even Chamberlain's sell out at Munich had been orchestrated by Agrat's sisters? Or even worse, what if one of them had infiltrated herself close to Churchill? Given the complexity of the nightmare they faced, she did not blame Curtis or Cody for indulging in a few vices.

Meeting Cody had been the most positive thing to come from taking over Project Samail. Although she would never admit it to him, she found him attractive and charming, although rough around the edges. Even that quality was due to his being a self-made man, which carried its own appeal. What appealed to her the most was his acceptance of her gift. Up until a few weeks ago, none of the men in her life, what few there were, could cope with her psychic abilities. Most considered her a freak or a nut and walked away. A few realized her ability made her vulnerable and manipulated that weakness to get her into bed, only to throw her aside once they had gotten what they wanted. This shunning was the reason she had suppressed her psychic ability for years and never admitted it to anyone. Bellingham and Curtis embraced her ability, and by extension her, as special. As much as that pleased her, she saw them mostly as father figures to replace the one who had abandoned her. The fact someone like Cody viewed her in the same light made her feel desirable.

Mumbling from Agrat's cage caught Lee's attention. She stepped away from the office to get a better view. Agrat was curled up in the corner, her back to the office, hidden in the shadows but mumbling as if carrying on a conversation. Lee approached the cage, slowly and quietly so as not to disturb Agrat. When a few feet from the bars she heard Agrat whisper, "The bitch is the most vulnerable."

"Who are you talking to?" Lee asked.

Agrat mumbled something incomprehensible and laughed.

She shifted her body to view Lee and spoke in a normal tone. "A friend."

Lee became excited. "Are you talking with one of your sisters?"

"Just a friend. Although one of my sisters is listening in."

Lee stepped up to the cage. "Which sister? Where is she?"

"How rude, my dear." Agrat unwound herself and slid across the floor to the center of the cage. "You want me to answer your questions but offer nothing in return."

"You know I can't give you anything."

"Not even a *quid pro quo?*" The succubus' reptilian face pouted.

"What do you mean?"

"I answer your questions, you answer mine."

Lee hesitated.

Agrat turned away. "Suit yourself."

"Ask your question," Lee blurted, instantly regretting it.

Agrat slithered a few feet toward the cage. The cold smile of the succubus' face made her want to cringe. "The sister who's listening in is Malalath, one of my younger siblings."

"Where is she?"

"*Quid pro quo.*" Agrat waved a taloned finger in front of her in admonishment. "Where am I?"

"In London."

"Don't insult me, little girl," Agrat snapped.

"You're in the basement of a secret facility in downtown London. I can't tell you more than that."

Agrat's head swayed from one side to the other like a cobra. When she finally spoke, her voice was taunting. "Malalath is in a castle in northern Germany run by the SS. I can't tell you more than that."

"Who is your friend?"

"Someone much like you."

"You mean she's psychic?"

"I mean my friend was chosen for her *special* abilities the same way you were chosen for yours."

"What's her name?"

"She never told me."

"Ask her."

Agrat chuckled. "I'll make a deal. You give me your name, and I'll introduce you."

"No."

"Fair enough." Agrat inched closer to the bars. "It's my turn. What will you do with me when you no longer need me?"

Lee was taken aback. For several seconds, she couldn't answer. "I... I don't know."

Agrat stared at Lee. "You really don't know, do you? How pathetic you all are at this game."

When Agrat coiled back toward her corner, Lee grabbed the bars in both hands and shook them. "Please don't go. I have one more question."

Agrat slithered up to Lee. "Go ahead."

"Where are Lilith and Naamah?"

"Lilith is nearby. Naamah is where she can do the most harm."

"Where's that?"

Agrat reached out her scaly hands and cupped them over Lee's. "That's for me to know and you to discover in due time."

Lee jumped as a pair of hands grabbed her shoulders. Cody pulled her away from the cage. Curtis wheeled by on her right as one of the guards raced up on their left, his Thompson aimed at Agrat.

"Back off!" Curtis yelled.

"No need for violence," Agrat cooed as she swayed back and forth, slowly receding back into the shadows. "I didn't harm the little girl."

"Are you okay?" Cody asked.

"I'm fine." Lee wanted to shrug off his hands but refrained. There was no need to treat him rudely because she was embarrassed. Instead, she patted his left hand and squeezed, then stepped away. "Thanks."

"What happened?" Curtis asked.

"I'll tell you in your office."

As the three went back to Curtis' desk, the British guard moved back to his station by the door, all the while keeping a wary eye on Agrat.

"So, what happened out there?" asked Curtis as he rolled behind his desk.

"I heard Agrat talking with someone, so I went to investigate. Agrat said she was talking to somebody with abilities like mine."

"You mean a Nazi psychic?" Cody asked.

"She didn't clarify. All I could find out was that Malalath was in a castle in northern Germany run by the SS, Lilith was nearby, and Naamah was somewhere she could do the most harm."

"That doesn't help us much," said Cody.

"Agrat actually provided intelligence we've not had before," said Curtis. "Lee, draft a report about what happened out there. Bellingham is on tour but will be back in two days. He'll be interested in what you found out."

"I will." Lee was still a bit shaken by her experience with the succubus.

Cody must have noticed. "I'll wait for you to write up the report and then walk you home when you're done."

"You don't have to do that," Lee protested.

"It's not a bother. Besides, if I have to stare at the walls of my hotel room much longer, I'll go as crazy as that thing in there."

"At least let me buy you dinner. There's a pub near my apartment that serves the best fish and chips in London."

"Deal."

"I don't mind taking care of things here while you're gone," Curtis teased. "You love birds run off and have a good time."

Lee cast Curtis a glare, part disapproving and part anger, which only made him smile. If Cody had heard, he didn't show it. He stepped aside and ushered her toward the exit.

As they left, Lee could not shake the feeling that Agrat was staring at her from deep in the shadows.

CHAPTER SIXTEEN

Wewelsburg Castle, Germany
7 June 1941

WINNIE SAT BEHIND the desk in the King Arthur Study Room. Malalath took her usual spot—an easy chair in the corner—where she slouched into the cushions and frowned. Her presence made Winnie's job that much more difficult because she now knew what she was dealing with, and it scared her. Winnie had always found it draining to reach out and psychically connect with others. After every session, she needed time to recover both physically and mentally.

The incident the other day when Dietrich made her channel through Lilith to forge a link with Agrat had been excruciating. The direct contact with Lilith had drained much more of her energy than she was used to, causing her to need an entire day of rest. Once the bond between her and Agrat had been established, reconnecting did not require any effort. Unfortunately, as a prisoner Agrat had no clue as to where she was being held and knew nothing about her captors or their plans. The few times she had channeled Agrat had been non-productive. The downside to being able to reach out and communicate with succubi was that it allowed her access to the deep recesses of their minds. She had gotten a glimpse of that inner Hell during the other day's session with Lilith. In her subsequent attempts to talk with Agrat and gather information, Winnie had been extremely careful not to delve too deep into the succubus' inner thoughts.

Winnie closed her eyes, cleared her mind, and psychically

reached into the nethersphere for Agrat. It took her only a few minutes to contact the succubus.

"It's good to hear from you again," said Agrat telepathically. "It's lonely here."

"I know."

"When are you getting me out?"

"Soon," Winnie lied. "First, I need to know where you are."

"I have no idea where I am."

"Those around you do. One of these times when we connect, I need you to engage one of them. I might be able to develop a psychic bond with one of your captors and figure out where they're holding you."

"Can you do that?"

"I won't know until I try," said Winnie. "Is there someone there who I might be able to connect with?"

"The bitch is the most vulnerable."

"*Who are you talking to?*"

"Like a sacrificial lamb bringing herself to the alter," Agrat said to Winnie and laughed.

Winnie sensed the woman's aura. "If that's the 'bitch' you're referring to, talk to her so I can make contact."

"*A friend.*"

"*Are you talking with one of your sisters?*"

"*Just a friend. Although one of my sisters is listening in.*"

"*Which sister? Where is she?*"

The woman's aura grew slightly stronger as she approached the cage. "The connection is still weak. Get closer."

"*How rude, my dear. You want me to answer your questions but offer nothing in return.*"

"*You know I can't give you anything.*"

Winnie had a good sense of the woman's aura. Now it was time to probe it.

"*Not even a quid pro quo?*"

"*What do you mean?*"

90

"*I answer your questions, you answer mine.*" A pause. "*Suit yourself.*"

Winnie sensed Agrat moving away from the cage. "What are you doing? I haven't linked in with her yet."

"*Ask your question.*"

"*The sister who's listening in is Malalath, one of my younger siblings.*"

"*Where is she?*"

"*Quid pro quo. Where am I?*"

"*In London.*"

"*Don't insult me, little girl.*"

"*You're in the basement of a secret facility in downtown London. I can't tell you more than that.*"

Agrat was getting useful intelligence from the woman. For some reason, though, Winnie could not make a psychic connection with her. Something about this woman was unique.

"*Malalath is in a castle in northern Germany run by the SS. I can't tell you more than that.*"

"*Who is your friend?*"

"*Someone much like you.*"

"*You mean she's psychic?*"

"*I mean my friend was chosen for her special abilities the same way you were chosen for yours.*"

That explains the unusual aura! This woman possessed psychic abilities similar to her own. If the woman had not been intent on questioning Agrat, she might have detected Winnie's presence in the conversation. If she did, and if she had a stronger ability or more experience than Winnie, the woman might be able to reverse the link and make a connection with her. Winnie realized she needed to work quickly and keep the woman occupied.

"*What's her name?*"

"*She never told me.*"

"*Ask her.*"

"No!" Winnie warned Agrat. "Don't let her know I'm

linked to you. Find out her name."

"*I'll make a deal. You give me your name, and I'll introduce you.*"

"*No.*"

"Good," Winnie said to Agrat. "Keep her talking."

"*Fair enough. It's my turn. What will you do with me when you no longer need me?*"

"*I... I don't know.*"

"*You really don't know, do you? How pathetic you all are at this game.*"

"*Please don't go. I have one more question.*"

Winnie sensed the woman grab the cage. She had one final chance to make the connection.

"Touch her," she ordered. "Make physical contact for a few seconds."

"*Go ahead.*"

"*Where are Lilith and Naamah?*"

"*Lilith is nearby. Naamah is where she can do the most harm.*"

"*Where's that?*"

"*That's for me to know and you to discover in due time.*"

When Agrat reached out and cupped the woman's hands, a flood of thoughts and emotions poured into Winnie's psyche. The negative feelings overwhelmed her—a lifetime of confusion, fear, guilt, hatred, abuse, shame, and self-loathing. For a moment, she experienced an emotional power surge that threatened to close down her own abilities. Winnie cut through the psychological chaff and probed the woman's aura, searching for the one thing they both had in common—psychic abilities. She sensed another aura, one that was powerful and focused, but not yet attuned to the netherworld. It connected with the woman's aura. No, it made physical contact with her, and was attempting to break the link. Winnie concentrated and went deep into the woman's psyche before it was too late, before the other person could—

The connection shattered like an exploding light bulb. For a moment, Winnie was aloof with no grounding in the real world. Panic set in as she feared being lost forever in the nethersphere. Then her surroundings began to refocus. Her heart raced, her skin felt damp and clammy, and her forehead dripped with sweat. An overbearing exhaustion closed in on her. Winnie struggled to remain awake. Gradually, her vision returned, beginning as a sliver of light penetrating the dark. After several seconds, she recognized the study hall at Wewelsburg and, standing in front of her, Malalath. The succubi looked concerned. She leaned across the table, clutching Winnie's hand and talking to her, although the young woman could not make out her words.

"Are you alright?" Winnie finally heard Malalath's question echo through the din. She held up a hand to signal she'd be fine, a gesture that drained most of her remaining energy.

"Do you need anything?"

"Yes," Winnie mumbled. "Take me back to my room so I can sleep. Then call *Obergruppenführer* Dietrich and tell him I've made contact with the British occultists."

CHAPTER SEVENTEEN

Westminster, London, England
7 June 1941

A S LEE HAD promised, the pub in Pimlico she had taken Cody to for dinner served the best fish and chips in London. Although, to be fair, he had eaten fish and chips only twice since arriving in the city, so he was not a fair judge. The most pleasant part of the meal was the company. After the incident earlier in the day with Agrat, Cody knew Lee needed human contact to connect her back to reality, and he had attempted to provide that by steering the conversation toward any topic other than work. It had worked like a charm. Lee had opened up, and the two of them had spent the next several hours chatting like normal people discussing normal topics during normal times. For a while, Cody had almost forgotten that he and Lee were fighting an occult war against Nazi Germany.

Reality had barged its way back into their lives after leaving the pub. Cody had wanted to walk her back to her apartment, which was in Covent Garden. To get there, they had to stroll through Westminster along the Thames, the area of the city most affected by the *Luftwaffe* bombing raid of 10 May, the largest of the war so far. The House of Commons had been destroyed in the raid, and Westminster Abbey had suffered extensive damage. The surrounding neighborhood had not fared much better. Dozens of buildings had been bombed out or gutted by fire, and several had collapsed, leaving piles of debris blocking the sidewalks and streets. In one section, the street had caved in, swallowing two cars and a lorry. Despite the carnage, Londoners carried on, picking up the pieces, burying the dead, and pretending as though the next raid would not be even more devastating. It was only after they had passed Downing Street that the bomb damage subsided.

"Sorry about walking you through all that," Lee said after several minutes of awkward silence. "We should have taken a cab. After so many months, Londoners have become accustomed to the Blitz. I forget how upsetting it can be for outsiders."

"I've seen combat and destruction. I've just never seen it used against civilians before."

"Believe it or not, you get used to it and adapt."

"I'm imagining what it would be like if Hitler launched the *Luftwaffe* against New York or Washington."

Lee frowned. "If we fail, that might happen."

Cody dropped the conversation, not wanting to sour their good mood. After several more minutes, the couple reached an apartment building a few blocks from Charing Cross subway station. Lee stopped by the front stairs. "This is where I live."

"I had a great time."

"The night's not over yet."

"I appreciate the offer," Cody said hesitantly. "Don't you think it's kind of late to come up for a drink?"

"I'm not inviting you up for a drink. I want you to spend the night."

For a moment, Cody had no idea how to respond. "I'm not sure where you think this—"

Lee placed her fingertips over his mouth, silencing him. "Don't over think this. I've spent every night of the past eight months with the specter of death hanging over my head. Two weeks ago, the Germans dropped their bombs a mile from here. And now I have succubi and Nazi occultists hunting me down. Who knows how much time I... how much time *any* of us have left. I want to spend that time with you."

Lee took his lapels between her fingers and held Cody in place as she pushed herself against him. She felt excited even through the thick wool uniform. "Are you coming up or not?"

"I'd love to."

"Good." Lee leaned forward and kissed him. Still holding Cody by the left lapel, she led him up the stairs and into her apartment building.

CHAPTER EIGHTEEN

The Kremlin, Moscow, the Soviet Union
8 June 1941

I T HAD TAKEN Levorov two days to find what he had been looking for. Considering how dangerous it was to have such items in your possession since the Revolution, he felt lucky to discover so quickly someone who still possessed them. It helped that Stalin kept on dismissing him from his duties to be alone with Naamah, which freed up Levorov's time. It also helped that he had the authority of the NKVD behind him, which expedited his search. Now, as Levorov sat behind his desk reading and drinking tea, several books about the occult and the supernatural were stacked on the floor beside his chair.

The books belonged to an old Ukrainian woman named Lyaksandra who lived in the suburbs of Moscow. Levorov had stumbled across her name in the NKVD's files quite by accident, although it turned out to be fortuitous. Lyaksandra had been widowed for years, her husband having been killed fighting alongside of Stalin while defending Tsaritsyn from White Russian troops. Prior to 1918, she had worked as a clairvoyant, making a modest living foretelling the future for bourgeois women seeking excitement in their monotonous lives. Such practices were frowned upon in the new socialist paradise. However, because Lyaksandra's husband had made the ultimate sacrifice for the Revolution, no efforts had been undertaken to reeducate her and no one from the security services had bothered with her until yesterday afternoon when Levorov had showed up at her front door.

As expected, she had been reluctant to let him into her apartment and had become wary about his inquiries into the occult, but an assurance that her cooperation would be of the utmost benefit to the Motherland, combined with a thinly veiled threat that the lack of cooperation would see Lyaksandra spending the rest of her life in the gulag system, eroded the last threads of resistance. She had eventually admitted to keeping banned books on the supernatural and agreed to let Levorov borrow them. Under normal circumstances, he would have ordered her to report to Lubyanka for questioning about her counter-revolutionary attitude, but in this instance, such action would have been hypocritical. It also helped that Lyaksandra reminded him of his grandmother Marina.

Levorov had never confided in anyone about his own experiences with the supernatural as a child growing up near the Ural Mountains. For months he had suffered from bad dreams, waking up to visions of his entire family being murdered, and remembering distinctly the image of their bodies strewn about. His mother had called him overly sensitive, while his father had written him off as being weak. Several doctors had diagnosed him as mentally unstable. Only Marina had believed him, comforting him and telling him he had become the victim of a *mapa*, an evil spirit that would sit on his chest at night, conjure up nightmares, and feed off the negative energy. One night, as the rest of the family slept, Marina had snuck into Levorov's room and used a spell to permanently drive away the *mapa*. As Levorov grew older, the memories of those events blurred until he convinced himself they were merely imaginations from his childhood. That changed in 1922. Tsarists from his hometown, angered by Levorov's participation in the Revolution, had stormed the family home, dragged everyone outside, and murdered them in the street. When Levorov later saw the photographs of the massacre site, they mirrored the images from his childhood nightmares.

Marx may have been brilliant a philosopher, Lenin an

ardent revolutionary, and Stalin a master politician, but none of them knew shit about the spiritual realm. Levorov knew from experience that demons existed in the real world. At this moment, one of them was threatening the existence of the Soviet Union.

The difficult part would be figuring out which demon and, more importantly, how to combat it. Lyaksandra's books were filled with myths and legends, some from around the world, most from Russia or its Slavic neighbors. He had been thumbing through them all last night and most of the morning, and still had not made a correct match. A dozen times he had told himself to take a break and get some rest, that his mind would be sharper after a few hours of sleep. Each time he continued to browse through the books, always hoping the next page would give him the answer. Levorov did the same thing again, only this time he swore to himself that he meant it. He would mark his place and come back after—

Levorov stopped upon an entry for *rusalka*. The text described them as fish-woman who lived at the bottom of rivers and lakes, usually the lost souls of jilted women who had drowned themselves out of grief or the unwanted children of unwed mothers cast away. He would have skipped the entry had he not noticed the colored painting accompanying the test which depicted the *rusalka* as mermaid-like in appearance with emerald eyes exactly like Naamah's. Not much of the legend corresponded to the current situation—*rusalka* could only stray from the water for short periods of time, and even then, they needed to always keep their hair moist or they would die. The danger of the demon centered on its ability to charm men and entice them to do the *rusalka*'s bidding, which usually ended in the victim's death. That part of the legend fit precisely what was going on between Naamah and Stalin. Nothing was mentioned about how to break the *rusalka*'s hold over its victim without killing the victim, or how to destroy the demon. Not that it mattered. Now that he knew exactly what type of demon he dealt with, he could cross reference *rusalka* with *Lyaksandra's* books and hopefully discover a way to deal with it. If his research led nowhere, he had at his disposal modern methods to manage this threat, no matter how demonic it might be.

Closing the book and placing it back on the desk, Levorov contemplated what he realized would be the hardest part of this whole scheme, and that would be getting Beria to believe him. Considering how enamored Stalin was of Naamah, unless Levorov had incontrovertible proof that she was a *rusalka* controlling his mind, no one within the party leadership would dare move against her. Even the thought of broaching such a subject with them seemed insane. He would have to conduct much more research if he hoped to produce evidence solid enough to convince them of the unthinkable. In the meantime, Levorov had to face the reality that he may never get the support of the others, and a time might come when Naamah would make her move and he would have to stop her on his own initiative. If and when that day came, he would need to be ready to move quickly and effectively because he would have only one chance to stop her.

Pushing himself out of his chair, Levorov made his way to the bedroom, got undressed, and slid into bed. Right now, he needed to sleep. Tomorrow he would visit his friend in the Red Army armory.

CHAPTER NINETEEN

Covent Garden, London, England
8 June 1941

C ODY DRIFTED OUT of his deep slumber feeling something he had not felt in a long time—contentment. He opened his eyes and had to squint. Morning sunlight poured through the bedroom window. Cody did not mind, enjoying the reassuring comfort and warmth it provided. He slid across the bed to move out of the beam. When he did, Lee cooed and draped a naked arm and leg across his body. Cody rolled to one side so he could wrap his arm around her.

"Good morning," he said.

"It is." Lee rested her cheek against his chest.

"What time is it?"

She shrugged. "Eight, maybe nine o'clock. Why?"

"Don't we have to be at work?"

"Considering all the hours we put in, no one is going to care if we're late one morning." Lee snuggled closer. "Besides, I don't feel like getting up right now."

Cody reached up and stroked the hair on the back of Lee's head. She smiled and sighed, running her fingers along his arms, pausing when she reached a tattoo on his upper right forearm of a square and compass, the tip of the former pointing down and the hinge of the latter pointing up, with a G in the middle.

"What's this?"

Cody glanced down at his arm. "You mean the tattoo?"

"Yes."

"It's the Masonic Symbol."

"You're a Freemason?"

"Was." Cody rolled to the side to look into her beautiful eyes. "I joined after I left home because a friend told me Masons looked out for each other and I'd land some good jobs."

"Did it work?"

Cody shook his head. "Not at all. All I succeeded in doing was wasting quite a few nights learning and memorizing the initiation rituals but, other than a few free dinners, I got nothing out of it. I haven't gone to a meeting in over ten years."

"You did get something else."

"What?"

"A good-looking tattoo."

Cody pulled Lee close and held her tight. They lay like that for close to ten minutes when Lee said, "I have something I want to share with you that I've never shared with anyone else."

"Is that possible after last night?" Cody joked.

"I'm serious." Lee sat up and rested her body on her right side so she could face him. "I'm part of Operation CROWLEY and am in charge of Project Samail because of my psychic ability, but if I had a chance to be normal, I would take it in a heartbeat."

"That's an interesting choice of words."

"What is?"

"Saying that you wish you were normal."

"I do. You of all people know what a curse having this ability can be." Lee closed her eyes as if trying to shut out bad memories. "I grew up in Norfolk in one of those small towns where everyone knows each other's business. I was about twelve when the dead started talking to me. At first, I thought it was nightmares, or I was going insane, until one of the dead explained it to me. The dead can sense people with my ability, and some of them who had once lived in town were trying to reach me to contact their relatives. At the time I was thirteen, open to new ideas and idealistic enough to want to help them out."

"Not everyone thought the way you did."

"No." Lee placed her head on Cody's chest. "When I tried to contact their relatives, nobody would believe me. Most people in town thought I was playing cruel jokes on those who had lost family members. The police investigated me, afraid I might be trying to swindle the relatives. None of the local kids would be my friend. Even worse, my parents didn't believe me. My father thought I was an unruly teenager trying to prank everyone, and every time I brought up the subject, he would slap me across the face and tell me to get my shit together. My mother thought I was nuts and had me admitted for psychiatric care when I was sixteen. The courts ordered me released when I was of age, but only because I had spent the last year telling the doctors I no longer heard voices. After that, I broke all contact with my family and moved to Manchester, figuring I'd be accepted in the city. I spent a year there being taken advantage of by people. I finally left Manchester and moved to London. I never told anyone here about my ability, but it didn't matter. My confidence had been shattered. I hopped around from job to job before finally joining the WAAF five years ago. The military gave me the self-assurance I needed. I was putting my life back in order when Bellingham pulled my file and drafted me into the occult war."

"I thought you volunteered for this assignment?"

"I did after a lot of cajoling on Bellingham's part."

"He can be persuasive."

"I know it's all for King and country, but I get tired of being a freak."

Cody winced. He had used that word during his first meeting with Bellingham, never realizing how painful it must have been for Lee to hear him say that. "I'm sorry when I used the term sideshow freak two weeks ago."

"Don't be. It's true."

"No, it isn't." Cody placed his hand on Lee's chin and lifted her head so he could make eye contact. "How much do you know about my past association with the supernatural?"

"Just that you're open-minded to the supernatural because your mother possessed psychic abilities similar to mine."

"Her abilities were a little more advanced. She could reach out into the nethersphere and seek out the dead. Like you, she had developed her abilities around twelve. She quickly learned that not everyone was accepting of her skills, so she kept her talent to herself and only used it in special cases, mostly when close friends whom she had trusted with her secret would bring a loved one to her who wanted to contact a deceased relative. My old man accepted it, though he never understood it. He was a banker. His world was all about economics and finance, so the supernatural never interested him.

"At least not until the Depression hit in 1929. In less than a month, we went from being middle class to living out of the back of our car. My old man couldn't find a job, I was thirteen and too young to work, and my brother was two years younger than me. The only skill my mother had was her psychic ability, so my old man hired her out to a carnival side show as a fortune teller. At first, she didn't mind. Like you, she tried to put a positive spin on the situation and hoped to use her skills to connect people with their relatives, maybe give them comfort since everyone's life had gone to Hell. Nobody in the Midwest wanted that. They wanted their fortunes told. When will I find a job? Will I find work if I move to California? Can you tell me which horse will win the Kentucky Derby? The asshole who ran the carnie made my mother go by the name Madame Divine and forced her to wear a turban when she performed. She made a lot of money, but it wasn't worth my mother becoming a circus freak."

Lee placed a hand on Cody's chest and patted him. "But

I'm sure she did that to make money so you and your brother could survive."

"She did, but we saw little of the money. My old man took it all and spent it on fancy clothes for himself and on entertaining his friends. 'We're in show business,' he used to say, 'so we have to keep up appearances.' Meanwhile, my brother and I ate our meals with the rest of the performers. I kept on trying to convince my mother to quit, telling her we could move to the coast where she could get a job as a psychic to the Hollywood stars, but she would only smile and call me a dreamer."

"What happened?"

"I ran away when I was sixteen. I figured I'd get a good job and then bring my mother and brother to join me so I could take care of them. You can imagine how that turned out. I spent three years begging and doing odd jobs before I finally joined the military. Once I got settled, I hunted down my mother and brother, but it was too late. Between being a carnie and my running away, my mother slipped into depression. Eventually, she gave up and passed on, not wanting to live any longer. My brother blamed it all on me and hasn't spoken to me since, not that I can blame him."

"What about your father?"

"I don't know what happened to him, and I don't care. When my mother died, he no longer had any income, and all his friends who he entertained had left him. My brother said he had gone off to Hollywood to break into the industry. I heard rumors a few years back he had become an alcoholic and was living in a flop house."

"I'm so sorry," said Lee. A tear ran down her cheek.

"Thanks, but don't be. The one thing I've learned is that nothing good can come out of these supernatural abilities, which is why I've avoided admitting to having any experience with them. The fact that Hitler is using the occult against us only proves my point."

"I hope you don't feel that way about me?"

"I wouldn't have spent last night here if I did."

Lee placed her head back on Cody's chest. "So, what happens now?"

"I don't know about you, but for me this is personal. The supernatural ruined my childhood and destroyed my family. If I can stop the Nazis from exploiting the occult, then maybe I can make some amends for leaving my mother as a teenager. And if I can turn the tables on the Nazis and make their lives Hell, then I'll have some payback for everything I went through as a child."

Lee chuckled. "That's how I feel... about getting some payback. I just never wanted to admit it. I thought it might make my look petty."

"There's nothing wrong with that." Cody patted Lee on the back. "And we're never going to make Hell for Hitler if we stay in bed much longer."

"I don't know." Lee rolled over on top of Cody and sat on his hips. "I don't think another thirty minutes will matter one way or another."

"Miss Harris," Cody joked. "I do believe you want to hinder the war effort."

"On the contrary," Lee responded, a seductive twinkle in her eyes. "I'm hoping to improve the morale of the troops."

CHAPTER TWENTY

Wewelsburg Castle, Germany
9 June 1941

DIETRICH AND LILITH arrived at Wewelsburg around noon after a morning flight out of Berlin. He was excited to hear that Winnie had made a breakthrough in her contact with Agrat, although he was aggravated over why Malalath wouldn't provide any details over the secure line. No matter. He had come to expect that, when dealing with succubi and humans with supernatural abilities, certain latitude needed to be shown to accommodate their quirks.

However, as the staff car pulled through the east gate into the courtyard and parked in the inner courtyard, Dietrich was not happy to see that only *Brigadeführer* Taubert and Malalath waited to greet them.

The *brigadeführer* greeted Dietrich. "*Obergruppenführer*, it's good to see you back here so soon."

"You're doing important work here," said Dietrich with a forced pleasantness.

Taubert snapped to attention at the compliment. "Thank you."

Lilith and Malalath hugged each other.

"Where is Winnie?" Dietrich asked. "I'm surprised she's not here to greet us."

"Yesterday's session tired her out more than usual, so I told her she could rest. She's waiting for you in the King Arthur Study Hall."

"We'll take it from here. Thank you."

Taubert saluted and moved to one aside as Dietrich and the succubi entered the castle.

When Dietrich entered the study hall, he was taken aback at how exhausted Winnie actually appeared. She slumped in her easy chair, her head lolled to one side and resting against the corner backrest. Winnie opened her eyes upon hearing them arrive. They looked tired and drained, with dark circles underneath the lids. She stood to greet him, clutching the armrests to support her weight.

"Sorry to be rude," she said.

Dietrich rushed forward and helped her sit back down. "Don't get up. Taubert told me your experience yesterday was tiring."

"It was, but we succeeded."

"*You* succeeded." Dietrich took one of the chairs against the wall and brought it over to Winnie, placing it in front of her. He sat down and leaned forward, resting his elbows on his knees. "Tell me what happened."

"I'd been channeling with Agrat for several days. The British are keeping her locked in a cage in a basement, so she's not able to provide us with any intelligence. Yesterday, while I was connected to her, the British woman wandered into the basement. I had Agrat touch her, and now I have a psychic link with the woman."

"Who is she?" asked Dietrich. "Who does she work for?"

"This woman has psychic capabilities similar to mine, so I haven't probed her mind yet. The only information I've been able to obtain came from those few times I've briefly channeled her since yesterday. Her name is Ashley Harris, although everyone calls her Lee. She's working with an American officer named Cody and some professor in a wheelchair who is an expert on the occult."

Dietrich frowned. This meant the British were farther along in their occult research than he or Himmler had thought. It also meant the Americans were showing an interest in their activities, which did not bode well. "How much do they actually know?"

"From what I can sense from this Lee woman, they're still in the dark about our efforts. They know about Lilith, Malalath, and Naamah."

"Is Naamah in any danger?" Lilith asked.

Winnie shook her head. "Agrat didn't tell them anything. All the British know is that you three are out there and pose a threat."

"They have no idea how much," mumbled Malalath.

Dietrich ignored her. "What else can you tell me about this woman?"

"That's it for now. I've only made contact with her three times since yesterday, and then only for a few moments before I tired out."

"Can you enter her thoughts and gather more information?" Dietrich asked.

"Yes, but there's a potential danger to doing that."

"What?"

"As I mentioned, this Lee woman has psychic capabilities similar to mine, though I'm not sure exactly what they are. I can sense the aura about her. If I try to probe her mind, she'll more than likely detect me."

"What will happen then?"

Winnie thought about the question for a moment. "The best-case scenario is that she'll shut me out, she'll close off her mind so I can't get access. At that point, we're right back where we started, only know the British will know we're actively working against them."

"And the worst-case scenario?" Lilith asked.

"If this Lee woman is any good, she could reverse mind probe me, and then she would know everything I do."

Dietrich leaned back into his chair. "We can't let that happen."

"There is another way that should work with much less

risk," said Winnie. "If I go in and just rest on her consciousness, like a fly on the wall, I should be able to see what she sees without her knowing I'm eavesdropping. If I do that while she's at a meeting, it'll be like I'm in the room with them. But it could take time. I can't channel her all the time without wearing myself out, four or five times a day for a few moments at a time. With luck, I'll be able to gather some useful information during one of those sessions."

"I need you to be honest with me," said Dietrich, locking his eyes on Winnie's. "What is the possibility Miss Harris is doing that same thing to you at this moment? While I'm talking with you, is she listening in on our conversation? Or even probing your mind without you realizing it?"

Winnie closed her eyes as she thought about her answer. Dietrich assumed she was scanning her own psyche for a British probe. After a few moments, she opened them again.

"It's possible, but highly improbable."

There's always a risk of having an intelligence operation being run against you, thought Dietrich. In this case, the risks were minimal. Even if the British successfully probed Winnie's thoughts and learned everything she knew, that would not give them much of an advantage. Winnie possessed no knowledge about the ultimate goal of Himmler's occult activities. She didn't even know the name of Naamah's target. The most information she could provide was the location and purpose of Wewelsburg Castle as well as some of the officers and psychics associated with it, most of which had probably been passed to the British already through informants and agents serving in Germany. This was one risk he felt worth taking.

"Keep up what you're doing," Dietrich told Winnie. "Don't take any unnecessary risks but, if an opportunity to gather intelligence arises, take advantage of it."

"I understand."

"Good. I'll talk to Taubert. If there's anything you need to make yourself more comfortable or to help in your recovery after a session, let him know and he'll provide it."

"Thank you," said Winnie.

"It's the least I can do considering what you're doing for the *Reich*." Dietrich stood, placed his chair back against the wall, and headed for the exit. Malalath opened the door for him and her sister. He glanced over his shoulder on his way out. "Let me know the moment you get anything that will be useful to us."

Malalath followed Dietrich and Lilith down the corridor. Once they were out of earshot, Dietrich stopped.

"I need you to do me a favor," he said to Malalath.

"What's that?"

"Keep a close eye on Winnie. If you think at any time the British have a psychic hold on her, or are running her against us, eliminate her."

CHAPTER TWENTY-ONE

SOE Headquarters, London, England
10 June 1941

BELLINGHAM READ LEE'S report for a second time as Lee and Cody sat across from his desk. For some reason, she seemed nervous, although Cody had no idea why. Nothing about Bellingham showed any emotion. The group captain flipped the pages one by one, studying each with a stoic expression. Finally, he closed the report and placed it on his desk.

"This is what happens when I go away," Bellingham said. "All the good stuff takes place."

"I don't know how good it is," said Lee. "I didn't get much out of Agrat."

"You actually got a lot more than you realized."

"It doesn't feel that way. I did a horrible job of questioning her."

"Don't be hard on yourself," Bellingham said in a fatherly tone. "You weren't talking to a downed *Luftwaffe* pilot. You were interrogating a succubus."

"It felt more like she was interrogating me."

"She was."

"And I gave up intelligence."

"You gave up information. More than I would have, but nothing the Germans don't already know or have surmised. Under the circumstances, you did well. Just be more careful in the future."

Lee visibly relaxed. "Thank you."

"What intelligence did we get?" Cody asked.

"For one thing, we know for certain that Himmler is actively using at least one psychic against us, although we have no clue about the extent of her capabilities. We can now take precautions against that type of espionage."

"And we learned that the SS is keeping Malalath in a castle in northern Germany," said Lee.

"That's more of a confirmation of prior intelligence." Bellingham stood up from his desk and crossed his office to a map of Germany hanging on the wall. He scanned it until he found the location and pointed to it. "We've been receiving reports from the underground for over eight months of unusual activity taking place at Wewelsburg Castle outside of Paderborn. Himmler has shown a special interest in this castle for years, although we're not certain why. From what little intelligence we've been able to piece together, the *Reichsführer* sees Wewelsburg as an SS version of Camelot, with him in the role of King Arthur."

"So that's the center of the Nazi's occult efforts?" Lee asked.

"At first we didn't think so," Bellingham replied. He walked back and took his seat behind the desk. "Initial intelligence described Wewelsburg as more of a research center for Germany's pagan roots and lost Aryan civilizations. That changed about three months ago when MI5 received a report from Berlin that Karl Vonnegut was claiming his work at Wewelsburg would eventually win Germany the war and ensure the Thousand-Year *Reich*."

"The same Vonnegut who arranged the meeting between Hitler and Steiner?" Cody asked.

"The same," said Bellingham. "We're also getting information that a special construction project is going on in the basement of the castle's north tower that has been green lighted by Hitler and has the highest authority with Himmler. Everything about this project is classified at the highest level.

From what we can tell, less than a dozen people inside Germany know its true purpose. There are a lot of good assets trying to find out what's going on at Wewelsburg, but so far, they've come up empty."

Bellingham paused for a moment. "Getting back to what Agrat provided us, she confirmed we're dealing with four succubi, which makes me more confident about the course of action we've taken."

"We still don't know where the other three are," said Cody.

"On the contrary. We know that Malalath is with the German psychic in Germany, so at the moment she poses no immediate threat." Bellingham picked up the report and thumbed through. "According to Lee, Agrat said 'Lilith is nearby.' Did Agrat give any indication whether she meant nearby her or nearby you?"

Lee shook her head. "That's exactly how she phrased it."

"Damn." Bellingham contemplated for a moment before closing the report and setting it down. "I would rather err on the side of caution and assume that Lilith is nearby us, so we'll need to take measures accordingly. What concerns me most is what Agrat said about Naamah being where she could do the most harm."

"That could be anywhere," said Cody, "from Buckingham Palace to Downing Street."

"What if she's somewhere in this building?" asked Lee.

Bellingham held up a hand. "We can speculate all night, but that's not going to help us. We know a succubus' spell can be broken and the demon contained. What we need to figure out is how to detect them. Once they take on human form, physically they're indistinguishable from humans. And if anyone becomes suspicious of them, the succubus glamours that person so they don't raise any alarms."

"But that only works on men, correct?" Cody asked.

"Yes."

"What about recruiting more women to Project Samail so

they can detect the succubi?"

"In theory that's a good idea," Bellingham admitted. "The problem is numbers. There are thousands of people they could be going after, and we would never be able to cover them all. It would only work if we could narrow down the list to a handful of potential targets."

"Maybe I should go back and talk with Agrat again," Lee offered.

"Good idea," said Bellingham. "But I'll do it."

"Didn't I do a good job?" Lee asked.

"You did, but that was a onetime deal. Agrat saw an opportunity and took it. I doubt she'll talk with you again. Hopefully, she'll be more open to matching wits with me."

"How will you prevent her from glamouring you?" Cody asked.

"Remember, her abilities are severely limited now that she's in her succubus form. Besides," Bellingham said with a grin, "you'll both be listening in to make sure I don't get into any trouble."

CHAPTER TWENTY-TWO

Lubyanka Prison, Dzerzhinsky Square, Moscow
10 June 1941

THE GAZ-M1 EMKA staff car passed through the Savior Tower and cut diagonally across Red Square, cruising past Lenin's Tomb and toward Gum Department Store. At the northeast corner of the Square, the driver turned onto Nikolskaya Street and accelerated. From the back seat, Levorov absentmindedly watched the city pass by, lost in his thoughts. What he was about to do was extraordinarily risky, so he had requisitioned a driver to ensure he would not be away from the Kremlin too long and hopefully would not be missed. It seemed unlikely anyone would notice. Stalin kept on dismissing him to be alone with Naamah. If anyone did ask where he had gone, Levorov could honestly reply he was taking measures to guarantee Stalin's personal safety. He would leave out the details, however, in case someone locked him up for being insane or shot him for treason. In truth, he had already resigned himself to the fact that either option would eventually be his fate.

Dark days lie ahead, and not only for Levorov. Stalin's inner circle felt war with Germany was imminent and the Soviet Union should be preparing to defend itself, or even strike first, yet no one could convince Stalin of this. He wouldn't even discuss the issue with them. Because of the climate of fear instilled over the last ten years, no one in the inner circle, not even Beria, had the courage to confront Stalin.

Levorov had lost considerable respect for Beria and the

others these past few days. It was their responsibility to advise Stalin and counsel him if they felt he made an error in judgment. Instead, since they had the most to lose, they chose not to take any action that might infuriate Stalin and threaten their position. Their cowardice meant Levorov would be the one who would have to put his life on the line for his country and, if he failed, would have to bear the consequences alone. It was the reason he had to proceed with such caution.

Ahead of him, Lubyanka Prison sat at the far end of Lubyanka Square. Built in 1898 as the main office for the All-Russia Insurance Company, it had been converted to NKVD headquarters in 1920. In twenty-one years, the building had become the most infamous and feared structure in the entire Soviet Union. A summons to appear before the NKVD at the prison rarely ended well, and few people consigned to the prison cells on the first floor ever saw freedom again.

The driver circled around the fountain located on the island in the center of the square and stopped by the building's main entrance. Levorov leaned forward.

"No need for you to come in. I'll only be a few minutes."

The driver physically relaxed. "Yes, comrade."

Levorov stepped out of the staff car, hoping he could generate that same fearful acquiescence with others.

Once inside Lubyanka Prison, Levorov found the file office of the Chief Directorate of Labor Camps and Colonies and entered. A counter sat five feet from the door, separating a small waiting area from the main part of the room which contained rows of shelves stacked with boxes and file folders. A young junior sergeant sat behind his desk in front of the center row of shelves, scribbling in a ledger.

"Yes?" The junior sergeant did not bother to glance up.

"Are you responsible for maintaining these files?"

The junior sergeant raised his head. Upon seeing the senior lieutenant glaring at him, he snapped to attention, knocking over the chair he had been sitting on.

"Sorry, comrade."

Good, thought Levorov. *He's intimidated. It'll make him easier to manipulate.* "Are you responsible for maintaining these files?"

"I am."

"And you have the authority to access them if necessary?"

"Yes."

"Good. I need your assistance."

The junior sergeant rushed from behind his desk over to the counter. "How can I be of help?"

"I'm dealing with a highly delicate security situation that must be kept strictly confidential." As he talked, Levorov removed his credentials from his jacket pocket and presented them to the junior sergeant. The junior sergeant's eyes widened. "You understand the importance of not confiding this information to anyone else, including your superiors?"

"Of course, comrade."

"Good." Levorov closed his credentials, slid them back in his jacket, and removed a sheet of paper which he unfolded and handed to the junior sergeant. "I'm looking for someone with a specific set of skills that are unusual and rare. I'm sure the best place to find such a person would be in the gulag system."

The junior sergeant took the sheet of paper and read it. His eyelids scrunched. "Are you serious?"

"Are you questioning me?" asked Levorov with a carefully planned balance of anger and intimidation in his tone.

"No!" The junior sergeant went white. "I'm... it's just I've never even heard of these skills before."

"Didn't I say it was unusual and rare?"

"Yes, y-you did."

"Will you be able to find such a person listed in your files?"

The junior sergeant thought about it. "As long as this skill set is listed in the person's records, I should be able to. When do you need this information?"

"That's the problem. I need it now."

Fear morphed into panic. "Comrade, t-there's no way I can get this information that quick."

"Have I chosen the wrong man for this job?"

"I can do this. Please realize this is a specific requirement that few people have, and there are tens of thousands of files to go through. And that's assuming the recording officer even listed such a thing. I'll work as fast as I can, but it'll take some time."

"Then I'll leave so you can get to work."

"Thank you, comrade."

Levorov turned to leave and then paused. "One more thing. For obvious security reasons, you realize there can be no written or phone record of what we discussed."

"Yes, comrade."

"Good. When you find someone, please bring their file personally to my office at the Kremlin. Is that clear?"

"Of course, comrade."

Levorov exited the office. As he closed the door, out of the corner of his eye he saw the junior sergeant lean against the counter and exhale. Levorov knew he would have no problems with this one.

UNFORTUNATELY, THE SAME could not be said of the Red Army colonel who waited outside Levorov's office when he got back to the Kremlin fifteen minutes later. He sat in a chair by the door, an angry expression on his pocked, stern face. The colonel jumped up when he saw Levorov approaching. His entire demeanor pegged him as a bully who was used to getting his way.

"Are you Senior Lieutenant Levorov?" the colonel demanded.

"I am."

"What is the meaning of this?" The colonel held up a piece

of paper and shook it. Levorov recognized it as the requisition for specific small arms he had submitted.

"I didn't catch your name."

"Excuse me?" asked the colonel.

"In the NKVD we like to know who we're talking to."

"I'm Colonel Tukarov. And I want to know—"

"Let's discuss this in my office." Levorov tried not to smile as Tukarov went livid. He opened the door and ushered the colonel into his office.

Levorov had barely closed the door when Tukarov waved the paper in the air again. "I want to know what this is."

"That's an acquisition request for certain military items," Levorov said as he crossed over to his desk and sat down.

"Don't you get smart with me, you little shit. Why does a bodyguard detachment need weapons like this?"

"My job is to ensure Stalin's safety. Considering the nature of the threats we face, I feel these weapons will allow me to do my job more effectively."

"What threats do you face?" Tukarov demanded.

"I'm sorry, but that type of information is on a need-to-know basis."

Tukarov snorted with derision. "You're something else."

"What am I?" asked Levorov, purposefully trying to goad the colonel.

"You're a senior lieutenant, and I don't take orders from lower ranking officers."

"I understand."

"Good," Tukarov replied smugly.

Levorov picked up the receiver of his telephone. "Please get me Marshal Stalin's office."

"What are you doing?" asked Tukarov.

"You said you don't take orders from lower ranking officers, and I respect the chain of command. I'm giving you the chance to explain to Stalin why you feel the Red Army needs these weapons more than his personal security service."

Levorov turned his attention to the phone. "Yes, this is Senior Lieutenant Levorov. Is Marshal Stalin available?"

"Wait!"

Levorov made eye contact with Tukarov and lifted his brows.

"I can arrange to get you everything you requested."

"Cancel this call, please." Levorov replaced the phone in its receiver, and then focused on Tukarov. "I expect everything on that list to be delivered to my office within the next twenty-four hours. I would also like some of your men to train mine in their usage. Can that be done, colonel?"

"I can do that."

"That'll be all." Levorov waited until Tukarov was halfway out the door before calling out. "One more thing."

"Yes?"

"I'm busy trying to protect Stalin from his enemies, both external and those within the party and the government. I assume you will take care of everything and will not have to bother me again."

"I will."

"That will be all, *colonel*."

As the door closed shut, Levorov allowed himself a grin of satisfaction. He enjoyed putting that pompous ass in his place. Tukarov did not seem like the type who would take such action lightly, but he would be compliant for the next few days and would get Levorov the weapons he requested. After that, it was fifty-fifty whether the colonel would suck up the insult to his pride or would try and make Levorov's life miserable. Not that it mattered. Hopefully, Levorov would have this situation resolved soon.

CHAPTER TWENTY-THREE

SOE Headquarters, London, England
11 June 1941

"ARE YOU READY?" Bellingham asked Curtis.

"As ready as I'll ever be," Curtis replied.

Bellingham spoke into the microphone he held in his hand. "Lee, Cody. Can you hear me okay?"

"We can hear you fine," Cody's voice came through the headphones draped around Curtis' neck.

"Is the recording device ready to go?"

"Yes."

"Hit the record button when I tell you to and then listen in. If you have any questions you want relayed, pass them to Curtis and he'll ask them. Lee, let me know if you get any readings off her."

"Yes, sir," Lee said through the headphones.

"Let's do this."

Bellingham and Curtis exited the latter's office and walked over to Agrat's cage. A microphone stand had already been placed three feet from the bars, and a chair three feet beyond that. Bellingham attached the microphone to the stand. A stirring came from the shadows in the rear of the cage.

"What do you want, human?"

"I want to talk."

The succubus' upper body emerged from the shadows. "Is that a microphone?"

"It is." Bellingham leaned closer to the microphone. "Begin recording." The group captain looked at his watch. "Conversation with the succubus Agrat, London, 9:30 AM, 11 June 1941. Group Captain Cedric Bellingham and Dr. Curtis Brown residing."

What passed for a grin distorted Agrat's reptilian features. "Am I going to be on the BBC?"

"Sorry to disappoint you." Bellingham sat down in the chair as Curtis pulled up alongside him. "I want to talk, that's all."

"I prefer to talk with the woman."

"Why?"

"She's more malleable."

"You mean inexperienced?"

"I mean she was weak. I enjoyed toying with her." Agrat emerged from the shadows and slithered over to the lit end of the cage.

Bellingham sensed her trying to glamour him as images of his dead wife flowed into his mind. The group captain focused his thoughts on his hatred for the creature in front of him, and the visions faded.

Agrat hunched down and studied Bellingham. "Your will is strong. I like that. You'd make a worthy adversary."

"Then why don't you talk to me?"

"She had something to offer. She was willing to trade information for answers." Agrat headed back to the shadows of her cage. "You, on the other hand, will offer me nothing."

"Will you answer one question?"

Agrat paused, thought for a moment, and then slinked back toward Bellingham. "You may ask it."

"One thing seems so out of place to me. You were sent to glamour General Wavell, and Naamah has her own target she is currently working against. Why not use Lilith and Malalath? That seems like such a waste of resources. Unless they've already succeeded in glamouring their targets, or their mission is still to come."

"You are good. The weakling never picked up on that."

Agrat paused. "What will you give me for the answer?"

"I won't give you anything."

"Then why should I answer?"

Bellingham chose his words carefully. "The souls of twenty-five million people are at stake."

Agrat tilted her head and stared at Bellingham. "Do you really think that concerns me? Those souls are part of a business arrangement between my Master and Hitler. I'll make a deal with you. I will tell you everything you want to know about the arrangement between my master and Hitler—how those twenty-five million souls will be provided, the ceremony that will take place to ensure Hitler's Thousand-Year *Reich*, every detail you want—on one condition."

"What's that?" Bellingham asked cautiously.

Agrat leaned forward, her black eyes focusing on Curtis. "I want his life."

"Stop wasting my time," snapped Bellingham.

"I'm not wasting your time. I'm serious. I'll tell you everything in return for one life. It doesn't have to be the doctor. How about one of those soldiers guarding me? What do their lives mean to you? I bet you don't even know their names."

Bellingham glanced over his shoulder at the two guards. One had gone pale from fear, and the other had wrapped his finger around the trigger of his weapon.

"You don't want to give up one of your precious British soldiers? Then give me Hess. He's now considered a war criminal by both sides. Or any German soldier you're holding as a POW. I'm not particular."

Bellingham stood up and yelled. "I've had enough of this!"

"Of course you have, Englishman." Agrat laughed, an evil sound that seemed more like a hiss. The laughter died off as suddenly as it began. She moved toward the edge of the cage, only now her voice sounded menacing. "You've had enough because you are all weak and pitiful. I offered to give you all the information you needed to stop my Master and Hitler from creating a Thousand-Year *Reich* for the price of one human soul, and you turned me down. Hitler has the strength of his will, which is why we are helping him to succeed. All you have is your humanity." Agrat spat the last word. "Your humanity will be your downfall."

For a moment Bellingham felt as though he had been punched in the gut. Not only because Agrat had outwitted him, but because she had pointed out the glaring truth. The Allies were in a war against evil and would need to up their game if they hoped to win.

"I see I struck a nerve," Agrat cooed.

Bellingham said nothing.

"I have nothing more to talk about." Agrat slithered away, pausing halfway across her cage. "That deal I offered is no longer on the table. You'll have to find a way to stop Hitler on your own."

As Agrat disappeared into the shadows, Bellingham stepped over to the microphone. "End recording."

Without another word, he departed the basement.

LEE AND CODY sat in an anteroom near the stairwell leading to the basement where the recording device had been set up. Per their previous arrangement, Lee closely followed the conversation for cues to pass along to Bellingham while Cody made certain the taping of the conversation went well.

Lee listened in as Bellingham provided the introduction to the recording.

"Am I going to be on the BBC?"

"Sorry to disappoint you. I want to talk, that's all."

"I prefer to talk with the woman."

"Why?"

"She's more malleable."

"You mean inexperienced?"

"I mean she was weak. I enjoyed toying with her."

Lee winced. She had been weak when talking with Agrat and had let the bitch get the better of her. Even though Bellingham had comforted her and told her not to worry about it, they both knew she had compromised information for little in return.

Cody reached out, placed his hand over hers, and lightly squeezed. The comfort of his touch felt good, although it did little to assuage her feeling of inadequacy. She forced a smile and continued listening in the conversation.

During the portion when Bellingham asked Agrat his question about Lilith and Malalath, Lee developed a slight headache and a wave of dizziness washed over her. It lasted only a moment, yet it occurred long enough for Cody to notice. He placed his hand over the microphone in front of her and whispered in her ear, "Are you alright?"

Lee nodded. "I'm over tired. I've been getting them a lot lately. I'll be fine."

Blocking out the discomfort, Lee concentrated on the conversation.

"I've had enough of this."

"Of course you have, Englishman. You've had enough because you are all weak and pitiful. I offered to give you all the information you needed to stop my Master and Hitler from creating a Thousand-Year Reich for the price of one human soul, and you turned me down. Hitler has the strength of his will, which is why we are helping him to succeed. All you have is your humanity. Your humanity will be your downfall."

"Dear God," Lee gasped.

"What is it?" asked Cody, his concern evident in his tone.

"Agrat is right. We don't have the strength of will as do the Nazis."

"Don't say that. We'll beat them."

"We won't be able to defeat them unless we become as inhumane as they are. And if we do, then what good is victory?" Lee had a tear in her eye. "We're facing the downfall of humanity."

Cody turned in his chair to face Lee and placed one hand on each shoulder. "What's gotten into you?"

Anger, fear, and disappointment in her behavior threatened to overwhelm Lee. Then, as quickly as these emotions raged, they subsided. The headache and dizziness cleared up. She shook her head to clear it.

"Sorry. I have no idea what got into me."

"Are you alright?"

"I am now." Her eyes expressed tenderness for Cody.

"You need some rest. I'll take you back to your apartment."

"Okay. You're probably right." Lee stood up and removed the headphones. "First, let's check on Bellingham."

CHAPTER TWENTY-FOUR

Wewelsburg Castle, Germany
11 June 1941

WINNIE AND MALALATH entered the King Arthur Study Hall. Winnie sat at the table while Malalath slid into the comfortable chair against the far wall.

"How many times is this?" the succubus asked, making no attempt to hide her irritation.

"This will be the eighth time channeling with her, not counting the initial contact."

"And you've not been able to connect so far?"

"I've connected every time," said Winnie. "I've just not been able to gather anything useful."

"I don't see why we keep wasting our time."

"We'll never succeed if we don't try."

Malalath shrugged off the answer and leaned back in her chair to rest, which suited Winnie. She did not want or need to explain herself. The psychic process could not be changed to suite Malalath's fancy. Because of the physical connection made between the British woman and Agrat while Winnie was linked to the latter, she now had a psychic bond to the British woman she could exploit at any time. However, because of the British woman's own psychic ability, it was not as simple as Winnie had originally predicted to attach herself to the woman's psyche and telepathically observe. Every time Winnie connected, it caused the British woman a mild headache and dizziness. Thankfully, she had not figured out yet that these symptoms were the equivalent of psychic welcome chime.

Winnie had to be especially careful to mask her presence, which drained her energy more quickly.

Placing her hands palm down on the table, Winnie closed her eyes and lowered her head. She concentrated on a quiet spot in the nethersphere, focusing on that location and allowing her mind to drain of all other thoughts and emotions. Once her mind was clear, she traveled from the quiet spot and narrowed her vision down to Europe, then England, and then London. Winnie formed a mental image of the British woman. The psychic energy directed her toward the woman's aura, like a river flowing along its banks, until the two were linked. Winnie sensed the woman's physical discomfort over the connection. Her lover was nearby, reaching out a reassuring hand. Winnie sat on her conscious, a telepathic voyeur.

The British woman was listening in on a conversation between Agrat and her boss whose name was Belford or Bellham or something like that. He had been asking about whom Lilith and Malalath had been targeted against, and Agrat had turned the conversation around, taunting the British that they would lose the war because their humanity prevented them from confronting the evil of Nazism. However, Winnie found it hard to maintain focus on what the two said because the British woman's aura interfered.

She switched her focus back on the woman. The disturbing aura came from the woman's intense emotions, the most prevalent being fear. Winnie found it hard to maintain contact, at least not without tightening her psychic hold, which would have alerted the woman to her presence. The disturbed aura bucked off Winnie's psyche, and she came crashing back into reality. Winnie bolted upright at the table and gasped.

Malalath jumped out of the easy chair and rushed over. "Are you okay?"

Winnie nodded. "The connection was broken before I was ready."

"What happened?"

"The British woman was listening in on a conversation between her boss and Agrat. Agrat was taunting him, telling him the British would lose the war because their humanity would prevent them from doing what was necessary to defeat Hitler."

Malalath grinned. "That sounds like my sister. Then what happened?"

"I don't know. The British woman became upset because she thought Agrat was right. It was that display of intense emotion that broke the bond."

"Can you reconnect?"

Winnie shook her head. "Not without resting for a bit."

"That's okay." Malalath rubbed Winnie's shoulder in an uncharacteristic gesture of kindness. "It's good to know my sister is still alive. Thank you."

"You're welcome."

"It's also good to know that the British are scared. Maybe they'll realize they can't win and get out of this war while they can."

Winnie nodded half-heartedly. The truth was she empathized with the British woman's fear that the Allies wouldn't be able to defeat Germany unless they become as inhumane as the Nazis. She harbored the same fear.

CHAPTER TWENTY-FIVE

Wewelsburg Castle, Germany
12 June 1941

A S THE STAFF car raced across the countryside for Wewelsburg, Himmler leaned to one side to look out the window at the castle on the cliffs above him. Wewelsburg Castle was symbolic of Germany. In 1933, both were once shadows of their former selves, with the rest of the world thinking their greatness had long since passed. Both had been rebuilt by National Socialism until the castle towered over the surrounding area and Germany dominated the rest of Europe. Soon, both would be the epicenter of a new millennium of greatness, the castle the center of his SS Camelot, the pinnacle of his achievements as SS *Reichsführer*, and Germany the center of a Thousand-Year *Reich*.

"You must be happy today," said SS *Obergruppenführer* Reinhard Heydrich, who sat beside Himmler.

Over the years, Heydrich had rapidly risen through the ranks to become the second most powerful figure in the SS and Himmler's right-hand man. The two men complimented each other perfectly. Heydrich was the man of action, the key to implementing the policies put into place by Himmler. Heydrich hated speaking in public because it made him uncomfortable, and preferred to work behind the scenes, letting Himmler be the public face of the SS. Even in looks they contrasted sharply, with Heydrich appearing as the quintessential Aryan SS officer—tall, blond hair, piercing blue eyes, and with an angular, chiseled face with a dueling scare on his cheek. What made them an effective team was their total commitment to Hitler, to the *Reich*, and to Operation STEI-NER.

"Why do you say I'm happy?" Himmler asked.

"We're about to fulfill everything we've been working toward these past twenty years."

"You're overly optimistic, but I appreciate your enthusiasm. We have a long road ahead of us, and we're going to run into setbacks."

"That's all they'll be is setbacks." Heydrich beamed with confidence. "In ten days, we put Barbarossa into play and are going to achieve everything the *Führer* has strived for—*Lebensraum*, the defeat of Bolshevism, and, after we provide twenty-five million souls, the assurance of a Thousand-Year *Reich*."

Himmler turned back toward Wewelsburg Castle, his eyes focusing on the North Tower. Heydrich was right. They were on the verge of greatness, of accomplishing what no one else in history had been able to. He should be proud of what they had achieved so far.

As their staff car pulled through the east gate into the inner courtyard, Himmler noticed ten more cars parked along the walls. Hopefully, the other participants in the conference had arrived. *Brigadeführer* Taubert stood in the center of the courtyard, stepping over to greet his guests as they disembarked.

"It's good to see you again *Reichsführer*, *Obergruppenführer*. It's been a while."

"It has," said Himmler. "Is everyone else here?"

"Yes. They're waiting in the *Obergruppenführersaal*. Follow me."

Heading to the opposite end of the courtyard, the three men passed through the door of the North Tower and entered the *Obergruppenführersaal*, the meeting hall for the highest-ranking members of the SS. The circular hall took up the entire first floor of the tower. Twelve columns rose from the floor's periphery, connecting to a groined vault ceiling. Eight windows, each half the height of the hall itself, sat in the recessed walls between the northernmost columns, allowing in enough sunlight that little artificial illumination was needed. Imbedded in the center of the white and gray marble floor was the twelve-spoked sun wheel, or *Sonnenrad*, laid out in dark green marble squares. It symbolized that the North Tower one day would be the center of the New German Empire.

Around the hall, the eleven SS *obergruppenführers* Himmler had called to attend this three-day conference in preparation for Operation BARBAROSSA socialized with one another. These were the officers designated to carry out the administrative policies in the East that would ensure Himmler was able to provide twenty-five million souls for the *Führer*: SS *Obergruppenführer* Karl Wolff, head of the *Personliche Stab* SS *Reichsführer*, Himmler's personal adjutant; SS *Obergruppenführer* Ulrich Greifelt, *Reichskommissar fur die Festigung Deutschen Volkstums (Reich* Commissioner for the Consolidation of German Nationhood), who would be instrumental in the planning and implementation of population relocation to allow for German colonization of Central and East Europe; SS *Obergruppenführer* Richard Hildebrandt, head of the *Rasse– und Siedlungshauptamt (RuSHA)* (SS Race and Settlement Main Office), who would oversee the forced evacuation and resettlement of the Slavic and Russian population in occupied territories as well as their utilization as slave labor; SS *Obergruppenführer* Werner Lorenz, head of the *Hauptamt Volksdeutsch Mittelstelle (VoMi)* (Main Office for the Welfare of Ethnic Germans), who would be responsible for the resettlement of ethnic Germans in the occupied territories and the Germanization of foreign children with Aryan features; SS *Obergruppenführer* Oswald Pohl, chief of both the SS *Hauptamt Verwaltung und Wirtschaft* (Main Office for Administration and Economy) and the Ministry of the Interior's *Hauptamt Haushalt und Bauten* (Main Office for Budget and Construction), who oversaw the organization of the concentration camps, including the distribution of detainees to each facility and the use of detainees for slave labor; SS *Obergruppenführer* Gottlob Berger, head of the SS *Hauptamt* (SS Main Office), the "father" of the *Waffen SS* responsible for implementing the force's recruiting structures and policies; SS *Obergruppenführer* Franz Breithaupt, head of the *SS Hauptamt–Gericht* (SS Main Office–Courts), who oversaw the formulation of the laws and codes for the SS and police groups, as well as the administration of the SS and Police Courts and penal systems; SS *Obergruppenführer* Maximillian von Herff, head of the SS *Hauptamt—Personnel* (SS Main Office— Personnel), the central recording office for all officers and potential officers in the SS; SS *Gruppenführer* Erich von dem Bach–Zelewski, *Hohere SS und Polizeiführer* (Higher SS and Police Leader) for Army Group Centre, who in the coming BARBA-ROSSA campaign would serve as HSSPF in the territory of Belarus, extending to the Ural Mountains; SS *Obergruppenführer* August Heissmeyer, head of the SS *Heissmeyeramt*, the office responsible for general inspections of the SS *Totenkopf;* and SS *Oberstgruppenführer* Kurt Daluege, head of the *Ordungspolizei* (*Orpo*), who possessed administrative, though not executive, authority over most of the uniformed police in Germany.

Upon seeing Himmler enter, the eleven SS *obergruppenführers* snapped to attention, extended their arms, and saluted *"Heil* Hitler." Himmler and Heydrich returned the salute and then mingled with the others, engaging in idle chatter and small talk. After several minutes, Taubert announced to the *Reichsführer* that everything was ready. Himmler led the way to the castle's west wing where the Great Hall, the meeting hall of the SS elite, was located. As the others took their seats at the conference table in the twelve leather-backed chairs emblazoned with SS runes and intertwined swastika motifs on the oak frames, Himmler took his position by a podium set up near the far end of the table. He waited for everyone to settle down before speaking.

"Gentlemen, we're about to launch the greatest undertaking in German history, if indeed not in all of history. The *Führer* has signed an order approving the invasion of the Soviet Union to begin on 22 June. The defeat of Bolshevism, one of the greatest enemies of National Socialism, is at hand."

A murmur of excitement made its way through the hall. Himmler allowed it for several seconds before continuing. "The *Wehrmacht* has been planning Operation BARBAROSSA since late last year and has incorporated five divisions of the *Waffen SS* into its three army groups. There are also four *Einsatzgruppen* that will follow the army groups and undertake special actions in the occupied territories."

"Excuse me," interrupted SS *Obergruppenführer* Greifelt. "What are the *Einsatzgruppen?*"

"They're paramilitary organizations under the command of the SS," said Heydrich. "Its members are recruited from the *Waffen SS*, the security services, and various police units. Four groups will be going into the Soviet Union, one assigned to each army group, with the fourth being allocated to 11th Army for operations in the southern Ukraine, the Crimea, and the Caucasus. Each group is tasked with mopping up the occupied territories behind the front lines, including the seizure of Communist Party offices and papers, the liquidation of Commissars and higher cadres, and the elimination of the Jews."

"Thank you," said Greifelt.

"Unfortunately," said Himmler, "none of us will be sharing in the glory of the *Einsatzgruppen* or the *Waffen SS*. Your task will be much more mundane. But as bureaucrats, you're used to that."

A wave of chuckling washed through the hall.

"Your task is much more important. Over the next three days, you are to develop the plans that will allow Germany to implement the *Lebensraum* policy put into place by Adolf Hitler. I'm not referring to a simple colonization that will allow us to exploit the natural resources of Central and East Europe. Starting in Russia, we will transform the East into German territory and make it part of a greater *Reich*. In order to achieve this goal, we are going to have to cleanse the East of its non-Aryan influences.

"With regards to Russia, Ukraine, and Belarus, once these regions have been purged of Bolsheviks, Jews, and the intelligentsia, the remaining population will be utilized as slave labor to run the farms that will feed Germany. Unfortunately, we will have to maintain this population for up to twenty years until farming in the region can be fully mechanized. So as not to drain vital resources, this population will be provided with only the barest minimum to survive. We will not waste education, medicine, or shelter on them. I will consider it a criminal offense and will hold the responsible official to account if one German goes hungry because we are feeding our slave labor. Remember, once our farms in the east are automated and self-sufficient, this segment of the population will be eliminated, so it would be a sin to squander resources on them now.

"The same holds true for the populations of Poland and the Czech region. Although they are not racially Slavic, and thus are more acceptable, they are of even less use to the *Reich* because they are not good laborers. These people we must treat with greater care because of centuries of breeding between them and Aryans. We should carefully comb through the Polish and Czech populations, searching for those who have more valuable racial qualities and Germanize them into the *Reich*. The remainder can be resettled in Siberia. Make no mistake, though. Those that cannot be Germanized or resettled must be eliminated."

Himmler paused for dramatic effect. When he resumed, he spoke slowly and deliberately, making eye contact with each officer seated at the table.

"We all remember what happened when the Jews and the intellectuals snatched defeat out of the jaws of victory in 1918 and cost us the last war, and how the Bolsheviks drooled over our crippled carcass. Our nation barely survived that betrayal. If we fail this time, the Jews, the Bolsheviks, and the capitalists in the west will tear Germany apart, leaving nothing left to rise from the ashes.

"I realize full well that I'm calling for the decimation of the Slavic race by thirty million. None of us can take any pleasure in that. But what we are about to undertake is not cruelty for cruelty's sake. It is not easy to put down a sick horse that can no longer till a field or euthanize a child that is mentally impaired and a strain on society. Those are difficult decisions that must be made. These are the same type of decisions we are about to make, although on a larger scale. We cannot let sympathy get in the way of our duty. Each and every one of us in this room has a responsibility that is far greater than our own personal desires or ambitions, and that is to ensure the prosperity, the very survival of the *Reich*. We must be tough, even if it goes against our nature. We must be resolute, even if we know what we're doing may not be understood by our wives, families, and friends back home. That is the reason we are all here. And I know every one of you will do what is required of him for the fatherland and for the *Führer*. Thank you."

With the meeting over, the SS officers retired back to the *Obergruppenführersaal* to discuss their roles in BARBAROSSA and how they could coordinate with one another to achieve their aims. After five minutes of making small talk, Himmler noticed Heydrich standing by one of the long windows, switching his attention from the view outside to those mingling around inside the hall, all the while nursing along a glass of wine. Himmler strolled over to check on his deputy.

"You seem pensive," said Himmler.

"I'm remembering this moment. It's not often you get to witness history being made."

"We've been making history for decades."

"Not to this extent," Heydrich replied, his tone philosophical. "This is one of those key moments in time, like the fall of Rome to the Visigoths or the edification of Muhammad, which will impact mankind for more than a Thousand-Years. And we're key players in the event."

"You find that humbling?"

"I find it invigorating." Heydrich beamed with confidence. "Someday, people from around the world will come here, like they do to Jerusalem and Mecca, to see where it all began."

Himmler nodded. Heydrich was right. They were living in a key moment… no, they were *making* a key moment in history, and he should take a few moments to bask in the event. Then the realization struck him, and he turned to his deputy.

"You haven't seen the vault yet, have you?"

"Not in its final form. The contractors hadn't finished their renovations last time I was here."

"Come with me."

Himmler placed his glass of wine on a serving table and crossed the hall, with Heydrich close behind. They exited the *Obergruppenführersaal* into the stairwell, descended one level to the basement, and entered the castles' Valhalla, or Realm of the Dead.

At first glance, the basement seemed nothing more than the stone cistern which was the room's original use. However, on closer look, it was obvious the vault had been remodeled to resemble a Mycenaean-domed tomb with twelve pedestals placed equidistant along the wall. A shallow sunken circle dominated the center of the floor and, in its center, a circular depression two feet in diameter and a few inches in depth. A two-tier rim with four small pedestals on the east, west, and north positions enclosed the depression. Directly above the circular depression at the apex of the curved roof, and directly beneath the center point of the *Obergruppenführersaal*, another version of the *Sonnenrad* had been carved into the stone. Three small windows located high in the walls, with the panes slanted down through the three-foot thick stone walls, provided minimal lighting. The only illumination came from a series of low-watt light bulbs positioned above each pedestal.

Himmler stepped over to the sunken circle. "Can you believe it? This is where it will all take place. This is where the *Führer* will inaugurate the Thousand-Year *Reich*."

Heydrich stepped over to one of the pedestals. "And this is where you and I will participate?"

"Yes."

"It's a shame we have to share such an honor with those bureaucrats upstairs."

"I don't intend to let them share in the glory."

"Really?" Intrigue twinkled in Heydrich's eyes.

"The honor to be around for the duration of the millennium should belong to those who worked hardest to bring it about. Besides you, me, and Deitrich, only the eight SS officers who generate the highest body counts will be included."

"What about Vonnegut?"

"That half-Jew?" Himmler practically spat the words. "I'd shoot myself before I would ever allow him to soil the Realm of the Dead."

Heydrich circled the hall before stopping beside Himmler in front of the depression. "Not that I care, but you know they will call us sadists for carrying out what we have to do to ensure victory?"

"Two of three generations from the losing side may do that," Himmler responded. "After that, once the world realizes we made the choices too difficult for weaker nations to make, then we'll be hailed as warriors. By the time the *Reich* comes to an end in a Thousand-Years, no one will even remember what happened here today."

CHAPTER TWENTY-SIX

**St. James Park, London, England
15 June 1941**

B ELLINGHAM STROLLED THROUGH St. James's Park on his
way to meet Prime Minister Churchill. Although it was a
two-mile walk from SOE Headquarters to the Cabinet's
underground war rooms, the distance did not bother him.
When the weather was good, he enjoyed the walk. Bellingham
always took the long route that swung by Hyde Park and
Buckingham Palace Garden before cutting through the center
of St. James's Park. God knows he could use the exercise and
fresh air. More importantly, this walk gave him some solitude,
providing the time he needed to clear his head and recharge his
social battery. He needed it this morning because the news he
had to share would not please Churchill.

Exiting the east end of St. James's Park, Bellingham crossed
Horse Guards Road and entered the Government Offices
building, otherwise known as the Number 10 Annex ever since
Churchill moved his residence and War Cabinet to the more
secure location during the Blitz. Ahead of him stood the guard
post protecting the prime minister's private residence and
office, with a Royal Marine on sentry duty and an RAF first
lieutenant waiting patiently. Both men snapped to attention
when they spotted Bellingham.

"Good morning, Group Captain," said the first lieutenant
as he saluted.

"Morning." Bellingham returned the salute. "I assume the
Prime Minister is below today?"

"Yes, sir. The Cabinet meeting ran long this morning. He's down there now reading the overnight intercepts. If you'll follow me, please."

Passing through the sliding steel door built into the blast wall opposite the sentry position, the two men descended the stairs into the basement. Bellingham hated coming down here. The atmosphere was dank and claustrophobic, the lighting poor, and the air heavy with must, cigarette smoke, and body odor. It reminded him of a tomb. As restrictive as he found his own office, this underground complex made him uncomfortable. He was grateful that he had not needed to visit the prime minister during an air raid because he knew he would rather take his chances topside with the bombs rather than sit it out down here.

The two men entered a steel door marked 65 Map Room, the nerve center of the complex. Half a dozen duty officers representing every branch of the armed forces sat along two long tables dominating the southern half of the room. An elevated platform ran between the two tables on which sat the colored telephones with flashing lights rather than ringers that connected the Map Room to the various services and other key locations. The entire southern wall was taken up by a world map on which the duty officers plotted the position of British convoys and surface vessels. Off to the right was a door that led to Churchill's quarters. The first lieutenant knocked on it.

"Yes?" asked a gruff voice from the other side.

"Group Captain Bellingham is here to see you."

"Send him in."

The first lieutenant opened the door and Bellingham stepped inside. The prime minister's room was even more claustrophobic than the rest of the complex, barely large enough to hold his single bed, small desk and chair, and serving table. The already minimal space was further restricted by the four cement support columns and wooden rafters that occupied the center area. The only features that signified this room as belonging to the most powerful man in the Empire rather than the cell for a prisoner were the war maps pinned to the walls and the smell of cigar smoke and scotch that hung in the air.

Churchill sat behind his desk reading a classified document. When Bellingham entered, he waved over the group captain and pointed to an easy chair whose fabric was frayed along the edges.

"Have a seat."

"Thank you, Prime Minister."

Churchill placed the document on his desk. "So, what is the status of our occult war? I hope we're doing better on that front than in North Africa."

"No major victories, but we're making progress. We got Agrat to talk. She's cagey, but she did let slip some information that either confirmed or filled in gaps in our intelligence."

"But she didn't provide any new information?"

"No, sir."

Churchill frowned. "What did she give you?"

"We've been able to confirm that there are three more succubi besides Agrat. One is still in Germany, we don't know the location of the second, and the third is in a place, and I quote, where she can do the most harm."

"Where she can do the most harm?" asked Churchill. "That could be anywhere."

"I know. We tried to get her to tell us more, but she took great pleasure in being cryptic. We've been trying to figure out an effective way to unearth the third succubus so we don't have any more incidents like with General Wavell."

"That's not what I'm worried about. I can replace a commander or a cabinet minister who's not performing well. Internally it's a major concern, but not a crisis." Churchill stood up and crossed over to the world map pinned to the wall opposite his desk, staring at it intently. "My fear is over the influence she can assert with people I have no control over."

"I assume you're referring to President Roosevelt."

Churchill turned to the group captain and nodded. "You know as well as anyone that England is hanging on by its fingertips. And even though I'm stuck in this bunker, that doesn't mean I have my head in the sand. I know there are powerful figures in the government and the royal family who feel I'm leading the Empire to destruction, and who want to replace me with Lloyd George so they can negotiate a peace accord with Berlin. Unless America gets into the war or Hitler screws up in a major way, we may not be able to hold out much longer. If that missing succubus has glamoured Roosevelt or one of his advisers and is using her influence to keep America out of this war, then we may have already lost."

"Granted that would be the worst-case scenario," said Bellingham. "But I don't think we have to worry about that."

"Why is that?"

"If Roosevelt or one of his advisers was being influenced by a succubus, the president would not have sent Major Williams to help us."

"Good point." Churchill returned to his desk. "What else have you learned?"

"We were able to confirm that the center of Himmler's occult activities is Wewelsburg Castle. We've not been able to determine what his exact intentions are, but Agrat was confident that what Himmler is involved in will win the war for Germany."

"Hitler may not need the occult for that." Churchill chuckled at his own joke, and then became contemplative. "Wewelsburg Castle. That's the triangular one on top of a hill in in the Paderborn District, right?"

"Yes, sir."

"We could send in a squadron of Mosquitos and level the place, make sure whatever Himmler is up to is over with."

"We could." Bellingham ended his sentence with an inclination in his voice.

"You disagree?"

"I'm not questioning the RAF's ability, Prime Minister. I'm questioning whether we would do ourselves more harm than good. We can easily destroy the castle, but unless we take out Himmler, the succubi, and everyone else involved in this project, then we will wind up only hurting our cause. They'll set up shop somewhere else, and it might take us years to find them again."

"You're right, of course. I hate inactivity."

"We can be proactive," said Bellingham. "Now that we know Wewelsburg is where everything is taking place, we can target the castle for an intelligence operation."

"Are you suggesting sending an SOE team to Germany to infiltrate Wewelsburg?"

"Much too risky," said Bellingham, shaking his head. "More than likely, they'd be caught and executed before they could get anywhere near the castle, and then all we'd have achieved is to lose several good men and women and tip off the Germans that we know about Wewelsburg. I had another, more unconventional way in mind."

"You definitely have my attention."

"Agrat mentioned the Germans have someone with abilities similar to Squadron Officer Harris who is working against us, although she would not explain what those abilities were. I want to do the same thing back to the Germans. With your permission, I would like to go outside the ranks of the military and recruit a psychic to spy on Wewelsburg."

"You mean have that person sit here in London and telepathically link into what's going on inside the castle?"

"Yes, Prime Minister."

"Why can't Squadron Officer Harris do that?"

"Her psychic abilities are limited. Miss Harris can only make a telepathic connection with the dead, and only if they reach out to her. I'm looking for someone who not only can initiate a psychic link but can do so with the living. If I can find that person, it will be almost as good as having an agent inside

Wewelsburg itself."

"How would you go about recruiting this person?"

"I'll have to go back to MI5 and Scotland Yard for help," Bellingham explained. "I'm sure they will have files on such people."

"Mostly con artists and lunatics who have had encounters with the authorities," Churchill snorted.

"It's not ideal, but it's the best place to start. The real problem, assuming we even come up with a list of potential candidates, will be not only finding someone with the abilities we need, but one who is willing to work with us and adhere to security protocols."

"It's war time," Churchill snorted. "Everyone is expected to do their part."

"Many of these people don't think that way. They're more independent in their thinking. Some of them don't affiliate with a nation or a political system as much as they feel a close bond with others like them. We could be acquiring a source of intelligence and a security risk in the same package. That's why I'm asking your permission before I proceed. Of course, I'll be fully responsible for whatever happens within my command."

Churchill stared at Bellingham for several seconds as he weighed his options, his face stoic. Finally, the Prime Minister asked, "I don't suppose there are any alternatives?"

"Well, we could go back to Plan A and have the RAF bomb them into submission."

"Permission granted," said Churchill. "Let me know if you need my office to apply pressure anywhere. And you won't be fully accountable for anything that goes wrong with this plan. I'm as responsible for approving Operation CROWLEY as you are for carrying out my orders."

"Thank you, Prime Minister."

Churchill shook his head. "What would Lloyd George and the Duke of Windsor say if they knew I was waging an occult war against Hitler?"

"If it weren't for you, we wouldn't be waging war against Hitler. We would be allied with him."

Churchill broke into a hearty laugh. "Thank God you're not a politician, Bellingham. You'd be sitting where I am right now."

"No offense, but the last thing I want is to be prime minister."

"I don't blame you. Many a day I feel that way myself."

Bellingham started to leave when Churchill called out to him.

"By the way, General Auchinleck is replacing General Wavell as commander-in-chief Middle East on the 21st. I'm flying out on July 3rd to meet with him and to inspect the troops, a combination strategy session to shore up our position in North Africa and a show of force to keep up morale. I want you and the Project Samail team to go along."

"Are you concerned the Germans might try a succubus attack on Auchinleck?"

"Not really, but it's better to be safe than sorry. It'll also give your team a chance to talk to those closest to Wavell. Maybe they'll be able to uncover something the Eighth Army investigators missed."

"No problem, Prime Minister. We'll be ready."

"Good. I'll have my staff provide you with the details later."

Bellingham made his way topside, grateful to emerge back into the sunlight and fresh air. He would need to take the long way back to Baker Street to clear out his head after being stuck underground. It would also give him time to plan out his new operation against the Nazis.

CHAPTER TWENTY-SEVEN

The Kremlin, Moscow, Russia
16 June 1941

"YOU DID AN excellent job, Comrade Tukarov. Stalin will be pleased." Levorov knew it was a lie, one calculated to stroke the major's bruised ego and keep him compliant. Stalin would not be made aware of the military's involvement unless Levorov's plan failed miserably. Then the major would be implicated so Levorov could redirect the blame away from himself. Judging from the expression of relief and satisfaction on the major's face, the false praise seemed to have worked.

"Thank you, Comrade Levorov."

"My men reported that the training went well. Please express my gratitude to whoever oversaw it."

"I will. If you need anything else, please feel free to contact me."

"Hopefully, we'll never need to use this equipment, but if we have to, I'll have you to thank." Levorov rose from his chair and escorted Tukarov to the office door. "Of course, all of this must remain highly confidential."

"Of course."

"If word of this leaked out, it would tip off our enemies to our methods and would cause the more jittery members of the Politburo to ask questions. The last thing either of us wants is a bunch of politicians nosing around."

"I understand. You can count on me."

"I know I can," said Levorov with a smile on his face and a

tinge of menace in his voice.

Levorov stood at the door and watched Tukarov leave. The major was a useful pawn, but now his usefulness had ended. At the first opportunity, he would have the major and anyone in the military involved in this project rounded up and shipped out to Siberia to ensure their silence. As for the two men assisting in its implementation, Levorov knew he could rely on them. They had worked for him in previous assignments and were not only dedicated to the cause and fiercely loyal to him, but also had things in their past they desperately wanted to keep buried, things that if known could easily make them among the millions of nameless victims in the gulag system. Levorov had these men reassigned to the Kremlin, and then pulled their records from the files, ensuring their loyalty and total commitment. Everything was falling into place nicely.

As he turned to go back into his office, he heard a voice calling him from down the hall. A man raced toward him. Levorov recognized him as the junior sergeant from Chief Directorate of Labor Camp and Colonies' file office. He clutched a briefcase in his hand. As he rushed up to Levorov, he panted from exertion.

"I'm glad I caught you. Do you have a minute?"

"I do." Levorov stepped aside and motioned for the junior sergeant to enter. When he did, Levorov followed, closing the door behind him. "How can I help you?"

"Believe it or not, I think I found just the person you've been looking for." The junior sergeant held the briefcase against his chest with his left hand and used his right to unlock the flap. Reaching in, he pulled out a file folder and handed it to Levorov. Levorov opened it and thumbed through the pages.

The file belonged to a young Romani girl named Tasaria who was approximately seventeen years old at the time of her arrest in 1939. Her entire tribe had escaped from Poland during the Nazi invasion and settled down west of Kiev where the NKVD rounded them up and imprisoned them on charges ranging from robbery to prostitution, most of which were more than likely trumped up. Tasaria's file photograph showed a terrified, inexperienced young woman confused about what was happening to her, definitely not a hardened criminal. Whoever had interrogated her had done their job well, because included on her profile page was a list of various "skills" she possessed, including the particular one he was interested in plus other related abilities. He had struck the motherlode. Unfortunately, Tasaria had been arrested two years ago, so it was quite possible she had not survived the gulag system.

"Do you know if she's still alive?" he asked.

"I checked on that," said the junior sergeant. "I asked about the entire tribe so I didn't draw any attention to her. According to the camp commander, most of the tribe died within the first six months of imprisonment, but Tasaria, her younger sister, and her grandmother are still alive."

"Excellent job."

"Thank you, comrade. Do you want me to have her brought to Moscow?"

Levorov thought for a moment. An inquiry about the girl followed by an order to transfer her to Moscow might raise suspicions, especially if anyone else knew about her special abilities. The chances were slim, but Levorov did not get where he was by taking too many of them. Besides, he had pushed his luck already with Tukarov. The woman had the skill set he needed, was still alive, and could be transferred to Moscow within twenty-four hours. There was no need to push his luck any further until events made it absolutely necessary.

"Let's hold off on bringing her here for now, although I want you to get a transfer order ready so we can send it at a moment's notice. Then contact the camp commander and tell him there is interest in Moscow in the tribe and advise him to take care of the survivors until further notice. And keep the contact between us personal. No phone calls and nothing in writing."

"Yes, sir. Is there anything else?"

"No. I'll keep the file, though. I want to study it some more."

The junior sergeant left and Levorov returned to his desk where he locked Tasaria's file in his drawer. Not a bad afternoon, he thought. Everything had come to fruition easier than expected. He only needed to wait for the right opportunity to present itself, and then he could intercede and save Stalin from his succubus.

CHAPTER TWENTY-EIGHT

The Soviet-Polish border, several kilometers west of Brody, Ukraine
22 June 1941

SS *BRIGADEFÜHRER* EMIL Otto Rasch sat in the passenger seat of his *Kübelwagen*, two hundred meters behind the row of *Panzerkampfwagen* IIIs and IVs of *Panzergruppe* One preparing to invade the Soviet Union. As part of Field Marshal Gerd von Rundstedt's Army Group South, *Panzergruppe* One was tasked with driving through Ukraine and taking Kiev. Rasch commanded *Einsatzgruppen* C, the special action responsible for the northern and central Ukraine. His unit would follow behind the *Wehrmacht* and cleanse those areas, but they would not deploy until later. With nothing better to do, Rasch drove to the front to watch the opening of Operation BARBAROSSA.

"Why are we here?" complained his driver, SS *Sturmmann* Weber. Weber had to yell the question to be heard over the sound of dozens of *panzer* engines warming up.

"To witness a historic event," answered Rasch. "Everything Germany has been working toward for eight years is about to come about. Soon Germany will have all the land it needs to become a great empire, and we won't have to deal with Jews and Slavs anymore. And we're a part of this. Someday, you'll be able to tell your grandchildren you were here when this all began."

Weber remained unimpressed, slumped down into his seat, and closed his eyes. *Fuck him*, thought Rasch. He wouldn't allow the little *arschloch* to get him down. Rasch stood up in the front seat of the *Kübelwagen* to get a better view.

Most of the softening up was beyond his line of sight. German artillery had been shelling the Russian positions since 0315 that morning, concentrating on fuel and ammunition depots, communication centers, and border defenses. German assault troops already had moved forward against lightly defended Russian border posts and bridges, eliminating the soldiers and opening the border for invasion. As the first rays of dawn crested the horizon dawn, *Luftwaffe* aircraft flew overhead, winging their way toward the Soviet airfields situated behind the front.

A few minutes after the fighters and bombers flew past, the commander of the lead *panzer* ordered his driver to move out. Up and down the line, *panzer* engines revved and crews closed the hatches to their vehicles, except for a few commanders who remained exposed in their cupolas. One by one, the *panzers* lurched forward, the rear panel of each draped with a large blood-red flag bearing a white circle and black swastika in order to be recognized by friendly aircraft. As Rasch watched the unit cross the frontier into the Soviet Union, he thought that right now over three million German soldiers and over three thousand *panzers* were advancing along a front that stretched from the Baltic to the Black Sea. The drive to create *Lebensraum* for Germany had begun.

Rasch slid back down into his seat and slapped his hand against the dashboard, jarring Weber awake.

"What's wrong?"

"Nothing," said Rasch. "Let's head back to camp. I want to finalize preparations for moving out."

CHAPTER TWENTY-NINE

The Kremlin, Moscow, Russia
22 June 1941

LEVOROV DROVE THE Emka staff car, racing through the streets of Moscow and maneuvering around what little traffic existed on the roads in the early morning hour. Beside him, his driver sat with his legs stiffened against the floorboards, one hand frantically clutching the door handle. Levorov ignored him. Time was of the essence, and he needed to get back to the Kremlin in a hurry, not be chauffeured around like some elitist. Russia was now at war with Nazi Germany and Stalin could be in imminent danger.

In front of the Hotel Moskva, a slow-moving truck blocked their path. Levorov accelerated around the vehicle and swung into the opposite lane, directly into the path of an approaching bus. The bus driver leaned on his horn to warn the offending car out of the way. To Levorov's right, his driver yelped, placed both hands against the dashboard, and locked his elbows. Levorov refused to give way and, at the last second, the bus swerved to its right and bounced onto the sidewalk, opening a space for Levorov to pass through. Accelerating even faster, he raced past the State Historical Museum and into Red Square.

Levorov scanned the area for signs of battle, focusing most of his attention on the Senate Building on the opposite side of the Kremlin wall behind Lenin's Tomb. He half expected to see German gliders littering the square, or smoke from fire fights billowing from the compound, indications that the *Wehrmacht* had launched a surprise attack against Stalin much like they had against the Belgian fortress of Eben-Emael to facilitate the May 1940 invasion of that country. Thankfully, everything seemed normal, which in itself seemed out of place considering that a few hours ago German troops had invaded the Soviet Union.

Entering the *Spasskaya* Gate so fast he ripped off the driver's side mirror on the abutment, Levorov swung around in front of the Senate Building, parked by the main entrance, and rushed inside. As he approached the door to Stalin's suite, the two guards posted out front snapped to attention. Both men remained professional but were tense and nervous.

"Is everything secure here?" asked Levorov.

"Yes, Comrade Levorov," answered the more senior of the two.

"Is Stalin still inside?"

"As far as I know. No one has come in or out since we took up our posts."

"Except that woman," said the other guard with a note of disdain.

"Of course," mumbled Levorov. He pointed at the senior guard. "Call in the rest of the security detail. I want everyone on duty as quickly as possible. Let no one into this suite other than the top leadership. Come and get me if anything out of the ordinary occurs. If you're not certain, get me anyway. I'd rather you be overcautious than allow something to happen."

The guard snapped to attention. "Yes, Comrade Levorov."

"Sir," asked the other guard. "What's going on?"

"Hitler has invaded the Soviet Union."

The expression of both guards changed from concern to determination.

"You can count on us," said the senior guard.

"I know." Levorov stepped past his men and pushed open the doors.

A sense of calm permeated Stalin's suite. There was no bustle or activity. In fact, Levorov saw no signs of activity. He stopped in the middle of the receiving room and called out, "Is anyone here?"

After a few seconds, a female voice came from the other room.

"The Marshal wants to be left alone."

Naamah, Levorov mentally spat her name. *It figures.*

"I need to speak to the Marshal immediately."

He heard a commotion from the other room, and a moment later Naamah came out, closing a silk robe around her body and tying the sash around her waist.

"Stalin does not want to see anyone right now. He's tired."

"This is an emergency. I need to see—"

"I said no."

Levorov surged toward Stalin's bedroom. "This is a state emergency—"

Naamah stepped in front of Levorov, blocking his path. The sultry voice became cold and sonorous. "You defy me and I'll make you regret the day that your bitch of a mother gave birth to you."

The sudden change in demeanor caused Levorov to back down, that and the fact an inner sense told him Naamah could carry out that threat. His hesitation lasted only for a moment. Levorov's hands bunched into fists.

"If you don't get out of my—"

A commotion from the entrance to the suite distracted Levorov. He glanced over his shoulder as Beria, Molotov, and Mikoyan barged into the room. They spotted the confrontation between him and Naamah and, surprisingly, seemed unfazed by it.

Beria nodded toward Levorov. "Where is Stalin?"

"In his bedroom, but *she* won't let me in to talk with him."

"We'll see about that." Beria approached Naamah, with Molotov and Mikoyan behind him.

Naamah took a step back, not out of fear, but to better position herself against the four men. "As I told this *krest'yanin*,

Stalin does not want to be disturbed."

"What gives you the right to interfere with us?" barked Molotov.

"I do." All eyes turned to the bedroom door. Stalin emerged wearing his uniform pants and a white shirt, buttoned up but not tucked in. He was barefoot. As he approached Naamah, the others backed away a few feet, including Levorov.

"What's going on out here?"

Molotov was the first to regain the courage to speak. "Hitler has broken our agreement and invaded the Soviet Union."

Stalin chuckled derisively. "Nonsense."

"It's true," said Mikoyan. "About three hours ago, shortly after three in the morning, the Luftwaffe began bombing cities in our sector of Poland. We also have reports of German artillery bombardments from as far north as Kronstadt and as far south as Sevastopol."

"Mikoyan," said Stalin in a fatherly tone. "You're making too much out of these reports. We've had exchanges of artillery fire between our sides before. It's a misunderstanding, not war."

"What about the reports of air raids on Polish cities?" Molotov asked.

"We're dealing with nervous commanders overreacting to these reports of artillery exchanges."

"Comrade Stalin," added Beria, "we also have intelligence indicating that German ground troops have crossed the border at several locations."

"Tell me, Beria. Has the NKVD cleared out the anti-Soviet partisans in Lithuania and Ukraine?"

"No," Beria replied in a low voice.

"There you go. There's your *invasion*."

"Comrade Stalin," said Mikoyan. "Please listen to reason. Every indicator points to—"

"Don't you dare presume to tell me what is reasonable!" Stalin yelled. All four men took a step back. "I built up the

Soviet Union based on strength and an iron will. There is no reason to believe Hitler would violate our pact, and I'm not going to be the one to start a war by listening to a bunch of cackling hens afraid of their own shadow. Is that clear?"

Beria and Molotov both nodded. Only Mikoyan remained resolute. Stalin glared at him. "I said, is that clear?"

"Yes, Comrade Stalin." Mikoyan's tone dripped with hatred.

"I want all of you out of here now." The four men obeyed. As they were about to exit the suite, Stalin called out. "Levorov, I'll hold you personally responsible if anyone disturbs me again."

"Understood."

"One more thing. If you ever talk to Naamah like that again, I will execute you myself. Is that clear?"

Levorov snapped to attention. "Very clear." He then turned to Naamah. "Please accept my apology."

"No harm done." Naamah smiled at him, though her expression reminded him of a snake closing in on its prey.

Once all four men had exited the suite, Levorov turned to the two guards.

"Stalin has demanded that no one disturb him until further notice. You are under orders to let no one other than the four of us into that suite no matter what the circumstances. And pass that order down to whoever replaces you."

"How far can we go to prevent anyone from entering?" asked the senior guard.

"Shoot to kill," Beria answered.

Both guards glanced at each other, not certain how to respond. Finally, the senior guard replied, "We'll do as ordered."

The four men walked until they reached the lobby of the Senate Building. Mikoyan spoke first.

"What the hell just happened back there?"

"I have no clue," said Molotov.

"It's that woman," said Beria. "She has too much control

over him. I think she's a German spy."

"Do you want to say that to him?" asked Levorov.

"No."

A Red Army senior lieutenant holding an envelope rushed past the group toward Stalin's suite. Molotov called to him.

"Where are you going?"

"I have an urgent message for Marshal Stalin."

"He's busy at the moment. I'll take that."

The lieutenant hesitated until Molotov extended his hand. He stepped forward, handed the envelope to the foreign minister, saluted, and left. Molotov opened the envelope.

"Maybe Stalin's right," said Mikoyan. "Maybe we are over-reacting and this is all just a minor border skirmish that will go away soon."

"I doubt that," said Molotov. "This just came in from our radio monitoring unit. Goebbels issued the following statement from Hitler half an hour ago over the radio. 'At this moment, a march is taking place that, for its extent, compares with the greatest the world has ever seen. I have decided today to place the fate and future of the *Reich* and our people in the hands of our soldiers. May God aid us, especially in this fight.'"

"We have to bring this to Stalin's attention," said Mikoyan.

"You heard him," argued Levorov. "He ordered that no one disturb him."

"This is different. He can't get mad if we bring him this. I'm willing to take the chance."

"I'm not," said Levorov, knowing who would suffer if Mikoyan was wrong.

"Levorov is right," added Beria. "He won't listen to us if we try to bother him now. The best course of action is to pull together more intelligence about what's going on and bring it to Stalin when we have enough evidence to convince him."

"What about our forces on the front?" Mikoyan asked.

"They're military units. They'll defend themselves if at-tacked."

"I'll go on the radio this afternoon," said Molotov. "I'll let everyone know we're at war with Germany and the country needs to defend itself. At least that way someone from the leadership is talking to the people."

"Good idea," agreed Beria. "We'll all meet back here at six."

Mikoyan and Molotov responded in the affirmative.

"Levorov," said Beria. "Keep an eye on Stalin. If he tries to leave and you can't stop him, stay with him as his bodyguard and let us know where he goes. If he wants to talk about the invasion, call us immediately."

"I will."

"And try to figure out a way to get that damn woman away from him," added Mikoyan.

Levorov nodded. The others did not know it, but he had a way planned. All he needed was the right opportunity.

CHAPTER THIRTY

Covent Garden, London, England
22 June 1941

ODY KNOCKED ON Lee's apartment door repeatedly, each time harder and more frequent, and still she did not answer. He glanced at his watch. It was a little after seven in the morning.

Bellingham had rung him at the hotel less than an hour ago to inform him about the German invasion of Russia and to tell him to pick up Lee and get to the office immediately. Cody had tried to call Lee beforehand, but the line was busy. He had assumed she was on the line with Bellingham and headed over, hoping to find her waiting for him. However, after two minutes of banging on her apartment door, Lee still had not answered. He reasoned she must have gone to SOE Headquarters without him and had started back toward the elevators when the apartment door opened.

"Do you know what time it is?" Lee asked. She stood in the half open doorway, wearing a bathrobe, the ends of which she clutched against her stomach. Her hair was tussled and her eyes were bloodshot with dark circles beneath them, yet he still found her attractive.

"It's a little after seven," he replied with a grin.

"I was being sarcastic."

Cody came back to the door and gently maneuvered Lee back into the apartment. "Can I come in?"

"It seems you already are," she said, irritated.

"I tried calling you and your phone was busy."

"I took it off the hook so I could get a good night's sleep, which I was doing just fine until you nearly battered down my door."

"Sorry, but Bellingham wants us in the office right away. Hitler invaded the Soviet Union five hours ago."

Lee's anger and annoyance changed to determination. She ran into the bedroom, yanking off her robe as she passed through the door.

"Wait here. I'll be ready in a few minutes."

THEY ARRIVED AT Bellingham's office only to find the group captain away at a meeting, so they sat by his desk and waited. The wait was not long. After a little more than twenty minutes, Bellingham rushed into his office. Upon seeing Cody and Lee, he said, "Good. You're both here. There's a lot to go over."

"What's going on?" Lee asked.

"I just came from the Cabinet War Room." Bellingham slid into his seat behind his desk. "The information coming in is still sketchy, but it appears Hess was telling the truth. Germany invaded the Soviet Union at 0330, and by all indications, the scale of the invasion is as massive as Hess claimed."

"Churchill must be frantic," said Cody.

"On the contrary. Short of America joining the war, this is the best thing that could have happened to England. With Hitler bogged down in the east, the pressure will be lifted off us for a while and will give us a chance to recover."

"What's the Soviet reaction?" Lee asked.

"That's the interesting part. According to what little intelligence is available, the only responses to the invasion have been from ground commanders who have taken it upon themselves to deal with local incursions. No orders have been issued from the Kremlin, nor have there been any public announcements yet about the invasion. Our Foreign Ministry reached out to

Molotov this morning and was informed that Molotov was unavailable but would get back to us as soon as possible. Based on the general reaction from Moscow, the government doesn't seem to think anything unusual is taking place."

"Do you think Naamah might be influencing someone in the Kremlin?" Cody asked.

Bellingham nodded. "I think Naamah probably got to Stalin himself."

"What are we going to do about it?"

"There's nothing we can do. Churchill doesn't want to share our knowledge of Nazi occult activities with the Russians, at least not yet."

Lee thought for a moment. "Should we question Agrat again?"

Bellingham shook his head. "I don't want to give her the satisfaction. Besides, even if she told us that one of her sisters was glamouring Stalin, what could we do? Tell Molotov the supreme leader of the Soviet Union is being sexually controlled by a Talmudic demon working for Heinrich Himmler, so they might want to eliminate the threat?"

Cody chuckled. "When you put it like that, it does sound crazy."

Bellingham shook his head in despair. "If the Soviets are dealing with a succubus, they have to manage this situation on their own."

CHAPTER THIRTY-ONE

Stalin's Office, the Kremlin, Moscow, Russia
29 June 1941

WHAT A DISASTER, thought Levorov as he stood to one side in Stalin's office and observed the briefing, if you could call the fiasco taking place a briefing. After isolating himself for seven days and allowing the Nazis free reign in the west, Stalin had finally asked to be updated on the military situation. Beria, Molotov, and Mikoyan had shown up with General Kirill Meretskov, the permanent advisor to STAVKA, the high command of the Russian armed forces. Noticeably absent from the meeting was Naamah, which explained why Stalin was more attentive than usual.

Meretskov relayed the litany of bad news all along the front, using a map spread across the table. Stalin stood on the opposite side and listened silently, hovering on the general's every word. The Marshal had his arms folded across his chest with a mixture of disgust, fear, and resignation on his face.

Levorov could not help but remember an incident that occurred during the struggle against the White Russians for control of Tsaritsyn. The day before the final battle, his commanding officer had related the story of the sacking of Rome by the barbarians and the resulting collapse of western civilization, wondering when the Visigoths appeared on the Seven Hills if the Romans realized they were witnessing the end of their empire and their way of life. Watching events as they played out, Levorov thought that sentiment was more apropos now than ever.

"Marshal Stalin," said Meretskov. "The enemy has made significant advances all along the front. In the north, they've already occupied the Baltic States and are pushing toward Leningrad. The only success we're having is along the Southwestern Front. General Kirponos has counterattacked and has significantly slowed the German advance on Kiev."

"What about here?" asked Stalin as he pointed toward Belarus on the map. "You've not reported on the Western Front."

Meretskov looked to the others around the office, seeking advice. Molotov and Beria avoided his gaze, only Mikoyan nodded for him to proceed. Meretskov took a deep breath to brace himself.

"Marshal Stalin, Minsk has been surrounded. Between the pocket west of the city and the Bialystok salient, three hundred thousand Red Army soldiers were captured. Belarus is wide open to the Germans, and they've already begun the push toward Smolensk."

Stalin studied the map. "What do we have in this area that can stop the Nazis?"

"We have nothing left in that sector, Marshal Stalin. The road between Smolensk and Moscow is wide open."

Stalin pounded the map table with his fist with such force everyone in the office jumped. "Lenin founded our state and now we fucked it up!"

"This is merely a setback," offered Mikoyan weakly.

"This is more than a setback." Stalin leaned across the map table and stared at Meretskov. "Who's in charge of the Western Front?"

"General Dmitri Pavlov."

"I want him relieved of command and brought back to Moscow immediately." Stalin switched his attention to Beria. "Once Pavlov is back in Moscow, I want you to personally see to his execution."

"Isn't that a bit much?" asked Meretskov.

"Are you questioning me?" Stalin's eyes bore deep into Meretskov.

"What should we do about the three hundred thousand prisoners?" asked Molotov.

"Nothing," barked Stalin. "They're as good as dead to me. If they were loyal Soviets, they would have fought to the last man instead of surrendering and opening up the front. They're all traitors to the motherland, and their commanding officers are fifth columnists. Better that they die in German camps. It'll save us the trouble of executing them when the war is over."

A stunned silence fell across the attendees. No one dared respond for fear of incurring Stalin's wrath. The uneasy silence was broken only when Naamah entered the office and sauntered over to the Marshal.

"What's going on?"

"We're having a classified briefing," said Meretskov. "Please leave."

"You will not tell her what to do!" Stalin yelled. "If you want to order someone around, try telling those useless generals on the front to do their job and quit retreating."

"Is that what this is all about?" Naamah pouted. "You're getting yourself so upset over a minor border skirmish."

"It's much more serious than a minor border skirmish," corrected Meretskov.

"Do not talk to her that way!" Stalin slammed his fist on the map table again, only this time everyone was prepared for the outburst. "I've had enough of this shit. I want everyone out. Now! And Beria, have the general sent to Siberia. Maybe a few years in the cold will teach him how to talk to a lady."

Meretskov went pale and attempted to stammer something unintelligible. Beria grabbed the general by the arm and pushed him toward the door. The others followed him out.

Stalin noticed Levorov standing in the corner. "I want you out, too."

"Yes, Comrade Stalin."

As Levorov followed the others, Naamah cuddled up beside Stalin and whispered something in his ear. Stalin nodded and then called out to Levorov.

"Yes?"

"Have my car brought around in an hour. We're going to spend some time at my summer *dacha*. You're going with us. It'll be your job to make certain we're not bothered while we're there."

"I'll take care of it."

Levorov exited the office and joined the others in the lobby. Two NKVD soldiers stood on either side of Meretskov, each one clutching an arm. Beria was issuing orders to his men.

"Take General Meretskov to Lubyanka Prison and put him in a holding cell."

"Y-you're not really going to deport me to Siberia, are you?" asked a visibly shaken Meretskov. "I didn't do anything."

"I'm detaining you for your own good because you can't keep your fucking mouth shut. You'll stay there for a couple of days until this shit blows over." Beria directed his attention to the NKVD soldiers. "Take him away."

Once the general had been escorted out, Beria turned to the others. "What do we do now? Based on what Meretskov said, the Nazis could be in Moscow in a matter of days."

Mikoyan sighed. "If we could separate him from that bitch, maybe we could talk some sense into him."

"That's not going to be easy," said Levorov. "Stalin asked me to get his car ready. He and Naamah are heading to his summer *dacha*, and he ordered me to go with him to keep everyone away, including all of you."

"Shit," said Molotov. "Once he's out there we'll have even less influence over him."

"There's nothing we can do about that right now." Beria thought for a moment and the placed a hand on Levorov's shoulder. "Do what Stalin ordered. Once you get to the *dacha*, stay close by. If he tries to go somewhere else, let us know immediately. We're going to formulate a plan and come out to the *dacha* tomorrow to try and talk some sense into him."

"And if we can't?" asked Molotov.

Beria did not respond, which told the others more than they wanted to know. "And Levorov, if an opportunity rises to separate Stalin from that bitch, take advantage of it. We'll cover your ass. Understood?"

"Clearly."

"You're a good man," Beria nodded.

Levorov rushed off to make sure Stalin's car was ready in time. After that, he would contact his special unit and have them surreptitiously go to the *dacha* and await his instructions.

CHAPTER THIRTY-TWO

SOE Headquarters, London, England
29 June 1941

CODY SET DOWN the book on his desk. Placing one palm over each eye, he rubbed backwards along his temples. "I'm getting hungry. It must be lunch time."

"Lunch?" Lee laughed. "It's half past four."

"Why didn't you say anything?"

"I thought you were onto some promising research and didn't want to disturb you."

"I wish. I wound up wasting another afternoon chasing a dead end. Some days I think we'll never find an answer to stopping the Nazis."

"We will." Lee reached out, clasped his hand, and squeezed gently. "Bear in mind we're doing something that's never been done before. We're not going to figure this out overnight."

"I guess you're right."

"Of course I am." Lee winced and brought her hand up to her face, massaging her forehead.

"Are you okay?" Cody asked.

"I got that headache again."

"Maybe you should have it looked at."

"I have a better idea." Lee stood up and took her jacket from the coat rack. "Come on."

"Where are we going?"

"Any place but here. You need to clear your head."

"Are you seducing me, Miss Harris?" Cody teased.

"No," she replied with a coquettish smile. "We need to get

something to eat and take in a movie. Anything to clear our heads and get our minds off the occult."

"That sounds good to me. Let me get my jacket."

As Cody was slipping on his jacket, Bellingham knocked and opened the door. He peered inside. "I'm glad I caught you."

"Is anything wrong?" Lee asked.

"No," said Bellingham as he entered the office and closed the door. "I have our flight itinerary for the prime minister's trip to Cairo. We'll be taking a Boeing clipper to Egypt."

"Like what you took to fly here," Lee said to Cody. "I can't wait."

"Trust me," Bellingham chuckled. "The journey won't be fun or easy. Make sure you bring something to read."

"I will."

"And make sure you bring your camera. We're staying at Mena House, right next to the Pyramids."

"How exotic," Lee said.

"Wouldn't it be safer for the Prime Minister if we stayed in the government quarter?" Cody asked.

"There'd be better security, but within a day half of Egypt would know Churchill is in town. Mena House is isolated from the rest of the city, so it'll be easier to keep his presence secret. That's the important thing. With the Germans getting so close to Cairo, we don't want them launching an air raid against him. Eighth Army will deploy more than enough troops around the hotel to keep him safe from commando raids."

"Okay," responded Cody, although he was not fully convinced.

"Have your gear ready and be out in front of headquarters at 2100 tomorrow night. A staff car will pick us up and take us to the airport. We should arrive in Cairo late on the second or early in the morning of the third. Churchill is meeting with Molotov on the fourth, your Independence Day. Sorry, there'll be no fireworks."

"That's fine. I won't mind the peace and quiet."

"Both of you," said Bellingham, "take the day off tomorrow and get some rest. You'll need it over the next ten days. See you tomorrow."

When Bellingham left, Lee jumped into Cody's arm. "This is going to be so romantic. I've never been to Cairo before. I hear it's beautiful."

"Like you." Cody kissed her. "Just remember, we have a lot of work to do while we're there."

"I know. But you know what they say about all work and no play." Lee straightened his necktie. "Which reminds me, we have a dinner and a movie planned."

"Shouldn't we pack?"

"We can go back to my place after the movie and pack. We'll pack your things in the morning."

The gleam in her eyes assured Cody they would spend the night doing more than packing.

CHAPTER THIRTY-THREE

Wewelsburg Castle, Germany
29 June 1941

"ARE YOU THROUGH for the day yet?" asked Malalath, making no effort to hide her boredom.

"Let me connect with her one more time," said Winnie. "Maybe this time we'll get lucky."

"You haven't for the past three days, why waste your time?"

"Dietrich has ordered me to."

"Dietrich is not here and won't know any better."

Winnie lowered her head. "Maybe you can afford to disobey him. I can't."

"That's true." Malalath said it with more disgust than sympathy. "I'm not going to waste my time. Call me if you get anything useful."

If only Malalath knew how much she hated channeling with the British woman. Most of it was due to the toll it took on her, for even a few minutes of connection required hours of rest. What Winnie would not admit to Malalath was sometimes she would be embarrassed when forming the link, like the night she connected with the British woman when her and the American were having sex. Usually, she wasted her time and drained her psychic energy for nothing but, as she told Malalath, she did not have the luxury of getting Dietrich mad at her.

Placing her hands palm down on the table, Winnie closed her eyes and entered the nethersphere, draining her consciousness of all other thoughts and emotions before mentally traveling to London where she focused her energy on the woman's aura. Once again, her American lover was nearby.

"Are you okay?"

"I got that headache again."

"Maybe you should have it looked at."

"I have a better idea. Come on."

"Where are we going?"

"Any place but here. You need to clear your head."

"Are you seducing me, Miss Harris?"

Not again, Winnie sighed to herself. At least this time she didn't catch them in the act.

Winnie was about to break the psychic link when their boss came into the office and said, *"I have our flight itinerary for the prime minister's trip to Cairo."*

Winnie nearly shocked herself out of the psychic connection. Churchill was going to Egypt, and he was bringing his occult warriors with him. She listened carefully to the details, remembering as much as possible.

Once Bellingham had departed, Winnie broke the psychic connection with the woman and jotted down the relevant information about the flight to Egypt. Then she raced out of the study to find Malalath and have her contact Dietrich with the news.

CHAPTER THIRTY-FOUR

Stalin's *dacha*, Kuntsevo, Russia
30 June 1941

L EVOROV PACED NERVOUSLY in front of Stalin's *dacha*. The compound gave him the creeps. He had always pictured *dachas* to be bright villas located in plush, spacious areas where the party elite could unwind. This place seemed more like a morgue. It was located approximately ten miles west of the Kremlin in the neighborhood of Kuntsevo and sat amongst a copse of dense trees that limited the sunlight, with the only access being an anonymous driveway which cut through the woods. Even the *dacha* was oppressive, the large, dark green building with small windows and a columned entranceway more reminiscent of the Soviet-style architecture dominant in Moscow than a vacation retreat.

Deep down, Levorov knew the setting was quite appropriate for the scene about to play itself out. In the next few minutes, he would either be a hero of the Soviet Union or one of its numerous anonymous victims.

Beria had called him an hour ago to warn him a delegation was coming out to talk with Stalin, and this would be the final attempt to get the Marshal to step up and lead the Soviet Union in the war against the Nazis. If he refused, Stalin would be removed from his position; a triumvirate composed on Beria, Molotov, and Mikoyan would replace him; and Levorov would be responsible for keeping Stalin under house arrest until the change in government could be enacted. Levorov had other plans. He knew the problem was not Stalin but Naamah and had arranged to permanently remove her.

Senior Sergeant Yurchenko exited the *dacha* and stepped up beside Levorov.

"Is everything ready?" Levorov asked.

"Yes. Andre is inside. Once the others arrive, he'll stay close by you and wait for your command. If we hear gunfire, Vladimir and I will join you with the special weapons."

Levorov paused a moment. "Are you sure you're up to this?"

"It's a bit unorthodox, but we've done worse."

"Thank you."

The noise of engines caught his attention. Levorov stopped pacing and watched as two staff cars came up the driveway, circled around the fountain in front of the *dacha*, and stopped by the entrance. Five men climbed out and gathered in a circle by the vehicles. In addition to Beria, Molotov, and Mikoyan were Minister of Trade Anastas Mikoyan and General Kliment Voroshilov. Voroshilov was the only person to ever have openly confronted Stalin, telling the Marshal that it was his military purges that had hurt the effort in last year's Winter War with Finland, emphasizing his displeasure with Stalin by slamming a platter of roast pig down onto the dinner table. His presence here as a member of the State Defense Committee and a former people's commissar for defense was understandable, but Levorov feared the general's presence might antagonize Stalin even further.

Levorov had no time to worry about that now. He stepped forward to greet the party.

"Is Stalin inside?" Beria asked.

"He's in his study."

"What about Naamah?"

"At the moment, she's in the garden. We have a few minutes at best."

"Let's do this," said Molotov.

Levorov led the way inside. Andre waited for them in the

main lobby. As the others gathered in the conference room at the rear of the *dacha* with the large picture windows overlooking the backyard, Levorov went to Stalin's study and knocked on the door.

"What is it?" said the gruff voice from the other side.

Levorov swallowed hard. Opening the door, he stuck his head inside. "I'm sorry to bother you, but something needs your attention."

"What?"

"Could you please come with me?"

Stalin sighed and followed Levorov. Andre fell in behind his boss. When Stalin stepped into the conference room, he stopped short, then glared at the others in the room who had gathered around the central table. Levorov moved to the right, positioning himself between Stalin and the others. Andre stood ten feet behind his boss.

"Why have you come?" Stalin asked guardedly. He glared at Levorov. "I thought I told you I wanted to be left alone."

Molotov stepped forward. "We're here to ask you to return to work. Russia needs you."

"No." Stalin crossed over to the windows looking over the backyard. "The Russian people need a leader. I can't live up to their expectations."

"Yes, you can." Voroshilov joined Molotov.

Stalin shook his head. "I should resign. I've failed as a leader. I've fucked around for a week and let the Nazis overrun our country. One of you should take over for me."

"There's no one more worthy than you to lead us," said Molotov.

"You still think so?" Stalin's voice wavered with uncertainty.

All five responded in the affirmative.

Turning from the window, Stalin stood straight and arched his shoulders back, having regained some of his lost confidence.

"You're right. Let's get back to Moscow."

"You're not going anywhere." The voice came from the entrance to the conference room, a voice so cold and angry it startled Levorov. Everyone turned to see Naamah standing in the doorway in a yellow summer dress and heels. Her eyes glowed red.

"Iosif, tell them to leave now if they know what's good for them."

Stalin's confidence drained away in Naamah's presence. His shoulders drooped again and he lowered his head. "Russia needs me," he mumbled.

"I need you," Naamah growled.

Keeping his left hand by his side, Levorov used it to motion to Andre, who slowly crossed the room and stood beside his boss.

"I want everyone out of here now!" demanded Naamah.

"You heard her," Stalin said sheepishly. "Please leave."

Beria stepped forward, placing himself between Naamah and the others. "Miss Naamah, you are under arrest for treason and for conspiring with Nazi Germany against the Soviet Union."

"Iosif, are you going to let him talk to me this way?"

"Lavrenti, stand down." Stalin spoke with no emotion in his voice.

Beria turned around to face Stalin. "Marshal Stalin, you are relieved of all party and military positions and are confined to house arrest until further notice. I'm afraid we have no other choice."

"We do."

Levorov reached out his hand to Andre, who opened his overcoat to reveal the Degtyaryov light machinegun concealed beneath the folds. Levorov took the machine gun and cocked back the bolt.

Voroshilov and the two Mikoyans jumped in front of Stalin. When Levorov aimed the machinegun at Naamah, Stalin cried out and went to protect her, only to be held back by Voroshilov. Naamah curled her lips back and hissed.

Levorov squeezed the trigger.

It took only ten seconds to empty the entire forty-seven-round drum into Naamah. Each bullet tore into her body, shredding flesh and muscle and forming small geysers of blood that sprayed across the conference room floor. The force of the barrage drove her back against the wall. Stray rounds tore chunks out of the wood and plaster. When the machine gun finally ran out of ammunition, the thing that used to be Naamah teetered for a moment before sliding down the wall, leaving a streak of gore before collapsing into a pile of pulp on the floor.

Beria moved toward the senior lieutenant and screamed, "Are you fucking insane! I'll have you executed—"

The moan that came from Naamah interrupted Beria's tirade. All eyes focused on what should have been a corpse. The mangled carcass struggled to its feet, using the bullet-ridden wall as support. It teetered for a moment, and then its coal black eyes focused on Levorov. It opened its mouth, but the lower jaw disconnected and fell to the floor. Even so, the voice that emanated from the mound of tattered flesh was deep and malevolent, echoing through the conference room.

"You'll regret that, human."

Naamah's body expanded, shedding the remaining flesh and muscles that slid off her, cascading down her scales to form a pool of human detritus around its snake-like tail. The bat-like wings unfolded, dripping with blood and gore. Her body coiled, ready to strike. She bore her fangs at Levorov, and her lower jaw unhinged and widened.

"I'm going to tear your soul from your body and watch it burn in Hell."

Levorov sneered back. "Not if you burn first."

Senior Sergeant Yurchenko and Vladimir rushed into the conference room, each carrying a flame thrower on their back. Naamah spun to the side and lunged, her unhinged jaws clamping over Vladimir's head. The man thrashed about and screamed in pain and terror, his cries muffled inside her throat. When she bit down, Vladimir's body tensed for a moment. Blood poured down his chest and back. A moment later, his headless body fell to the floor.

Yurchenko blasted Naamah in the face with a jet spray from his flamethrower. Fire engulfed her head and upper body. She fell back against the wall. The attack had burned her badly, but the scales had protected her. Yurchenko sprayed her again, holding the trigger for a few extra seconds. As he kept up the assault, he retreated several feet back and to her left side so that, when she whipped her tail at him, the appendage struck empty space. The move made Naamah vulnerable, exposing her back.

Yurchenko directed the stream against her wings, which ignited. She trilled in agony and flung herself around the room, rubbing against the floor and wall to extinguish the flames. It did little good, for Yurchenko followed her death throes across the room, maintaining the stream.

By now, the entire southern half of the conference room was an inferno. Voroshilov and the two Mikoyans rushed Stalin through the rear exit into the garden, with Andre providing protection. Levorov and Beria stayed behind to watch, although they moved out of the path of destruction.

After a minute of being consumed in flames, Naamah ceased the frantic slithering and slid to the floor. Only then did Yurchenko stop his attack and step back. Naamah's entire body burned except the tip of her tail that still twitched. A pitiful hiss escaped from her charred throat. After several seconds, the tail stopped moving and slumped to the floor. The only sound came from the fire raging around them. Beria motioned for Levorov and Yurchenko to join him outside.

Stalin sat on a stone bench in the middle of the garden, slumped over, his arms resting across his knees. Voroshilov and the trade minister tended to him. Molotov stood several feet behind him, shaking. Andre had rushed off to get help. Upon seeing the NKVD officer approach, Mikoyan walked up to them.

"What the fuck happened in there?"

Beria was at a loss for words.

Levorov answered for him. "We killed a *rusalka*, or what the west refers to as a succubus."

"Don't fuck with me, lieutenant," said Voroshilov. "*Rusalka* are myths."

"Then how do you explain what you just saw." Levorov motioned toward the conference room.

Voroshilov backed down.

"Wait a minute," mumbled Stalin. He stood up, but immediately grew dizzy. Voroshilov and the trade minister each grabbed an arm to steady him. Stalin brushed them away and staggered over to Levorov.

"Are you telling me I've been under the influence of a succubus?"

"Yes. I believe Naamah was sent here by the Nazis to distract you and prevent you from making the proper decisions that would counter the German attack on the motherland."

"But... but I did everything willingly."

"Naamah controlled your will. She told you what to do and made you think the decisions were yours. That's why you were conflicted whenever she was not around."

"Are you sure it was the Nazis who sent Naamah?" Voroshilov asked.

Beria was aghast. "Are you defending them, Comrade General?"

"No. But using that... that thing in there seems extreme even for Hitler."

"I'm certain it was the Nazis," said Levorov. "But there is a way to be certain."

"How?" Beria asked.

"There's a young woman in one of the gulag camps who

can help us. Her name is Tasaria. She's Romani. She also claims to be a necromancer, a person who can talk to the dead. I've already tracked her down and have informed the camp commander to have her ready to be brought back to Moscow."

"You did all this behind my back?" Beria asked with a tinge of menace in his voice.

"I showed initiative on your behalf." Levorov wanted to point out that he also made Beria look good in front of Stalin but knew better than to press his luck.

"You did well," said Stalin. "Better than any of us here did."

"Thank you, Comrade Stalin."

Beria grinned, although Levorov wasn't quite certain if it expressed approval at his subordinate's actions or was a warning that Levorov would eventually get what he deserved.

"What do we do now?" Stalin asked.

"I recommend we fly Tasaria to Moscow and have her contact Naamah's spirit as soon as possible. Once we know who sent Naamah against you, and what type of war they're waging against us, we can respond accordingly."

"Do it." Stalin turned to the others. "I want to get back to the Kremlin right away."

"You've been through a lot," said Voroshilov. "You're still disoriented and weak. Don't you think you should wait before going back to work?"

"Russia needs me. I've abandoned her long enough." Stalin headed for the eastern exit of the garden, then paused after a few feet. "Comrade Levorov, find out who did this to me. If it was Hitler, I'll teach that bastard and the Germans a lesson they'll never forget."

CHAPTER THIRTY-FIVE

Lotzen, Germany
30 June 1941

R EINHARD HEYDRICH STOOD outside the office car of
Himmler's private armored train, sipping from a mug of
real coffee, and admiring the pine forest that surrounded them.
He understood why Himmler had chosen this location to
establish *Hochwald*, his headquarters in the east. These woods
were quiet and far removed from the war. Unlike most of the
sprawling wartime complexes composed of underground
bunkers and massive cement structures, *Hochwald* consisted of a
simple wooden shack which supported Himmler's command
train when he visited the region.

Despite the peaceful surroundings, Heydrich knew the
serenity was merely a façade. Twenty miles to the west sat
Wolfschanze, Hitler's command center on the Eastern front from
where he oversaw BARBAROSSA. Thirty miles to the east
was the border between German- and Russian-occupied
Poland, and beyond that the region where *Einsatzgruppens* A and
B operated, cleansing Poland, the Baltics, and Belarus in order
to create *Lebensraum*.

Himmler stepped out of his private car and joined Heydrich on the platform.

"Is my staff car ready?"

"It is. Our luggage is stored away and the driver has been
briefed on the itinerary."

"Excellent. Where are we going today?"

"Augustowo and Grodno." Heydrich removed a folded

piece of paper from his pocket and handed it to the *Reichsführer*. "Here are the latest tallies for the *Einsatzgruppen*."

Himmler read the figures and frowned. "Less than ten thousand eliminated in over a week of combat? That's unacceptable."

"At this rate, it'll take fifty years to reach our goal."

"What's the problem? Did all the Jews and Commissars retreat when we attacked?"

"It's the men," Heydrich explained. "The special actions are taking a serious toll on them emotionally."

"We all have to do things in war we don't like. Even you and I." Himmler motioned for them to walk. "We'll have to admonish the commanders to push their men harder or step aside and let those who aren't quite as sensitive take over."

"I agree. I think with a little prodding the commanders will—"

"*Reichsführer!*" Heydrich and Himmler turned to see an SS *hauptsturmführer* from the communication car rushing up to them. He held a sheet of paper which he handed to Himmler. "This urgent communique just arrived from Dietrich in Berlin."

"Thank you."

The SS *hauptsturmführer* saluted and raced off as Himmler read the sheet. After a few moments, he said, "This is interesting."

"What is?" asked Heydrich.

"MARLENE has finally proven her usefulness to Operation *Hexen*. Churchill is flying to Cairo this week and will meet with Foreign Minister Molotov. She was able to provide a rough itinerary of his flight and where the prime minister will stay. And he's taking his occult team with him."

"This is good news. It'll counter losing Hess."

"Tell the driver we'll be heading to *Wolfschanze* instead, and let the military commanders know our plans have changed. If we can shoot down that plane, it'll change the course of this war."

"Maybe we shouldn't be so hasty," said Heydrich.

"Go on."

"According to this, Churchill and his entourage are leaving tonight. Assuming Hitler approves an assassination attempt, this gives us little time to prepare an intercept. And we're going to have to go through the *Luftwaffe*, which poses its own set of problems. Trying to find a blacked-out aircraft at night with what little information we have is going to be next to impossible. Plus, our time to do this is limited. Once that plane reaches central Africa, we have no way of getting it. And you know how Goring is. If his *Luftwaffe* fails to shoot down Churchill, which will probably be the case, he'll blame the SS for not providing him with accurate intelligence. If by some miracle the *Luftwaffe* does succeed, then that fat bastard will hog all the credit."

Himmler nodded his approval. "What are you suggesting?"

"That for now we pretend we haven't seen this communique. Call Dietrich on a secure line and have him send Lilith and Malalath to Cairo to assassinate Churchill and his occult warriors. If they succeed, you tell the *Führer* you received the communique with little time to seek advice and made a command decision. If they fail, you tell the *Führer* that Lilith and Malalath went after Churchill on their own to avenge Agrat. In either case, the potential gains far outweigh the risks."

Himmler considered his options for several moments before speaking. "You're right. That is the best course of action. Call Dietrich and tell him what we're planning. I'll talk to the *hauptsturmführer* and make sure the communications car knows we did not receive this message until later."

Heydrich suppressed a grin. He knew damn well Himmler asked him to place the call to Dietrich so that, in case things went horribly wrong, the *Reichsführer* had an additional scapegoat. Not that it mattered. It was the nature of the job. Heydrich knew that, given what the regime was trying to accomplish, they would either emerge victorious or would all hang together.

As Himmler walked away, Heydrich went off to arrange the assassination of Winton Churchill.

CHAPTER THIRTY-SIX

Lubyanka Prison, Moscow Russia
1 July 1941

MOSCOW LAY IN total darkness as a result of the blackout conditions imposed on the city following the German invasion. Levorov raced through the streets on his way to Lubyanka Prison, this time driving the staff car himself. Without headlights, navigating the city streets was difficult. Thankfully, there was little traffic to contend with, partly because it was almost midnight and partly because people had evacuated Moscow out of fear of a German occupation.

Levorov had been at the Kremlin guarding Stalin during his late-night strategy meeting with Russia's military leadership when the call had come through from Lubyanka Prison that Tasaria had arrived. Expediting her, as well as her younger sister and grandmother, from the camp to Moscow had been Stalin's highest priority, and Stalin's signature on the order sped up the process. In just over twenty-four hours, the three Romani had been yanked from their camp and flown into the capital. When Captain of State Security Primakov, the prison's night shift commander, called less than an hour ago to let him know they had arrived, Levorov excused himself so he could begin Tasaria's interrogation immediately before the young woman could have time to adjust to her new surroundings. Levorov didn't even call his driver back to duty, preferring to drive himself rather than waste time.

When Levorov pulled up in front of Lubyanka Prison, the night shift commander and an NKVD private stood on the sidewalk to greet him.

Levorov climbed out of his car and shook Primakov's hand. "Thank you for calling me despite the late hour."

"I knew how important her arrival is to you," said Primakov. "Slava will take care of your car. I'll take you to see the prisoner."

Three minutes later, after discussing certain preparations with Primakov, Levorov entered Tasaria's holding cell. The space was small, seven feet wide and fifteen feet deep, and was spartanly finished with a cheap cot that had not yet been provided with a mattress, a desk, and a heater. For Tasaria, it probably seemed like a luxury hotel compared to the gulag.

She lay stretched out along the slats of the cot. His entrance had not disturbed her, so Levorov grabbed the metal door and slammed it shut as hard as possible. Rather than be startled, the young woman shifted her head to look at the door, then went back to sleep.

"Get up," Levorov ordered.

Tasaria continued to lie there.

Levorov placed his foot on the foot of the cot and shoved, slamming the end against the rear wall. Tasaria stirred.

"Get up, you Romani whore."

Tasaria rolled off the bed and stood. If the young woman had ever been attractive, two years within the gulag system had taken it away from her. Long, unkempt black hair framed a gaunt, sallow face. She was emaciated and dirty, and her shoulders slumped forward. Levorov did not know what smelled worse, her body or her prison garb. He could tell by examining her that Tasaria had once been a proud and resilient woman until the gulag system had beaten those qualities out of her. He saw it in the way she bore herself with a passive defiance and in the hatred burning deep in her sunken brown eyes. It would not be easy keeping this one under control.

"Are you Tasaria?" he asked.

"What do you want? Why did you bring us to Moscow?"

"I'll ask the questions. Once again, are you Tasaria?"

The young woman shrugged, though her gesture was barely perceptible. "My name is Tasaria."

"Your clan left Poland to escape the Nazis and was eventually arrested near Kiev, is that correct?"

"If you know so much about me, why do you keep asking me questions?"

"To make certain I brought the right person here. I would hate to think I wasted the state's time and resources bringing you here for nothing. Trust me, that wouldn't be good for you or your family. May I proceed?"

"Sure."

"Is it true you're a necromancer?"

Tasaria went rigid upon hearing the word and her expression hardened, but she did not answer.

"I think I've found the right Tasaria." Levorov allowed himself a brief chuckle. "I need to know if your abilities are real or if this just a parlor trick the Romani use to fool the peasants."

"You don't know what you're getting yourself into."

"I know exactly what I'm getting into. Do you have those abilities?"

Tasaria shook her head. "The powers you are asking about are evil and dangerous."

"That's why I need them." Levorov moved closer to Tasaria so he stood only inches from her. He made direct eye contact and spoke each of the next five words slowly and deliberately, emphasizing each one. "Do you have those abilities?"

Tasaria lowered her head and nodded.

"Excellent," Levorov said with a faked pleasantry. He stepped away and headed back toward the cell door. "You see how easy this can be if you cooperate. Which brings me to why you're here. I need you to use your abilities to help out the state with a delicate matter."

"Go fuck yourself."

Levorov laughed. "What language coming from a young lady. No wonder the Romani are reviled throughout Europe."

"Laugh all you want. After what you did to me and my family, I'd rather die than help you."

"So be it."

Levorov spun around and knocked three times on the cell door, then stepped back into the room. The metal door swung open. Primakov entered the room holding Tasaria's grandmother by the arm, and then shoved her to the floor at the end of the cot. A second guard came in, clutching her younger sister by the hair. Levorov moved behind the grandmother. When the old woman tried to stand, he pushed her back to the floor with his boot. Tasaria moved to help her family, but the glare Levorov flashed her stopped the woman in her tracks.

"This one here is useless to the state. We feed and house her, but she's too old to work." Levorov pointed to the sister. "She, on the other hand, is quite valuable. I have a brothel unit on the front that needs new blood. I could get some good money for her if she's a virgin, though I doubt that considering what whores you Romani are."

The sister struggled until the guard placed his meaty hand around her throat and applied pressure.

"Please don't," begged Tasaria.

"I'm going to ask you one final time." Levorov unholstered his Makarov pistol and placed the barrel against the back of the grandmother's head. The old woman wept when she felt the metal. "Will you use your abilities to help us?"

"Yes!" yelled Tasaria. She then dropped to her knees and cried, repeating the word three more times through her sobs.

Levorov slid his Makarov back into its holster. Primakov grabbed the grandmother, yanked her to her feet, and led her out of the cell. The other guard followed. After they left, Levorov sat on the cot in front of Tasaria.

"I promise that as long you cooperate, you, your sister, and your grandmother will remain here in Lubyanka and will be safe. You might even earn your release if all goes well. But you double cross me once, and there'll be no second chances. I'll shoot your grandmother in front of you, send your sister to a brothel unit, and ship you back to your camp. Is that understood?"

Tasaria nodded and whimpered, "Yes."

Levorov patted her on the shoulder in a false gesture of reassurance. "I know you've been through a lot, but I need you to put your necromancy skills to use right now. It's important."

Tasaria looked up at him and wiped her eyes. "I need the body of whoever it is you want me to talk to."

"You can't just *talk* to them from the beyond?"

"That's a different set of skills. I can only talk to the dead if I can touch the deceased's body." Panic set in on Tasaria. "Please tell me you have the body."

"I do, but...."

"What?"

"It's not in the best of shape."

"That doesn't matter," she said with a sense of relief. "As long as there's some part of the human body remaining, I can contact the spirit."

"That's the other problem," said Levorov. "It's not exactly human."

CHAPTER THIRTY-SEVEN

The Kremlin basement, Moscow, Russia
2 July 1941

*A*T LEAST THE *Russian pig allowed me to freshen up and get a change of clothes,* Tasaria thought as she sat in the backseat of the staff car as it raced through Moscow. It had been the first time in almost two years since she had experienced such luxuries as a cold shower and clean garments, and she felt spoiled by it. It gave her a sense of hope that maybe her life, and the lives of her surviving family members, would finally change for the better.

She quickly squelched those feelings. Hope had died a long time ago, and she could not afford to harbor any false illusions. If she was lucky, she could make herself useful long enough for her grandmother to die in relative peace in a jail cell rather than in the squalor of a gulag, and for her sister to find a way out of this Hell.

After driving for close to thirty minutes, Tasaria leaned forward to talk with Levorov, who was driving. "Where are we?"

"The eastern suburbs of Moscow."

"Why are we here?"

"This is where the body of the one to be necromanced is located."

Tasaria sat back and said nothing. Eventually, Levorov turned off the main road into a side lane that led to a stadium. She watched nervously as he drove around to the back of the structure, parked in front a flight of stairs, and stepped out.

Tasaria waited for the officer to open the door. When he did not, she let herself out and joined him. They descended the stairs to the base of the stadium wall and entered a pair of metal doors. Inside the building, they walked to a door at the far end of the corridor that descended several flights underground. For a moment, she thought Levorov had taken her someplace isolated to execute her.

When they emerged from the stairwell through a pair of wooden doors, Tasaria realized Levorov had taken her to an underground complex. A corridor with an ornate tile floor flanked with faux marble columns led to a spacious, circular conference room. More marble columns supported an ornately carved domed ceiling. A circular conference table with thirty seats dominated the room. Something lay on the portion of the table closest to the corridor, covered by a white sheet.

What startled Tasaria most was the presence in the room of two people. The first she recognized as Stalin. The other was a frightening looking man with a round head, prominent nose, and evil blue eyes staring out from under a pair of *pince-nez* glasses.

Tasaria glanced over at Levorov. "What are they doing here?"

"They have a special interest in this matter."

"I... I usually don't do this in front of others."

Beria stepped over and took Tasaria's hand. His touch sent a shiver down her spine.

"Don't worry, my dear. You'll do fine."

"Let's begin," said Stalin gruffly.

"Where's the body?" Tasaria asked.

"Over here."

Levorov stepped over to the table, took hold of the sheet, and whipped it aside. Naamah's charred corpse lay on top of it. To Tasaria, it looked like a giant snake with a human torso. The tail had curled up underneath the body, the last three feet so charred it looked like jerky. The skin had seared off the chest and arms, leaving behind scorched muscles, and the facial features had shriveled around the snake-like skull, revealing its fangs.

Tasaria lifted the two burnt appendages that dangled from the shoulder blades. "Are these wings?"

Levorov nodded.

"What is this thing?"

"It's a *rusalka*."

"A succubus?" She dropped the wings and stepped back from the table. "You want me to necromance a succubus?"

"Can you?"

"I've never tried it on a...."

"Demon?" said Beria.

Tasaria nodded. "I guess there's a first time for everything. Let's begin. Please give me some room."

The Russians moved back as Tasaria stepped over to the table. When she placed her hands on Naamah's chest, she recoiled from the feel.

"Is everything okay?" Levorov asked.

She nodded. "I need access to its chest. I can make a better connection with the dead if I can hold the heart or brain."

Levorov joined Tasaria. Placing his hands where the sternum should be, he pressed against the charred skin until it gave way, allowing his hands to penetrate into Naamah's chest. He pulled them out and wiped off the gore on the sheet.

"Go ahead."

Tasaria slid her hands inside the succubus' chest. She had done this before on numerous occasions and had learned to deal with the sensation, but this time was different. Closing her eyes so she did not have to look at the hideous face, Tasaria felt around until her fingers brushed against a tough, gristle-like object she assumed was the demon's heart. She wrapped her hands around the organ and clutched it tightly.

The sensations that assaulted Tasaria's psyche overwhelmed the young woman—physical torment, emotional anguish, mental trauma. A psychic wail cut through Tasaria's soul, startling her. She wanted to release the heart and break the link, but knew if she did, she would never have the courage to reconnect.

"Is this Naamah?" she asked.

Who are you?

"My name is Tasaria. I'm a necromancer. I want to talk with you."

Are you with him?

"With who?"

Levorov. He's the one who did this to me.

"He's the one who burned you?"

He destroyed my body. Now I cannot go back to Hell and am stuck wandering the nethersphere forever. I can sense his presence near you.

Tasaria felt the fury rage inside Naamah's spirit. "They want me to ask you some questions."

Why should I help you? You're with them.

"I'm not. They're threatening me. They'll kill my grandmother and sister if I refuse."

They'll kill your sister?

"Yes."

I understand your desire to protect your sister. A long pause ensued. *Ask your questions.*

"Who are you working for?"

I think they've figured that out by now.

"Please answer me."

I'm working for Himmler. One of my sisters was supposed to control General Wavell in North Africa and make sure he lost to the Afrika Korps. I was tasked to do the same thing with Stalin, to distract him long enough so the German invasion would succeed.

"Why?"

Hitler made a deal with Hell. My Master would ensure the Thousand-Year Reich if Hitler could provide him with twenty-five million souls. This is where Hitler plans to get them. Not only will he turn East Europe and Russia into a German Empire, but he plans on cleansing the area of everyone who doesn't fit his concepts of racial purity or who pose a threat to his rule. Once that number is reached, the rest will be used as slave labor or driven into Siberia.

"You're okay with this?"

Naamah laughed. *For one with such a gift you are so naïve. I could care less about your kind. You are nothing to me. My Master made a deal with Hitler and asked me and my sisters to help him fulfill his part of the bargain. There is no emotion involved in this. Or at least, there wasn't. After what they did to me, it'll give me great pleasure to watch the Germans place Levorov, Stalin, and that rapist Beria against a wall and execute them. I only wish I could be there to see it in person.* Naamah paused again. *You're Romani, aren't you?*

"How can you tell?"

I sense much more than you realize. Naamah expressed an emotion that seemed almost sympathetic. *It's a pity. Your people will suffer under the Germans as much as the Jews will. I want to go now.*

"Wait! One more question."

Just one.

"How can we stop the Germans?"

The only way you can stop Hitler is to defeat him before he provides my Master with the required souls. Even if you're in the streets of Berlin, once he has killed twenty-five million people his reign will be ensured.

"What are the details of this arrangement?"

I agreed to only one more question.

"I'm the necromancer, so I'm in control here. I'll say when we're done."

So be it, little one. Stay connected as long as you want.

Tasaria was bombarded with images of what was transpiring on the front. Men being shredded by explosives and bullets, or being burnt alive in tank fires, or dying slow and agonizing deaths from their wounds. Women and children being indiscriminately killed by aerial bombs or lined up along ditches and shot in the head. And the souls of all those butchered—German and Russian, soldier and civilian, men and women, saint and sinner—being dragged into Hell in a literal river of the dead, their lives having become little more than chits for a nightmarish body count. Thousands of these visions invaded her senses at once, and she saw each with clarity. It terrified and repulsed Tasaria. She let go of Naamah's heart to break the connection, and immediately her mind cleared. Her head spun, and she fell to the floor.

When a pair of hands touched her shoulders, she screamed and flailed her arms.

"It's alright," said Levorov in a surprisingly soothing tone. "It's over now. Let me help you up."

As Levorov helped Tasaria to her feet, she said, "I talked with Naamah."

"We heard. You spoke both sides of the conversation, half of it in her voice." Beria brought over a chair and Levorov maneuvered her into it. "What happened at the end? What caused you to scream and break contact?"

Tasaria explained the visions she had witnessed. When finished, each of the three men around her were pale.

"Make contact again," demanded Beria. "We need to know more details about what Hitler is planning."

Tasaria lowered her head and shivered, uncertain if she could deal with such an emotional trauma so soon.

"It won't work," said Levorov, coming to her defense. "Naamah made it clear she doesn't want to talk any longer. Trying to reconnect the link will only hurt Tasaria, and we may need her in the future."

"We need to know *now* the details of what Hitler is planning," demanded Beria.

"It's irrelevant," said Stalin. "We know enough. That madman is going to turn Poland and Russia into a slaughterhouse. How he's going to do it is not important. We need to stop Hitler before he succeeds. We'll have to drive the Nazis out of the east and wipe Germany off the map."

Beria nodded.

"You realize," asked Levorov, "that by doing this we run

the risk of helping Hitler achieve his body count?"

"I do. But if we do this violently enough and show no mercy, hopefully we can defeat the Nazis before the death count reaches twenty-five million."

Stalin broke away from the others and approached Tasaria. She feared the worst. Instead, he placed his left hand on her shoulder.

"You have done Russia a great service. Thank you."

"You're welcome."

"Comrade Levorov will escort you back to Lubyanka. We'll arrange better accommodations for you and your relatives later. But first, I need to speak with him alone. Would you mind waiting out in the corridor?"

"Of course."

Tasaria exited the conference room. Only when the door closed behind her did she fall against the wall and breathe a sigh of relief. She didn't know what bothered her more, having made such a nightmarish connection with a demon, or having to cooperate with the monsters who had wiped out her family. But what was it Naamah had said? *Your people will suffer under the Germans as much as the Jews will.* Which meant that, to keep her sister and grandmother alive, one way or another she would have to help out the butchers of her people.

Crouching against the wall, Tasaria placed her face in her hands and cried.

STALIN WAITED FOR the door to close before returning to Beria and Levorov. "I'm concerned about what Naamah told Tasaria about a succubus having been sent to distract General Wavell in North Africa."

"Why is that?" asked Levorov.

"General Wavell was replaced over a week ago after the disaster at Halfaya Pass, yet the British have not yet warned us about the threat to Russia from a succubus."

"Perhaps it's a coincidence," said Levorov. "Maybe Churchill removed him because of his poor performance, and they don't know about the succubus."

"Or maybe they've joined forces with the Nazis," added Beria. "We still don't know the reason why Hess flew to England back in May."

"Exactly," said Stalin.

"What do you need me to do?"

"Molotov is flying to Egypt tomorrow for a secret meeting with Churchill to discuss an Anglo-Russian strategy against Hitler. I want you to go with him. If the British bring up the subject, you're the best man to ask questions and coordinate our response. If they don't, then I want you to find out as much as you can about what the British know."

"How far do you want me to go to get that information?"

"Use your discretion. Don't do anything to jeopardize our relationship with the British."

"Can I bring Tasaria with me?"

"Do you think that's a good idea?" asked Beria. "I'm not sure where her loyalties lie."

"She'll do as she's told as long as we have her grandmother and sister in custody," said Levorov. "Right now, she's the only person with any psychic abilities we have available. I'd hate to run into a situation where she could be of use but she's back here in Moscow."

"Good point," agreed Stalin. "You can take her, but she's your responsibility. I'll let you arrange with Molotov the details of your departure. Is there anything else?"

Levorov and Beria shook their heads.

"Then take Tasaria back to Lubyanka and get her ready for the trip."

Levorov saluted and headed for the door. As he opened it, Stalin called out.

"One more thing. Good luck. You're going to need it."

CHAPTER THIRTY-EIGHT

Venice, Italy
2 July 1941

THE CAR THAT picked up Dietrich and the succubi at the airfield made its way along the causeway connecting the mainland to Venice as the last rays of the setting sun rippled along the water. Per Dietrich's orders, the SS driver had used a Fiat borrowed from one of the locals rather than the typical German staff car, and everyone had dressed in civilian clothes, hoping to remain inconspicuous. All three wore Greek fisherman's caps per the recognition code Dietrich had arranged with their contact. However, even in slacks and jackets, and with their hair tucked under their caps, they stood out much more than him. He knew they would attract attention, but with so little time to prepare that could not be helped. No one would ask questions out of fear of running afoul of the OVRA.

Once on the island of Venice, the driver dropped Dietrich and the succubi off on the outskirts of the Santa Croce *sestieri*. The three made their way on foot through the back streets and canals of Venice until they arrived at Piazza San Marco. The Basilica di San Marco stood opposite them along the east quadrant of the square. The three made their way along the northern arcade toward the basilica where they stepped into the northern most portal of the Italo-Byzantine façade and waited in the shadows, trying to appear as casual as possible. Dietrich knew they had little chance of that, so instead he scanned the square, looking for anyone who might have an undue interest in them.

This entire operation had been thrown together too haphazardly for his liking. Heydrich had called only two days ago to inform him Churchill and his occult team would be in Cairo on the fourth, which gave Dietrich precious little time to make the necessary preparations. It would have been easy if he could have flown into Egypt, but Heydrich had specifically warned him not to involve Goring or the *Luftwaffe*. Thankfully, the restriction didn't apply to the other branches of the armed forces. Admiral Donitz was more amenable to allowing Dietrich the use one of his U-boats to infiltrate the succubi into Egypt without asking prying questions, thus the reason for their trip to Venice.

Arranging for contacts to meet them in Egypt and escort them to Giza had been more complicated, and Dietrich was still uncertain if someone would be there to greet Lilith and Malalath when they landed. If not, then this assignment would end in failure before it could fully get underway. The uncertainty gave him the excuse he needed to disobey Heydrich's instruction to not accompany the succubi on their mission, allowing him to claim he needed to be on the ground to make decisions if the plans failed to pan out. If this mission was successful, Dietrich assumed Heydrich and Himmler would forgive him for not following their orders. If it failed, he would rather die in combat than be placed against a wall and shot like a criminal.

After fifteen minutes, a man entered Piazza San Marco from the canal side of the square and headed straight for the basilica. He looked like a seafarer, with a weathered face and calloused hands. His hair and beard had not been washed in weeks. He wore a dirty white turtleneck, dark slacks, and combat boots. Even without the uniform jacket, everything about this man exuded military bearing. Dietrich presumed he was the commander of the U-boat that had been ordered to ferry them to Egypt.

The man stopped one hundred feet from the basilica and scanned the five portals. Upon seeing Dietrich and the succubi in their Greek fisherman caps, he nodded and walked straight toward them.

"That man is an idiot," Malalath said. "If there are any British agents around, he'll lead them right to us."

"Do you want me to glamour him so he's not so obvious?" Lilith asked.

Dietrich agreed with them, but right now he needed to concentrate on the primary task.

"No. As long as he can get us to Egypt without being detected, that's all I care about."

The man walked directly up to them and stopped. At least when he spoke, he kept his voice quiet so no one else could hear.

"Are you the party that chartered my boat?"

"Yes," Dietrich answered, and then gave the counter signal. "How much is it to take us to Greece?"

"I thought you wanted to go to Egypt?"

"I do," said Dietrich, abandoning the effort to remain covert. "I'm Werner Dietrich."

The man extended his hand. "*Kapitän* Hoecker of U-275."

Dietrich took it and pulled the captain in close to him. "Don't use your rank in public. I don't want anyone to know we're on a military mission."

"What's the big deal? I thought the Italians were allies."

Dietrich ignored the captain's lack of tradecraft and common sense. "Is everything arranged per my instructions?"

Hoecker nodded and leaned in closer, talking in a low voice so no one else could hear. "My boat is submerged five miles offshore. I have a launch that will take us to it. That will give us plenty of time to get you to Egypt by midnight tomorrow. Do you have the coordinates where you want to land?"

"I'll give them to you once we're aboard your ship."

Hoecker nodded. "Do you have any gear?"

"No. The people we're meeting have everything we need."

Hoecker noticed Lilith and Malalath. "My crew hasn't seen women in weeks, let alone women as nice as them. Are you sure you want to bring them along on this trip?"

"We can handle ourselves," sneered Lilith.

Hoecker shrugged. "Suit yourself. Follow me."

The group made its way across Piazza San Marco to the waterfront. Hoecker led them to a motor launch that sat amongst the gondolas and other small craft. In the back sat another submariner dressed in a blue shirt and slacks whose eyes widened when he spotted Lilith and Malalath. Once everyone was on board, the sailor started the launch, backed it out into the canal, and headed for the U-boat waiting offshore.

CHAPTER THIRTY-NINE

Mena House, Giza, Egypt
3 July 1941

B ELLINGHAM HAD NOT been exaggerating when he warned
them the trip to Cairo would not be fun or easy. Lee only
wished he had told her and Cody how exasperating the journey
would be.

Lee had been excited when she had heard they would be
traveling aboard a Boeing 314 clipper, anticipating a luxurious
flight. The realization this would not be a dream trip struck
when she saw their plane had been painted black to mask its
presence at night from German fighters, and when the pilot
informed them that they would be flying under complete radio
silence and with no filed flight plan to maintain secrecy, which
meant they would also be susceptible to any RAF fighters that
might stumble upon them. That had been before they even
lifted off.

With the Germans controlling most of Europe and North
Africa, the flight had to circumnavigate Axis-controlled
territory. Taking off from Lyneham RAF base outside of
London around midnight, the clipper flew to Gibraltar, landing
before dawn so the plane could be hidden and refueled. They
departed Gibraltar after dusk, flew down West Africa to
Takoradi in Ghana, followed the Central African supply route
to Khartoum in Sudan, then headed north along the Nile until
they reached Cairo late on the morning of the third. From
there, a motorcade of staff cars and armored vehicles whisked
Churchill and his party to Giza.

On the plus side, Mena House far exceeded her expectations. She had anticipated elegance, and instead got exotic. The grounds were a forty-acre oasis located ten kilometers outside of Cairo and a kilometer from the pyramids of Khufu and Khafre. The archaeological wonders dominated the skyline, providing a panoramic view more picturesque than a postcard or painting. Just as magnificent was the hotel itself. Built in the mid-19th century as a royal lodge for the Khedive Ishmail, it was purchased by an English couple in the 1920s who renovated it into a luxury hotel. Terraces and patios lay spread around the grounds.

When Lee entered her room, she was excited to see it included a balcony with a scenic view of the pyramids. She rushed over to the balcony door and slid it aside, stepping out.

"This is gorgeous."

"What is?" asked Cody as he placed her duffel bag on her bed.

"This view." Lee raced back into the room, grabbed Cody's hand, and led him back onto the balcony. She wrapped her arm around his waist and leaned her head against his shoulder. "Have you ever seen anything so beautiful?"

"They're nice."

"Nice?" Lee gently punched him in the stomach. "You're so unromantic."

"You didn't say that the other night." Cody kissed her on the forehead.

Lee stepped away and crossed over to the far side of the balcony, placed her hands on the rail, and admired the view.

"As a kid, I dreamed of traveling the Middle East and Asia and seeing the sites of the ancient world. Giza was always on top of my list."

"So, this is a dream come true for you."

"One of many." Lee glanced over her shoulder and smiled. "Bellingham said he doesn't need us until tomorrow morning. Let's see the pyramids."

"Now? I thought you were tired after the flight?"

"I am. But I don't want to miss the opportunity to see them up close. Please?"

"Can I at least drop off my stuff in my room before we go?"

"Sure. We'll meet back here in fifteen minutes." Lee rushed over and hugged him. "Thanks."

BELLINGHAM ARRIVED AT the prime minister's suite. After having his identification checked by the guards, he was ushered inside. Churchill stood on the balcony admiring the pyramids, a cigar in one hand and a sifter of Johnny Walker Red Label whiskey in the other. Bellingham crossed the sitting room and stopped at the balcony doors.

"You wanted to see me, Prime Minister?"

"I did. Join me." Churchill raised his hands slightly. "May I offer you a Cohiba or some whiskey?"

"No, thank you. I don't drink." Bellingham stepped up beside the Prime Minister.

"You're a wise man. It's one of many bad habits I've taken up, but at my age, it would be too hard to quit. Besides, I've taken more out of alcohol than it's taken out of me."

"You have a good excuse, sir. You're running a war."

"That's as good enough reason as any." Churchill raised his sifter in a toast. "To the success of our missions."

Bellingham nodded. "Here, here."

Churchill drank a swig of whiskey and puffed on his cigar. "I've arranged for your people to meet with anyone who might have knowledge about the German occult activity against General Wavell."

"Thank you."

"Tell them a staff car will pick them up out front at 0800 and will take them to Cairo."

"I will."

"You're welcome to join the delegation tomorrow that's meeting with Molotov."

"Are you going to discuss occult activities with the Soviets?"

Churchill took another sip of whiskey. "Not unless they bring it up first. If Stalin is waging an occult war against Hitler, I'll help him in his effort. If not, this is one area of cooperation with the Russians I would rather avoid. If they don't already have an occult warfare capability, I don't want to be the one to give it to them."

"I understand."

"That'll be all," said Churchill.

Bellingham excused himself and was halfway across the suite when Churchill called after him.

"There's one more thing. Tomorrow night I'm hosting a dinner here for Molotov. I would like it if you and your officers attended."

"We will, Prime Minister. Thank you."

As Bellingham left the suite, he thought tomorrow night's dinner would be a pleasant way to cap off an uneventful trip.

CHAPTER FORTY

Shepheard's Hotel, Cairo, Egypt
3 July 1941

S O FAR, NOTHING about this trip had impressed Levorov. For all of Stalin's talk about how important this meeting with the British would be, the only delegates were Molotov, three experts from the Foreign Ministry, and himself acting as the minister's bodyguard. The rest of the delegation was excited about staying at the Shepheard's Hotel, one of the finest in the city, and getting the opportunity to see Cairo.

Levorov could not have cared less. He had the sole responsibility for defeating Hitler's occult efforts against Russia, and he would not be able to do that here in Egypt. Nor did it help his mood that the Latvian capital of Riga had fallen on the first, opening the way to Leningrad, and that Hungarian troops in Ukraine had pushed past Lvov. That afternoon, Stalin had spoken to the Russian people for the first time since the invasion, issuing his call to destroy the enemy. While all this was going on at home, Levorov was unpacking his bags and preparing for a conference in Cairo.

A knock sounded on the door. He was surprised to open it and find Molotov standing there.

"Comrade Levorov, do you have a moment?"

"Of course." He stepped to one side to allow the foreign minister into his room. "How can I help you?"

"I wanted to talk with you about why Stalin sent you along on this trip, and why I want you here."

"Thank you, but there's no need for that. I do as I'm ordered."

"But you're not happy about it."

Levorov became embarrassed. "Am I that obvious?"

"Yes," Molotov said forcefully, but then his tone softened. He walked over to the window and looked out over the city. "Don't worry about it, though. I understand your frustration. You're a soldier, not a diplomat, and with the motherland in danger, you would rather be fighting the enemy than escorting me on overseas trips. The truth is, you're not here so much to protect me but as one of my experts."

"What am I an expert on?"

"The occult." Molotov turned from the window. "You figured out it was a succubus controlling Stalin, and you knew how to deal with it. And you were smart enough to seek out Tasaria, who provided us with valuable intelligence about Hitler being behind this."

Levorov chuckled. "I guess that does make me the Soviet Union's best expert on occult warfare."

"It makes you the Soviet Union's *only* expert on occult warfare. Which is why you're here. One of the topics I intend to bring up with Churchill is whether Hess warned him about Germany using the dark arts against us."

"Even if Hess did tell the British, do you think Churchill will admit it?"

"Probably not. But if he does, I want you there to get as much information out of him as possible."

"You can count on me."

"I know." Molotov headed for the door and paused on his way out. "Worst case scenario, this entire trip is a waste of your time, and in two days you'll be back in Moscow fighting Nazis. See you at 0800 tomorrow."

CHAPTER FORTY-ONE

Off the coast of Egypt
3 July 1941

HOECKER DRAPED HIS hands over the handles of the periscope as he rotated it in a three-hundred-and-sixty-degree arc. Once he completed the first circle, Hoecker did it again, this time stopping three-quarters of the way through the sweep.

"Do you see anything?" Dietrich asked.

Hoecker moved away from the eyepiece and shook his head. "Sonar, do you have any readings?"

"No contacts, *kapitän*."

Dietrich checked his watch. Eight minutes until midnight. "They'll be expecting our signal soon."

Hoecker flashed Dietrich a dissatisfied glare that reminded him who was in command of this boat. Yet he also took the hint.

"Down periscope. Bring us to the surface. I want two men topside looking out for British warships. Tell the men to be ready with the raft. We're sitting ducks here in the shallow water, so I want to put our people on shore and get out of here as fast as possible."

Activity bustled through the conning tower as the crew followed Hoecker's orders. A few minutes later, the U-boat surfaced. Hoecker climbed the ladder, opened the hatch, and emerged onto the exterior deck of the conning tower. Dietrich followed. By the time he joined Hoecker, the captain was already scanning the coast with a pair of binoculars. A full moon hung high in the sky, casting a light glow on the darkened coast half a mile away. As one of the lookouts exited from below, he handed Hoecker a signaling lamp. The captain flashed the recognition signal toward the shore. Neither man saw a response.

"What's our location?" Dietrich asked.

"We're at the exact coordinates you gave me, which should put us halfway between Port Said and Lake Bardawil."

Hoecker sent the recognition signal again, and still received no answer.

Dietrich checked his watch. "We still have two minutes."

"Your contacts better be on time. I can't stay exposed like this for too long."

The next few minutes seemed interminable. Hoecker fidgeted and constantly checked around him. Dietrich looked at his watch. It read one minute after midnight.

"Try again."

Hoecker flashed the recognition signal a third time. Nothing.

"It looks like your friends stood you up." The captain turned to his lookouts. "Get below. Prepare to dive."

"You can't leave yet."

"Yes, I can. We're sitting ducks up here. For all I know, your contacts gave our position to the British and a destroyer is bearing down on us as we speak. Now get below."

"Then put us ashore."

"Without a guide? You wouldn't survive two days in the desert. I'm taking her down, so if you don't get below, you'll have to swim to shore from—"

"*Kapitän*," called one of the lookouts. "I see a light on shore."

Hoecker raised the binoculars and scanned the shore.

"What do you see?" Dietrich asked.

"It's the recognition signal." Hoecker used the signal lamp to flash the confirmation code and switched to his binoculars. A few seconds later, he received the appropriate response. Leaning to one side, he spoke down the open hatch.

"Get the raft up here now, and the two women. Dietrich will join them on the aft deck."

Dietrich felt a sense of relief. He offered Hoecker his hand. "Thank you."

The captain shook it half-heartedly. "I'm only doing my job. Now, if you'll pardon my being rude, I want to get you off this boat and ashore as quickly as possible so I can get out of here."

Dietrich understood completely.

THIRTY MINUTES LATER, the raft carrying Dietrich and the succubi came ashore on Egyptian soil. One sailor held it in place as the passengers climbed out. As they did, five men in *jellabiyas* approached. Four of them stopped twenty feet away from the raft, two carrying Enfield rifles and two carrying Thompson submachine guns. The fifth approached the party, pausing when ten feet from them.

"Are you *Obergruppenführer* Dietrich?" he asked in flawless German.

"I am."

The Bedouin stepped forward. "I'm Ahmed. Mufti Al-Husseini sent me. Welcome to Egypt."

"This is Lilith and Malalath." When Dietrich turned around to introduce the succubi, he noticed the crew of the raft had already pushed away from shore and were heading back to the U-boat.

Ahmed waved his hand. One of the men carrying an Enfield stepped forward, slung a burlap bag off his shoulder, and dropped it in the sand in front of Dietrich.

"What's this?"

"A *jellabiya* for you and *hijabs* for the women. So you can blend in. If you travel across the desert dressed like that, you'll draw attention to yourselves. We have three camels waiting for you on the other side of the sand dune." Ahmed stepped back with the rest of his men. "Hurry before a British patrol stumbles across us."

CHAPTER FORTY-TWO

Mena House, Giza, Egypt
4 July 1941

THE DAY'S MEETINGS with General Wavell's staff had not gone as anticipated. That was not entirely true, thought Lee. It had gone as anticipated since she and Cody had not expected to get any useful information out of them.

Everyone had reported that the general seemed distracted by his infatuation with Agrat. The men described her as stunningly attractive or seductive, while the few female officers interviewed had nothing nice to say about Agrat, with the word bitch being used frequently. All that had proved was the succubus had the ability to temporarily glamour men and had no influence on women. However, no one provided any information that could help them predict, discover, or deter the threat. The only thing that saved the day from being a complete loss was, having completed all their interviews early, and with little to draft up in the way of reports, Cody had been able to convince the driver to take them on a tour of Cairo.

Dinner was infinitely better. How often does a woman like herself get to dine in one of the finest restaurants in Cairo with Prime Minister Churchill and Soviet Foreign Minister Molotov? Bellingham sat at the head table with the prime minister. She and Cody sat at a table on the other side of the dining hall with some of the staffers from the British General Headquarters, spending the evening chatting each other up on what daily living was like in wartime Cairo and London. Only after dessert had been served and the event began to wind down was

Bellingham able to break away and join them. The others at the table politely excused themselves when the group captain sat down.

"How did your day go?" Bellingham asked.

"Not well," answered Cody. "We spent four hours interviewing those who were closest to General Wavell and still know nothing more than we did when we arrived."

"I was afraid of that."

"Did you have any better luck?" Lee asked.

"A lot of strategy was discussed. London and Moscow agreed to diminish Nazi influence in the Middle East by jointly invading and occupying Iran, which will offset the setbacks caused by Agrat. But the Russians made no mention of any occult activities."

"So, this whole trip was a dead end for us," said Cody.

"Not necessarily. I have one more thing I want to try." Bellingham watched the main table as Churchill and Molotov stood up and made their way toward a private hall to carry on further discussions. "Excuse me, please."

When Bellingham left, Cody stood up and offered his hand to Lee.

"Where are we going?" she asked.

"To see the pyramids in the moonlight."

"When did you become such a romantic?" she giggled.

"You don't think I've been romantic up to now?" he asked with feigned indignation.

"You've been passable."

"Well, if you'd rather not—"

"I didn't say that." Lee took his hand and rubbed her fingers against his palm. "I can't think of anyone I'd rather see them with."

The couple exited the dining room, crossed the lobby, and stepped outside. Arm in arm, they made their way around to the side of the hotel to the balcony overlooking the pyramids. Three British soldiers sat at a table in one corner of the balcony sharing a bottle of wine. A Soviet officer stood by the open window to the dining room, smoking a cigarette.

Cody led her to the far end of the balcony. They stopped in the shadows and rested their arms on top of the wall. The pyramids sat on the hill, towering over the hotel, the moonlight bathing their surface in a soft glow.

"Have you ever seen anything so beautiful?" Lee asked.

"I saw the Great Wall of China once."

"You never told me that."

"It never came up."

"When you see something like this it's hard to believe the rest of the world is at war."

"Don't think about that."

Cody wrapped an arm around her waist and pulled her close. Lee snuggled against him.

After several minutes, Cody asked, "Do you want to head back to the room?"

"Not yet. I want to enjoy this as long as I can."

LEVOROV WISHED THE day would be over so he could go back to his room and sleep. He wished this whole damn trip would be over so he could get back to Moscow and do something productive. Stalin had sent him to this meeting to gather what information he could about England's knowledge of Germany's occult activities. He had spent all morning and afternoon listening to Molotov and Churchill plan grand strategy, work out the details for the joint annexation of Iran, plot out a two-front war against Germany, and discuss supply lines and means of communication. Yet at the end of the day, he had picked up no new information of interest to him.

Even when Molotov had raised the subject of Hess' flight to England and what intelligence he had passed to London, Churchill had replied with the standard answer that Hess had wanted to make peace with England so Hitler could concentrate all his efforts against the Soviet Union. Levorov knew the prime minister was not telling the truth. He could tell by the slight change in manner, by the brief formal façade that masked the lie. No one else picked up on it. He would not have either if he had not been trained to look for things like that. If Levorov could get Churchill alone in a cell in Lubyanka for a few days, then he would be able to get some useful information out of him. As of now, he had wasted two days for nothing.

When dinner started to break up, Levorov felt a sense of hope that maybe now he could go back to the hotel and get some sleep. His hopes were dashed when Churchill ushered Molotov toward a private room off the main dining hall.

"Before you go, let's have a private conversation over some whiskey. There are certain things I want you to pass along to Stalin that are for his ears only."

"It'd be my pleasure." Molotov turned to Levorov. "Wait here. I shouldn't be long."

Levorov nodded, although judging by the stern expression on the foreign minister's face he must not have done a good job concealing his frustration. As the two men disappeared into the private room, Levorov stepped over to the open window overlooking the pyramids and lit up a cigarette. He had a feeling he would go through several of these before the delegation headed back to the hotel.

BELLINGHAM CROSSED THE dining hall, his attention focused on the gentleman in civilian clothes who had accompanied Molotov all day. He bore himself like a military officer, not a diplomat, so Bellingham assumed he was the foreign minister's bodyguard, probably NKVD. The group captain watched as he followed Churchill and Molotov to the private hall and was relieved when the foreign minister dismissed him at the door.

Like a dutiful officer, the Russian hovered nearby, stepping over to the open windows overlooking the pyramids and lighting up a cigarette. He could not have planned it better.

Bellingham stepped up to the Russian. "It's a beautiful night, isn't it?"

"Yes." The Russian did not make eye contact.

"It's so peaceful and quiet out here in the desert. Not like in London and Moscow."

"You've been to Moscow?"

"No."

"It's been quiet there lately. Everyone is evacuating as the Germans get closer."

"That's why we're here. To make sure the Germans don't take Moscow or London."

"That's easy for you to say. Moscow doesn't have the English Channel protecting it."

Being friendly did not work, so he decided to be more direct. "I'm Group Captain Bellingham."

"Pavel Levorov."

"You're Molotov's bodyguard, correct?"

For the first time, Levorov looked at him. "Why do you say that?"

"Your bearing seems more military than civilian."

The faintest hint of a grin pierced Levorov's lips. "I guess I have to work on blending in."

"It's fine. You're among friends here." Time to go for broke. "Is Marshal Stalin feeling better?"

Levorov turned to face Bellingham. "Why do you think Stalin is ill?"

"Sorry. That was another assumption on my part. When no one heard from Stalin for the first week after the invasion, we thought the Germans had launched a commando raid against the leadership that had succeeded in either killing or incapacitating them. It caused a lot of concern in London that Hitler might try the same thing against the prime minister. But when Stalin resurfaced a week later, I assumed he must have been sick. I hope he's recovered."

"Stalin was never sick. The invasion took us all by surprise. We needed time to coordinate a counterattack."

"It took over a week. Someone must have been really distracting Stalin."

Levorov studied Bellingham for several seconds. "*Nothing* distracted Stalin."

"Sorry if I offended you."

"You didn't offend me." Levorov flicked his cigarette out the window. "I have things to attend to."

Bellingham watched the Russian walk away. At least he had confirmed one thing on this trip—the Russians knew about Hitler's occult war. Now all he needed to figure out was what role they intended to play in it.

CHAPTER FORTY-THREE

The Pyramids, Giza, Egypt
4 July 1941

DIETRICH WONDERED IF he would make it. When he started climbing the southern slope of Khufu, it did not seem that high. In college, he had seen photos of tourists sitting on the summit enjoying the view. How difficult could it be? At first, it seemed no harder than climbing a flight of stairs, except in this case each stair was three feet high. He began to feel the physical strain halfway up the slope. By the two-thirds point he could barely breathe, and his heart felt like it would burst.

Lilith and Malalath accompanied him and both women had already reached the summit several minutes ago. Common sense told him to stop at this level and circle around to the front since this would make as good a vantage point to survey the area as the summit. Pride told him to push on. After catching his second wind, Dietrich continued climbing.

It did not help that he lugged a Thompson submachine gun Ahmed had given him slung over his shoulder, or that he began the climb already exhausted. After having been met by Ahmed on the coast, they had traveled all night by camel to Ismailia, a town north of the Great Bitter Lake, where some locals gave them shelter. After a few hours of rest, the party set off mid-morning for the long trek to Giza, arriving less than an hour ago. Ahmed and his people had set up camp two miles south of Giza and let the Germans go on ahead on their own with their camels; the Egyptians would wait until dawn and, if Dietrich and the succubi returned, would lead them back to the same location on the coast where Hoecker's U-boat would pick them up three days from now. If not, then they were on their own. Dietrich got the distinct impression that Ahmed believed the Germans were on a suicide mission. He was even beginning to feel that way.

After several more minutes that seemed like hours, Dietrich finally reached the apex of Khufu. Lilith and Malalath stared down at the Mena House more than five hundred feet below them. Although the grounds were dark, the lights inside the hotel blared, and little attempt had been made to black them out. He was surprised at the lack of security, but figured the British's complacency made them careless. If Heydrich had known how easy this would be, he could have saved a lot of trouble and sent in a flight of Heinkels to do the job. That would have made his life much easier. But then Dietrich would not have the satisfaction of watching Churchill and the others die. That knowledge gave him the burst of energy and confidence he needed.

"Is that them?" Malalath asked. "Are those the bastards who hurt Agrat?"

"Those are the ones," Dietrich replied.

"Then let's send them to Hell." Malalath began to climb down from the top of Khufu when Dietrich grabbed her arm. "What's wrong?"

"We can't storm down there. There are too many soldiers. Remember what they did to Agrat."

Malalath stiffened. "What do you suggest?"

"We're going to have to wait until things quiet down, and then we'll sneak up on them."

"Typically human," snorted Malalath. "We should have brought more people with us."

Lilith chuckled. "Why do that, sister, when they're already here?"

Malalath smiled malevolently. "I never thought of that."

"Thought of what?" Dietrich asked.

The succubi ignored him and descended along the southern slope of Khufu. Dietrich followed but was less sure of his footing and soon fell behind. By the time he caught up with them, the two succubi were on the open ground to the west of the pyramid. Lilith stood erect, her arms stiff by her side and her palms parallel with the desert. She moved across the sand in a spiral pattern, slowly increasing the circle.

"What's going on?" Dietrich asked.

Malalath placed her forefinger across her lips.

"Don't silence me. I'm in charge here."

"No, you're not. You're not even supposed to be here with us." The menacing tone in Malalath's voice warned Dietrich to keep silent.

Lilith stopped and spun around to face Malalath. "I was right. This is the location."

"Good."

"What location?" Dietrich asked.

"The cemetery for the workers who built the pyramids," said Lilith.

"You mean the slaves?"

Malalath snorted. "It sounds typical of his kind."

"They were not slaves," said Lilith. "The workers were skilled artisans who took pride in their work. To show his appreciation, the pharaoh allowed those who died to be buried alongside the project. Hundreds of workers are buried here."

"How do you know all this?"

Malalath laughed. "Who do you think convinced the pharaoh to build this?"

Lilith motioned for the others to stand back. Malalath escorted Dietrich to the base of Khufu. Crouching in the center of the open space, Lilith used her hand to draw twenty-five symbols in the sand in five lines of five, each symbol three feet in length.

פ ה ג ה ר

ה ט י א ה

ג י ס י ג

ה א י ט ה

ר ה א ה ף

When Lilith was finished, she joined the others and waited.
The wait was not long.

The sand around the incantation undulated, slow slight
rises at first, soon becoming swells that fluctuated more rapidly,
like waves rippling across a pond. A low rumble echoed off the
pyramid behind them, growing louder as the swelling became
more intense. After a few seconds, the desert floor collapsed,
leaving a gaping hole a hundred feet in circumference. An eerie
silence fell over the area.

Dietrich was about to ask what had happened when he
heard the noise emanating from the pit. It sounded like bolts of
leather being rubbed against one another, followed a few
moments later by moaning. A hand appeared from out of the
pit, or what at least looked like a hand. It appeared more
skeletal than human. The fingers moved in an awkward, jerky
manner. The hand imbedded itself in the sand and pulled. A
second later, a mummified corpse emerged from the pit and
crawled onto its knees. It staggered to its feet, swaying back and
forth. Shards of soiled bandages hung loosely off the body that
had long since dried out and become leathery. Twisting its
head to one side, the empty eye sockets focused on Dietrich, as
if it could see him. For the first time in his life, Dietrich knew
true fear.

He nearly wet himself when other mummies extricated
themselves from the pit. First a few, then a dozen, until finally
hundreds of these ungodly creatures surrounded the pit. All of
them stared at Dietrich. He wanted to go for his Thompson but

was afraid of the reaction that would cause.

Lilith moved along the side of the pyramid. As she did, her army of the dead followed her every move. She stopped at the corner of the northern slope and faced the horde.

"*Meyn knekht, ton ir farshteyn mir?*"

The horde straightened up, as if coming to attention.

Lilith pointed to Mena House at the base of the hill. "*Hargenen! Sper keyn eyner!*"

As one, the army of the dead surged forward.

CHAPTER FORTY-FOUR

Mena House, Giza, Egypt
4 July 1941

ONE MOMENT LEE was enjoying the view of the pyramids bathed in the soft moon light, and the next she was hunched over the balcony wall, clutching her head against the pain. For a moment, she thought she might be suffering from a stroke. Then she heard the voices, hundreds of them, anguished and afraid, calling out to her. Lee did not know what language the voices spoke. She did not need to. The emotions behind the voices were overwhelming. The fear they generated in her was almost as crippling as the psychic link.

Lee felt Cody's arms wrap around her. She turned her head toward him. He spoke, but Lee could not hear him with all the voices raging in her head. She tried to focus her thoughts, concentrating on Cody's voice, and pushing back the other psychic influences. After several moments, she could make out Cody screaming, "Someone get a medic!"

"No," Lee squeaked.

"You're having a stroke."

Lee shook her head and instantly regretted it as the pain spiked. It took every ounce of effort to restrain the uncontrolled voices.

"I'm fine. I'm having a connection with the dead."

"Are you sure you're alright?"

"No." Lee glanced up at Cody, terror in her eyes. "We're all going to die."

★　★　★

"IT'S BLOODY COLD out here," griped Private Taylor. He stood on the crest of the hill overlooking Mena House, with the Khufu Pyramid one hundred feet behind him.

"What did you expect?" asked Lance Corporal McLean.

"It's the bloody desert. I thought it was supposed to be hot in the desert. I saw a news clip of some blokes frying an egg on a tank."

"I told you it gets cold at night." McLean did not attempt to hide his irritation. "So quit your complaining before—"

"What the bloody hell is all the noise?" asked Sergeant Wayne as he approached. "You're supposed to be on guard duty, not pissing and moaning like a bunch of old ladies in a pub."

"Why are we up here in the first place?" Taylor asked. "Why aren't we down there with the rest of the guards?"

"Because someone has to stay up here to make sure the press and the spies don't get a vantage point."

"If you ask me, it's a waste of time."

"Nobody bloody asked you," Wayne said as loud as he could without yelling. "Now unless you want to be guarding these pyramids for the duration, I'd advise you to shut—"

A noise came from the west side of the pyramid. It sounded like sand shifting, followed a few seconds later by something dragging along the desert floor.

Taylor looked at the sergeant. "Commandos?"

Wayne motioned for the others to talk softly. "They're making way too much noise to be commandos."

"Then what is it?" McLean asked.

"Let's find out." Wayne raised his Thompson submachine gun and moved toward the western side of Khufu. Taylor and McLean unslung their Enfield rifles from their shoulders and followed behind, weapons ready to fire. As they drew nearer the structure, they heard a female voice from around the corner.

Meyn knekht, ton ir farshteyn mir? Hargenen! Sper keyn eyner!

"Bloody sod," whispered Taylor. "They're Jerries."

"That's not German. It sounds.... Jesus Christ!"

The horde of mummies emerged around the corner of the pyramid fifty feet in front of them.

"It's like a bloody monster movie," Taylor gasped.

"This can't be real," added McLean.

Wayne aimed his Thompson and fired, spraying the three mummies in front of him. The bullets tore into their bodies, punching their way through desiccated flesh to harmlessly imbed themselves in the creatures beyond. Two of the bullets ripped off a right arm, which separated from the shoulder in a cloud of dust. When the sergeant's weapon ran out of ammunition, he had not taken down a single mummy. Wayne reloaded, fumbling with the empty magazine. A dozen of the horde broke away and stumbled toward the humans.

Upon seeing the things coming toward him, Wayne became flustered and dropped the new magazine onto the sand. He knelt down to retrieve it. Taylor and McLean aimed their Enfields and fired. One bullet struck a mummy right where its heart should be, puncturing the leathery muscles with no effect. The other caught a second mummy between the eyes. It drilled a hole in the forehead and passed though the rear of the skull, generating a small cloud of dust but inflicting no damage. They maintained fire despite its ineffectiveness.

The pack of mummies drew closer.

"Come on, sergeant," called Taylor.

Wayne grabbed the magazine and loaded it into his Thompson as the closest mummy reached him. He stood to fire. The mummy knocked the weapon out of Wayne's hands and lunged, sinking its teeth into his neck and biting down on the carotid artery. Blood sprayed across the mummy's face, soaking into the dry skin. It whipped its head to one side, tearing a chunk from Wayne's neck. The sergeant screamed and dropped to his knees before falling forward, bleeding out into the sand.

McLean rushed to help the sergeant when a second mummy grabbed him around the throat and squeezed, crushing the lance corporal's larynx. McLean fell backward onto the sand, gasping out his final moments.

Taylor panicked, for a moment uncertain whether he should help his dying mates or run for help. The hesitation cost him his life. Ten mummies surrounded him. Taylor swung the butt of his rifle, striking one of the creatures in the head and knocking loose its jaw. Three grabbed the rifle and wrestled it out of his hands while the remaining six dragged him to the ground and ripped him apart.

The rest of the horde surged over the top of the hill and converged on Mena House.

"DEAR GOD," DIETRICH mumbled under his breath as he watched the undead rip apart the three British soldiers.

"Is the Thousand-Year *Reich* developing a conscience?" Lilith asked snidely.

"That's no way for a soldier to die."

"Death is death. Besides," said Lilith as she cast a disapproving glare at him, "it counts toward the final tally."

Dietrich could not take his eyes off the death of the three soldiers. He knew that image would haunt him forever.

Lilith and Malalath turned and headed for the southern face of Khufu. "Follow me."

"Where are we going?"

"While they distract the guards, we're going to hunt down Churchill and kill him."

THE SOUND OF gunfire coming from the pyramids caught everyone's attention at Mena House. Bellingham stepped out onto the balcony, followed by several British and Russian personnel. They all gathered around Cody and Lee.

Levorov was the last to emerge onto the balcony.

"What's going on? Are the Germans attacking?"

"Not with all that screaming," answered Bellingham. "Someone give me a pair of binoculars."

A waiter brought the group captain a pair kept behind the bar for sightseeing. Bellingham raised them to his eyes and scanned the hilltop. It took him only a few seconds to spot the horde of mummies surging over the crest and descending toward Mena House. Alerted by the battle taking place on the hill, the soldiers guarding the hotel's perimeter were responding to the threat and had already formed a defensive line, although they were outnumbered.

"What do you see?" Levorov asked. Bellingham passed him the binoculars. When he scanned the ridgeline, all he could manage to say was, "Fuck."

"That sums it up quite accurately."

Levorov passed the binoculars to Cody. "What do we do now?"

"I think our first order of business is to get the prime minister and foreign minister to safety."

"I couldn't agree more."

The two men rushed back into the dining hall and made their way to the private room where Churchill and Molotov were holding their discussions. They barged in without the civility of knocking first. Molotov shot out of his seat and berated Levorov.

"What is the meaning of this outrage? How dare you—"

Bellingham cut him off. "Mr. Prime Minister, Mr. Foreign Minister. We need to evacuate you from the building immediately."

"Does this have to do with the gunfire we heard a few

minutes ago?" asked Churchill. "Are we under attack from the Germans?"

"I wish it was that simple." Bellingham raced over to Churchill. "There's no time to explain. Please, come with me."

As the prime minister rose from his chair, Levorov ran up to Molotov and ushered him out of the room. The other three members of the Russian delegation and Molotov's bodyguards were already rushing over to him. Surrounding the foreign minister, they escorted him across the dining hall and headed for the main lobby. Churchill exited the private room but headed toward the balcony instead of the exit.

"Sir, we need to get you to safety," said Bellingham.

"You should know me well enough by now to realize I don't run away from danger." The prime minister stepped out onto the balcony and joined the others. "Would somebody kindly tell me what's going on?"

Cody handed him the binoculars. "You won't believe it unless you see it for yourself."

CAPTAIN MARTIN STOOD at the center of his line of one hundred troops along the northern boundary of the Mena House grounds. A part of him wondered if he had lost his sanity. The murmuring from his men and the sense of terror that permeated the line assured him he was sane, though he wished it was an illusion.

The officer inside him kicked in. His Majesty required him to perform his primary task, which was to protect Prime Minister Churchill, even if the enemy was an army of the undead.

"Listen up. This is no different than fighting Jerry outside of Tobruk, only this enemy doesn't shoot back. Line up your shots and make every bullet count."

"Don't fire until we see the grey of their eyes, sir?" Lance

Corporal Williams joked.

Awkward chuckles made their way up and down the line. Martin appreciated the attempt to boost morale, but still had to play the hard ass.

"If you were as good as firing a rifle as you are your mouth, you could defeat these things by yourself."

More chuckling spread along the line, but this time it sounded more confident. Martin stood behind Williams and tapped his shoulder.

"Steady, lads. On my command."

The horde of mummies shambled down the hill toward the hotel grounds. Martin waited until the undead were fifty meters away before yelling, "Fire!"

A fusillade of rifle and submachine gun fire erupted along the line. Scores of bullets slammed into the undead. Several of the mummies were pushed back by the force of the attack but pressed ahead once the initial folly stopped. The soldiers continued the barrage. Bullets punched through bodies with no effect. Arms and chunks of heads and torsos were blown off, yet the nightmare continued to surge ahead. The only mummies that had been stopped were those whose legs had been shot off.

The horde approached to within twenty meters.

"Aim for their legs," Martin called down the line. "If we can't kill these bastards, at least we can slow them down."

The soldiers followed orders. Those brandishing Thompsons were more successful, the massed firepower easily blasting away shriveled legs. Dozens of the undead fell to the sand where they then dragged their bodies toward the hotel. A dozen more tripped over them and stumbled, struggling to stand again. Most of the horde merely flowed around them. The soldiers carrying Enfields had much less success, dropping only a few of the undead. The horde had approached to within ten meters, diminished by only a few score of mummies.

One of the creatures bore in on Williams. He fired repeatedly at its face, each round blowing away a chunk of skull.

Only when the head had been completely shot away did it collapse. The other soldiers noticed what had happened and shifted their aim to head shots. When they ran out of ammunition, each raised the butt of their rifle above their shoulder and rushed forward, slamming the hard surface into the nearest mummy's face. Martin withdrew his Colt. 45 and moved forward with his men, emptying four rounds into the face of one of the undead until its head disintegrated, then shifted to another. The line succeeded in taking down another thirty mummies before being overrun.

Three of the undead clutched onto Martin's uniform and dragged him down. Williams spun around to help, clubbing them in the head with his Enfield. He succeeded in shattering the skull of one when five more overwhelmed him. Along the line, British troops fought hand-to-hand against the undead, only to be taken down by their sheer numbers. Three broke free and retreated toward the hotel, where those on the balcony waved for them to make it to safety. A dozen others dropped their weapons and ran into the desert.

The horde pushed past the line of dead British troops and headed for the hotel.

CHURCHILL LOWERED THE binoculars. He bowed his head and closed his eyes, saying a prayer for the brave men who had just died.

"We have to get you out of here *now*," Bellingham urged.

"Where are we going to run to?"

"It doesn't matter. We have to get you to a safe location. We have no way of stopping them."

"There might be a way," said Cody.

He stepped back into the dining hall, with the others following behind him. They watched as Cody made his way to the bar on the opposite end of the room, gathering cloth napkins from those tables he passed by. Once behind the bar, he shoved the napkins into an empty ice bucket, removed a bottle of vodka from the shelf, and poured its contents onto the napkins. Grabbing a second bottle of vodka, he removed the cap and fed one of the alcohol-soaked napkins into the opening.

"You're making firebombs?" Lee asked.

"We know bullets can't stop them," Cody answered as he prepared a second bottle. "Those things are dried out and covered in bandages. I bet they burn like a bonfire at a state fair when you light them up."

"That makes sense to me." Churchill rushed behind the bar to help, which prompted the others to join in.

As Lee walked by, Cody stopped her.

"Find some crates or boxes we can use to cart these things outside."

"You got it."

Churchill held up a bottle of Johnny Walker and sighed. "What a waste of good whiskey."

MOLOTOV'S PARTY EXITED the hotel lobby and raced over to the five vehicles parked out front, heading for the car waiting for them. As Levorov opened the rear passenger door for the foreign minister, gunfire broke out along the southern border of the hotel grounds.

"What's that?" asked the driver.

"The hotel is under attack by German commandos," Levorov lied. "You have to get the foreign minister back to Cairo at once."

The driver nodded.

"Don't try and escape via the hotel exit. You'll more than likely be ambushed. Make your way across the desert and pick up the road a few kilometers to the east."

"Yes, comrade."

"Aren't you coming along?" Molotov asked.

"I'm going to stay here and find out as much as I can about these things."

"It's suicide."

"I'll find out what I can and escape before they overrun the place. It's not too far to Cairo, so I can make it back there on my own. But you need to leave now."

Levorov closed the door before Molotov could protest and banged the roof twice. The driver accelerated rapidly, kicking up a small cloud of sand and gravel. Levorov closed his eyes and turned his head to avoid getting it in the face. The other two staff cars fell in behind the first. At first, Levorov thought the driver was going to attempt to escape via the main road since he headed up the driveway. At the last second, the convoy turned left, raced across a grassy field, and headed into the desert.

Levorov waited long enough to make certain Molotov got away before heading back inside the hotel.

AS EACH PERSON finished making a firebomb, they handed it to Lee who placed it in one of the three wooden milk crates she found in the kitchen. An embassy secretary stood by the open door to the balcony, updating them on the mummies' progress.

When the first crate was full, Cody lifted it and took it outside. Churchill, Lee, Bellingham, and three other soldiers joined him. The rest stayed behind the bar and made more firebombs.

"Where are they now?" Cody asked the secretary as he placed the crate on the ground.

"They're passing through the tree line bordering the road." She struggled to maintain her composure. "They're about a hundred meters away."

"You did well. Go back inside." Cody glanced over at the prime minister. "I really think you should be heading for safety, sir."

"I didn't run from the Boer, and I'm not going to run from those things."

Bellingham, who stood behind the prime minister, shrugged. Cody knew better than to argue.

"Does anyone have a lighter or matches?"

Churchill withdrew a book of matches from his jacket pocket. One of the soldiers produced a lighter. Cody picked up the milk crate and led the group off the balcony and into the grassy area, stopping near the tree line. He picked up one of the makeshift firebombs in his right hand and flicked on the lighter with his left, holding the flame underneath the bottle. The alcohol-soaked napkin ignited with ease. Cody waited several seconds and then, rushing forward, tossed the firebomb.

The bottle burst against one of the undead, splashing liquor across three of the creatures, which instantly ignited. Flames engulfed them, spreading rapidly along the dried bandages and consuming the desiccated flesh and muscles. On either side of him, the three soldiers each threw a firebomb. Two erupted amongst the horde, while one fell short and exploded in the grass. They continued until all twelve bottles had been expended, then fell back to the balcony.

By now, at least thirty of the mummies burned furiously, those stumbling against them also bursting into flames. Yet the horde still surged toward the hotel, reaching the wall surrounding the balcony.

"Why didn't that stop them?" Cody asked.

"Because they don't feel pain," answered Lee.

"But it should dry up the muscles and prevent them from walking."

"Their muscles are already desiccated." As she spoke, half a dozen mummies crumbled into ash as the fire consumed their bodies. "You see, it'll stop them, but it takes longer."

A British soldier ran out into the balcony carrying the second wooden crate of firebombs. Cody and the four soldiers lit and lobbed them at the horde gathering around the wall. More of the undead ignited. Being packed together against the wall, the fire spread quickly. For a moment, Cody thought they had contained the threat.

A few of the mummies pushed open the gate in the wall and staggered through. They made it only a few feet before crumbling into ash. A steady stream flowed through the gate and spread out across the balcony, converging on the group standing by the dining room. Cody ushered everyone inside and slammed shut the doors. As he ran down the length of the wall, closing and securing all the doors and windows, he called out to the others.

"Push the furniture against the doors. We need to keep them out as long as possible."

The soldiers did as ordered.

Bellingham placed himself in front of Churchill. "Mr. Prime Minister, we have to get you out of here now. I insist."

"Please," Lee pleaded. "Britain needs you."

"Very well," Churchill huffed. "Lead the way."

Bellingham turned to a British officer standing ten feet away who wore a revolver in a holster strapped around his waist.

"What's your name?"

"Major Foad, sir."

Bellingham pointed to the revolver. "Is that thing loaded?"

"It is."

"Then lead the way." Bellingham gently nudged Churchill toward the exit by the bar. "Lee, Cody, you're with me."

LILITH LED DIETRICH and Malalath to the east of Mena House so they could approach the hotel undetected. As they descended the hill and crossed the *Al Ahram* Road connecting the hotel and pyramids to Cairo, they saw a convoy of three vehicles pull away from the main entrance and enter the driveway. Red flags with gold hammers and sickles in the corner fluttered from each fender. She assumed it was the Russian delegation attempting to escape. They would have to pass right by her, at which point she and Malalath could—

Lilith cursed when the convoy veered left at the last moment and made its way across the desert. She contemplated chasing after them, but that would detract them from their primary goal of assassinating Churchill. The remaining two vehicles parked out in front of Mena House assured her he was still inside.

"They're escaping," said Dietrich.

"It's just the Soviets," Lilith reassured him. "Churchill is still inside. Those are British trucks out front."

"Good. Let's make sure he doesn't get away." Dietrich unslung his Thompson and aimed, but Lilith lowered the barrel.

"That'll make too much noise and alert them we're here. We have another way. Wait here and stay under cover."

Lilith and Malalath crossed the rode and maneuvered into the driveway. Once far enough away from the German so he would not be detected, the succubi ran toward the two vehicles.

Lilith waited until they reached the light generated by the lamps before yelling, "Help! Those things are after us!"

As expected, the five British soldiers guarding the remaining vehicles left their positions and rushed to assist the women. They did not live long enough to regret their mistake. Two of the soldiers each took one of the succubi and moved them toward the hotel while the other three kept guard. In one swift motion, Lilith and Malalath snapped the necks of their two rescuers and then turned on the other three. Taken aback by what had happened, none of them had time to react. Lilith head butted the closest soldier, crushing his skull and killing him instantly. Malalath punched the other in the chest with such force his heart ruptured. He dropped to his knees, staring at her in shock as his life drained away.

The fifth soldier stepped back and raised his Enfield, aiming at Lilith's head. She surged forward and slapped the rifle out of his hands, wrapped her right hand around his throat, and squeezed shut his larynx. He struggled to break the hold, punching her arm and face, but her grip was too strong. After several seconds, his face turned blue and panic set in. The soldier writhed around, frantic to get free, until his body went limp. Lilith maintained her hold for several moments to make certain he was dead, then threw the body aside as if it were a toy.

Lilith and Malalath continued down the driveway and entered Mena House.

"DAMN IT," DIETRICH swore as Lilith and Malalath disappeared inside Mena House. They were going rogue.

It did not bother him being alone in Cairo surrounded by dozens of British soldiers. That he could handle. He found it unsettling, though, to have a horde of resurrected mummies tearing their way through every human in the compound and the only two who could control them had left him behind. Common sense told him to follow the Russians across the desert into Cairo and sort everything out later. His sense of duty told him he needed to get in the middle of the fray and make certain Churchill did not make it out alive, even if meant he met the same fate. It took only a few seconds for Dietrich to decide.

He rushed down the driveway toward Mena House.

LEE AND FOAD led the way out of the dining hall and toward the front entrance. Churchill followed a few yards to her rear, with Cody and Bellingham on either side of the prime minister for protection. She rushed into the main lobby, glancing over her shoulder to make certain the others were behind her, and walked into someone rushing in the opposite direction. Lee yelped.

"I'm sorry," said Levorov, holding her shoulders. "Are you alright?"

"You startled me, that's all."

"Did Molotov get away safely?" asked Churchill.

Levorov nodded. "I came back to see if I could be of any help."

"I'm glad you did," said Bellingham. "We must get the prime minister out of here. Those things have already reached the hotel."

"Follow me." Levorov turned back toward the entrance. "There are two staff cars waiting outside we can use to—"

"Oh God," Lee moaned. She stopped and leaned against the wall.

Cody ran over to her. "What is it?"

Lee did not answer. A psychic feeling momentarily overpowered her senses. It was not the dead trying to contact her, or the anguished outcry of the undead reaching out. This was more like an awareness of an extremely powerful, evil force nearby, like experiencing heat when close to a fire. She had experienced this before, although not as powerful and malevolent, back in London when talking with Agrat.

Lifting her head, the sensation spiked as Lilith and Malalath walked into the lobby. She pointed toward the two women.

"They're succubi!"

"Split up!" ordered Bellingham. Placing his hands on Churchill's back, he rushed the prime minister across the lobby and down the corridor leading to the private bar. Cody and

Foad followed.

Lee stood in the center of the lobby, waving her arms to get the attention of the succubi. The one on the right with auburn hair spotted her. When their eyes met, Lee felt an awkward sensation, as if they somehow knew each other. For a moment she could not move. Then Levorov grabbed her upper arm, knocking her off balance as he pulled her back toward the dining hall.

ENTERING THE HOTEL lobby, Lilith saw the group of humans gathered at the far end. She recognized Churchill as two of the men took off with him down a side corridor.

"That's her." Malalath pointed at the female. "That's the one who Winnie connects with."

"Are you certain?"

"I'd know her aura anywhere."

"Then the bitch is yours."

Malalath smiled and took off after Lee and Levorov.

Lilith turned down the corridor and went after Churchill.

CHURCHILL AND BELLINGHAM rushed into the private bar. Cody closed the door and secured the lock while Foad grabbed a chair, the back of which he jammed against the handle.

"That's not going to hold her for long."

"We only need enough time to get out of here," said Bellingham as he looked around the bar. "Where's the exit?"

Churchill checked behind the bar. "It looks like we came through the only one."

"Damn!" Foad removed the revolver from its holster pocket and centered himself in the middle of the room, aiming at the door.

"That's not going to do any good," warned Cody.

"Do you have a better idea?" Foad asked.

"I do." Cody stepped over to the wall off to the right. "Bellingham, grab some of those tablecloths. Foad, come with me."

Dietrich ran into the hotel lobby and immediately knew this was a bad idea. He could hear the yelling coming from the opposite side of the hotel from those still inside. The first wisps of smoke filtered into the lobby accompanied by the distinct smell of burning wood and flesh. Ahead of him, the two succubi reached the reception desk and split up, heading in separate directions, seemingly oblivious to the chaos going on around them.

Once again, common sense told him to turn around and make his way back to the meeting point with Ahmed. Instead, he darted into the hotel and followed after Malalath.

When Lee and Levorov returned to the dining hall, pandemonium had broken out. The mummies had reached the closed doors and windows. Those who had stayed behind had shoved tables and chairs against the doors, which temporarily halted the surge. The sheer weight of the horde pressed against the doors and barricades, which bulged under the strain. Flames from those mummies on fire had spread to the wooden frames and jambs, which in turn ignited the curtains. In seconds, the southern wall of the dining hall became a conflagration.

The barricade collapsed, and the doors and windows shattered. The mummies pushed into the dining hall, shoving past the debris. Their numbers were fewer, many having been consumed by fire, and half of those that remained had burst into flames. Yet there were still close to one hundred left, way too many to battle their way through.

Those entering the dining hall overran the few British soldiers inside, dragging them to the ground and tearing them apart. The others staggered across the dining hall, those in flames setting fire to everything in their path.

Levorov shook his head. "No fucking way."

"No arguments here," said Lee.

The two raced back out into the corridor and stopped. Malalath entered the other end, blocking their escape. Her eyes connected with Lee, and a sardonic smile pierced her lips.

"Just the person I was looking for."

Levorov pushed Lee back into the dining hall.

Malalath laughed and yelled after her. "You can't get away from me, little one."

Levorov assessed the situation, not that he had many options to choose from. Trying to sneak past the succubus would be only slightly less dangerous than fighting their way through the mummies to escape via the balcony. That left him with only one choice. He pointed to the private dining hall where Churchill and Molotov had their meeting.

"In there."

The two raced inside. As Levorov shut the door, he noticed Malalath crossing the dining hall toward them. He had seconds, at best. Spinning around, the Russian searched for an escape route or weapon. The only other exit was through a series of windows along the exterior wall, but the fire outside had already burned its way along the grass and bushes, creating a flaming barrier that blocked their escape. As for weapons, he could choose from among the forks and knives on the single dining table or the cues mounted by the pool table located against the far wall.

Lee had already taken two of them from the mount and tossed one to Levorov. He caught it as the door burst open and Malalath barged into the room.

Holding the cue like a baseball bat and swinging around, Levorov cracked it against the succubus' head. The end of the cue snapped off and sailed across the room, having done nothing to Malalath other than piss her off.

Malalath lashed out with her right arm, her knuckles slamming into Levorov's chest. His vision blurred, first from the pain as three of his ribs cracked, and then when he banged his head against the pool table. When Levorov tried to stand, his vision went black and he collapsed face first onto the floor.

Malalath turned her attention to Lee. The woman had backed up against the wall, brandishing the pool cue like a club and ready to strike. Malalath laughed.

"You know what the best part about the hunt is, little one? The kill."

LILITH REACHED THE door to the private bar and kicked it open. As she stepped inside, she noticed Churchill against the opposite wall, defiant even in the face of death. The other three humans formed a semi-circle in front of her. They had no weapons. Instead, each stood by tablecloth draped over something tall and wide, approximately the size and shape of a man.

"You know this is futile," she scoffed. "If you give up now, I promise to kill each of you quickly."

"I don't think that's going to happen," said the human with the American accent.

Lilith approached him menacingly. "And how are you going to stop me?"

"With the one thing that makes you vulnerable."

Each human grabbed the top of their tablecloth and pulled it down. For a second Lilith was going to taunt them until she realized what the American was talking about. A succubus' vulnerability was its own reflection, and they must have set up mirrors around her.

Instinctively, Lilith turned her back on the humans and crouched.

As DIETRICH APPROACHED the far end of the main lobby, he paused, pressed himself against the wall, and peered around the corner down the corridor that Malalath had taken. He could not see her. A pair of large ornate doors sat in the center of the left wall of the corridor, with a single plain door opposite it and another at the end. Malalath must have entered one of these.

Making his way down the corridor, his Thompson at the quick ready, Dietrich paused to try the knob on the door on the right. It opened, revealing a linen closet lined with shelves packed with tablecloths and napkins. He stepped down to the double ornate doors. The outer surface bubbled and smoke leaked from under the bottom jamb. He was about to move on when he heard Malalath's voice on the other side. Grabbing the knob, he quickly let go because the metal was too hot to handle. Wrapping his hand around the tail of his jacket, Dietrich opened the door.

A blast of heated air burst through the open door, raising the temperature in the corridor by twenty degrees and driving Dietrich back against the wall. Black smoke billowed out and filled the corridor. From the quick view he got before he had to turn his head, the entire dining hall was in flames. However, that was not what caused him concern. The horde of mummies had made their way inside the dining hall and, upon seeing him in the doorway, the closest lumbered toward him. Without Lilith or Malalath there to protect him, they saw Dietrich as nothing more than another human to be eliminated.

The three closest mummies staggered into the corridor and surrounded Dietrich, blocking his path to the main lobby. He backed down the corridor, raised the barrel, placed it against the first mummy's head, and fired four rounds. Its skull fragmented into dust and bone shards. Stepping back three feet, he did the same to the second and third mummy. Before Dietrich could make his escape, another five pushed their way into the corridor and bore down on him. Using the same method, he eliminated two more before the Thompson ran out of ammunition. Reaching into his satchel, Dietrich removed a full magazine and reloaded, stepping back a few feet as he did to keep distance between him and the undead. He fired into their heads, taking down five or six with each magazine. For every one that collapsed, two more took its place. By the time he loaded his last magazine, close to thirty bodies lay scattered along the floor, with another forty or so pressing down the corridor toward him.

Dietrich backed into the door at the far end of the corridor. He had been so intent on taking down the mummies he had not realized he had retreated into a trap. Reaching behind him for the handle, it refused to turn. The damn thing was locked. The pack was only three meters away. He might be able to pull this off, but only if everything worked perfectly.

Raising the Thompson, Dietrich emptied his last magazine into the faces of the five closest mummies. Four of them dropped to the floor and the fifth staggered back into the throng. It bought him precious seconds. Turning ninety degrees to his left, Dietrich slammed the stock of the Thompson repeatedly against the knob until it broke off. The door popped open a few inches. Dietrich pulled it open and raced outside when several pairs of dead hands grabbed him, yanking back into the building. The pack swarmed round him. He punched and kicked, trying to break free. Dietrich cringed as the leathery hands tore at his clothes and dug into his flesh. One of the mummies leaned forward and clamped a decayed jaw around his neck.

Dietrich closed his eyes and prayed the end would be quick.

★   ★   ★

LEE SWUNG THE pool cue at Malalath's head when she lunged. In one rapid motion, Malalath grabbed the cue in her right hand, yanked it from Lee's grip, and tossed it onto the floor. Her left hand cupped around Lee's neck and drove her back into the wall.

Lee had the breath knocked out of her. She struggled to break free. Malalath tightened her grip, applying pressure to the woman's larynx. Lee stopped resisting and tried to check the panic welling up in her as she was being strangled.

"Don't worry," Malalath chuckled. "I'm not going to kill you right away."

"Do what you want, but I won't tell you anything."

"I don't need you to talk, you silly bitch. We already know everything we need to."

"Bullshit!"

"You work for an organization called the SOE out of a building on Baker Street. Your unit is called Project Samail. Stop me when you heard enough."

Lee clutched Malalath's hand and attempted to break the grip, but the succubus was too strong.

"The American, the one you've been fucking like a little whore, was assigned to you as a liaison from the States."

Lee swung at Malalath's face. The succubus caught the punch with her free hand and twisted, snapping Lee's wrist. She cupped the wounded hand against her chest.

"It's a pity the American had to get involved. Right now, my sister is probably gutting him like a pig."

"Fuck you!" Lee spit in Malalath's face.

The succubus used her free hand to wipe away the spittle. "And I know all of this because of you."

Lee stopped fighting. "What do you mean?"

"Remember back in London a few weeks ago when Agrat touched you?"

"Yes."

"Agrat did that to link you to our own psychic. She's been tuning into your ability and listening in on your conversations. How do you think I know so much about you? How do you think we knew Churchill would be coming to Cairo, and your team would be with him?"

"N-no," Lee stammered, not wanting to believe it.

"All of this is because of you." Malalath motioned toward the burning dining hall and the flames crawling up the exterior of Mena House. "Because you're a child playing an adult's game. Just because the dead can talk to you doesn't mean you're as powerful as me or my sisters. You got both your prime minister and your boyfriend murdered."

Lee felt the fury rage inside her. She kicked out at Malalath, her foot harmlessly slamming into the succubus' shin.

"It seems I struck a nerve," said Malalath. "How does it make you feel knowing this is your fault?"

"About the same as you feel knowing your sister is crippled without wings stuffed in a cage in London."

Much of the arrogance drained away from Malalath. Her left hand tightened around lee's throat as she raised her right and balled it into a fist. "Time to die, little one."

"Do you know what your problem is?"

"What?"

Lee smiled. "You talk too much."

Having regained consciousness, Levorov came up behind Malalath and jammed the broken end of his pool cue into the base of her skull. She stiffened and relaxed her grip. Lee broke free and ducked to the right, gasping for air. Levorov shoved the cue as hard as he could and drove the jagged end into Malalath's brain. The succubus spun around to attack but, being disoriented from the wound, she lost her balance and fell back against the wall.

Using her foot, Lee snapped the tip off her pool cue and drove the shaft into Malalath's chest. The jagged edge scraped against the succubus' heart and penetrated out back, piercing the wall. Lee placed all her weight on the cue's bumper and pushed, driving it into until only the grip showed, pinning Malalath to the wall.

Levorov stumbled over to Lee. "Are you okay?"

"I've been better." She clutched her throbbing hand against her chest. "We need to get out of here."

The two crossed to the door leading to the dining hall and opened it. A hundred mummies staggered across the dining hall, blocking their escape either to the balcony or the doors leading to the main lobby. By now the entire southern half of the hall had become an inferno. The flames had already spread across the ceiling of both the main and private dining halls. Sections of the ceiling crashed down, crushing the mummies beneath and creating more blockades to their escape. Behind them, part of the ceiling collapsed, landing between them and Malalath.

Levorov and Lee both knew they were trapped.

Malalath laughed. "I guess I'll get to watch you die after all."

CODY GRINNED. HIS ploy had worked. They had set up several of the ornamental room dividers and covered them with tablecloths, pretending they were mirrors. Lilith had fallen for it, although that would only last for a few seconds. Hopefully, it was all the time they would need.

Each brandishing one of the scimitars taken from the wall, Cody and Bellingham lunged at the crouching Lilith, as Foad moved around to her front holding a spear. Cody lifted the weapon above his head and aimed for her neck. Bellingham swung downward, slicing his blade deep into her abdomen. Lilith jerked up from the pain, causing Cody's aim to be off. His scimitar lodged in her back between the shoulder blades.

Bellowing in agony, Lilith sprang upright. Cody and Bellingham stumbled back, their scimitars still imbedded in the succubus.

Foad lowered his spear and charged. Lilith vented her fury on him. She deflected the spear with her right hand, grabbed the weapon, and shoved Foad back, using the shaft to pin him against the wall. Her body expanded until the skin shredded off with a horrendous tearing sound, knocking the two scimitars to the floor. The wings emerged through her back, leaving shredded cloths and shards of flesh dangling from their edges. The snake-like tail unfurled, ripping away her legs. Lilith curled the tail in front of her and wrapped it around Foad, pinning his arms against his chest and tightening the grip. Foad's face turned red and he screamed. His upper body exploded, spraying blood and organs across the wall and ceiling.

Rushing forward, Cody and Bellingham grabbed their scimitars. Cody sliced his into the root of Lilith's left wing with such force that the appendage was severed from her body. She bellowed and spun around. Cody ducked, but her right wing slammed into him, knocking the weapon out of his hand and throwing him back against the wall. He slid down and hit the floor, stunned.

Holding his scimitar like a sword, Bellingham rushed Lilith. She hissed and slithered toward him, grabbing his arm and twisting. He dropped his weapon.

"I've had enough of you two," Lilith hissed.

Clutching both arms, Lilith lifted Bellingham off the ground and pulled him toward her. The more he struggled, the tighter her grip became until he thought his humerus would shatter. Lilith opened her mouth. An ungodly crunching came from her maw as she unhinged her lower jaw, widening her mouth. She leaned forward to swallow Bellingham's head.

No one had noticed that Churchill had circled around the room and retrieved Foad's spear. As Lilith lowered her mouth over Bellingham, the prime minister rammed the spear into it, lodging the weapon in the back of the succubus' throat. She released the group captain, who rushed over to Churchill and moved him to the safety of the far corner.

Lilith hacked and thrashed her head around but could not dislodge the spear.

Having regained his composure, Cody picked up his scimitar and charged. When Lilith reached up to pull out the spear, Cody sliced off her hand. Lilith emitted a gargled howl. She slithered to the side to confront him.

Bellingham rushed back, grabbed hold of the spear, and dug it deeper into her throat until it ruptured out the back of her neck. He pushed back until the point imbedded into the wall, pinning Lilith like a bug in a display case. Stepping back, he picked up the second scimitar.

Cody and Bellingham drove their weapons into Lilith's abdomen to the hilt and twisted, gouging out her insides. Blood flowed from the wounds. She swiped at Bellingham with her remaining hand, but he withdrew his scimitar and sliced it off below the elbow. When Lilith swiped her tail at Cody, he sliced off a three-foot segment.

Both men kept up the assault, slashing and gouging. Blood and chunks of flesh washed around their feet. Lilith trilled and defended herself as best she could, but it was no use. Her struggling tapered off until she hung limp on the spear.

Bellingham walked over to Lilith. Placing his foot against her tattered chest, he grabbed the spear and yanked it out of her throat. Lilith fell back against the wall and slumped to one side. Her eyes glazed over and her lower jaw moved, though it was barely perceptible.

Cody stepped up and, holding the scimitar like a baseball bat, swung it into her neck. The blade sliced halfway through. When he tried to remove it, the weapon was stuck. He twisted the handle until the blade pulled free. Lilith gurgled, and blood flowed out of the neck wound. Cody swung the scimitar again. This time Lilith's head lobbed off her body.

DIETRICH BRACED HIMSELF for death. Instead, the mummies suddenly dropped all around him. There was no time to ask why, not that he cared. Whatever happened had spared his life. Dietrich raced through the door and across the lawn to a small copse of trees.

The fire that engulfed Mena House lit up the night sky and reflected off the pyramids. As he watched, the roof and upper walls caved in around the dining hall. He felt certain Malalath could not have survived that.

Sirens echoed from the other side of the hotel. Dietrich knew the police and fire brigade would be here in a few minutes, so he had to move now unless he wanted to spend the rest of the war as a POW. The funny thing, for a moment he contemplated giving himself up as preferable to having to tell Himmler and Heydrich he had failed.

Racing across the hotel compound and crossing the main road, Dietrich backtracked to the pyramids. With luck, he would make it back to Ahmed's camp before the British found him.

"WHAT THE...?" LEVOROV left his question hanging.

Every mummy in the dining hall and those still outside on the balcony suddenly collapsed.

"Who cares what happened?" Lee bolted through the door into the dining hall. "Let's go now while we still have a chance."

Levorov did not need to be told twice.

"Nooo!" Malalath screamed after them, her tirade cut off when the ceiling of the private dining room collapsed, crushing her under its weight.

Lee and Levorov dashed across the dining hall, dodging chunks of falling debris and bounding over the flaming corpses. Lee tripped halfway across the hall and fell on top of a mummy, yelping when the flames burnt her skin. The Russian doubled back and pulled Lee to him, pushing her toward the exit a moment before a huge section of ceiling crashed down on the spot she had been. Once in the corridor, their escape became easier since there were only corpses to contend with. The couple rushed through the lobby and out the main entrance. They could hear sirens in the distance coming from the direction of Cairo.

"Let me see your hands," said Levorov.

Lee held them out.

"Some first- and second-degree burns, but you'll be fine. And no bones have broken through the skin. Hopefully, they sent an ambulance along with the fire brigade."

"Let's hope so." Lee glanced around the parking lot and became concerned. "Have you seen Cody?"

CHURCHILL JOINED CODY and Bellingham to watch Lilith's final death twitches. Once the body had gone lifeless, the group captain prodded Churchill toward the door.

"We need to get out of here while we still can."

The three men made their way through main lobby and outside. Upon seeing Cody, Lee ran over to him, threw her arms around his neck, and kissed him.

"I thought I'd lost you," she said.

"It's going to take more than a couple of old hags to take me down."

"Good." Lee hugged him tight with her good arm, her head against his chest, her tears wetting his shirt.

Levorov took advantage of the distraction to wander off into the night.

Bellingham stepped over to Churchill. "How are you holding out, sir?"

Churchill smiled. "It's been a long time since I've been in a good fight."

"Thank God they're dead."

The prime minister became somber. "I hate that we had to destroy such a beautiful hotel in order to kill those things."

"I'm sure we can provide the owners financial assistance to rebuild."

"Maybe," Churchill chuckled. "But it'll be the last time I'm invited."

Bellingham paused for a moment. "You know that glass of whiskey you keep on offering me that I refuse?"

"Yes?"

"I think I'm ready for one or two of those right now."

CHAPTER FORTY-FIVE

Stalin's Office, Moscow, Russia
7 July 1941

THE NIGHT HAD been full of surprises for Levorov, beginning with the unnerving phone call from Beria an hour ago telling him to be at Stalin's suite at the Senate Building at midnight.

When he arrived at the Kremlin, half expecting to be met by an armed guard that would escort him to Lubyanka, Beria greeted him with a warm smile and a friendly handshake.

His third surprise was being led not to the Marshal's office but to his private quarters where Stalin, Molotov, and Mikoyan sat around a table drinking vodka. Beria joined the three men, then motioned for Levorov to have a seat. As he did, Beria filled a glass with vodka and placed it in front of Levorov.

Stalin raised his glass in a toast. "To Comrade Levorov, the only man I know to have killed two succubi."

Everyone took a drink. With a sense of embarrassment, Levorov joined in. He could tell the others had been drinking for a while now.

Stalin emptied his glass and refilled it. "I've read your report and had a long conversation with Vyacheslav, although I found the former lacking."

Levorov became uncomfortable. "Did I not provide enough information?"

"You did on everything except how you saved Vyacheslav's life. He told me personally how you rescued him from the attack by the mummies, and only after you knew he was safe did you return to gather intelligence."

"You're a hero of the Soviet Union," said Mikoyan.

"And I owe you my life," added Molotov.

"Thank you."

"There was one other thing you left out of your report," said Stalin. "You never offered an assessment of how we should proceed in this occult war."

"That's a policy decision which I'm not qualified to make."

"We disagree," said Beria. "You are the expert on occult activities and warfare, which is why we brought you here. Vyacheslav feels we should engage the British and work together to fight the Nazis on this front. We want to know how you would proceed."

Levorov took a long sip of vodka, using the time to contemplate his answer. He was not completely certain if they wanted his advice so they could consider it for future foreign policy or if they wanted to see whether they could trust him to follow the party line. This issue was too important for him to play politics with.

"With all due respect to the foreign minister," said Levorov as he placed the glass back on the table, "I think we should wait on reaching out to the British."

"Do you think they knew about the German attempt against Stalin," Beria asked.

"I'm not sure, but at this point it's irrelevant. We know the Germans have conducted similar operations against the British, and after Cairo, we also know the British are aware of those efforts. It's now up to the British to contact us and explain what happened. Once they've done that, and once we know what information they intend to offer and what measures they propose to deal with it, then we can make our decision. We also want to make certain we gather as much intelligence as we can but reveal as little as possible. I wouldn't want our Allies knowing our full capabilities."

"You don't trust our Allies?" Stalin asked.

Levorov dodged the question. "I'm looking ahead. Once we defeat Germany, we'll be facing challenges from other nations, some of whom may be our current allies who we won't see eye to eye with."

Beria nodded his approval at the answer. "What do you propose as the next step?"

"Based on what Naamah told us, Himmler has put together an occult army at Wewelsburg. We need to do the same thing."

"You mean like the necromancer who obtained the information from Naamah?"

"Yes, but her powers are limited." Levorov leaned forward in his chair. "We need to build up a force made up of anyone who has any type of psychic or paranormal abilities and use those abilities any way we can against the Germans."

"Where would you find these people?" Mikoyan asked.

"The same way I found Tasaria. I'd start by going through the NKVD files. I'm sure once we have a few people with such capabilities, they'll be able to direct us to others who can help."

"Excellent suggestion," said Stalin. "You can begin tomorrow."

Levorov was confused. "I don't understand."

Stalin turned to Beria. "You didn't tell him?"

"I was saving that honor for you."

Stalin laughed. "Comrade Levorov, you are now in command of the Soviet Union's first occult warfare unit."

"What is its title?"

"We don't have one yet," said Beria.

Levorov thought for a moment before proposing, "How about the *Bogatyrs*? They were legendary Russian warriors who protected the motherland from monsters."

"Perfect!" Stalin slapped his hand on the table, then raised his glass. "To Comrade Levorov, head of the *Bogatyrs*."

"To the defeat of Germany," added Mikoyan.

"To the death of Hitler," chimed in Molotov.

"And Himmler," said Beria.

As the five men swilled down their vodka, Levorov made a silent toast, hoping what he was about to undertake did not send all of Europe to Hell.

CHAPTER FORTY-SIX

Lotzen, Germany
10 July 1941

DIETRICH STOOD AT attention in front of Himmler's desk. The *Reichsführer* ignored him, instead reading the written report Dietrich had typed up of what had transpired in Cairo, deliberately thumbing back and forth through the pages. What bothered him most were the others attending this meeting: Heydrich, Vonnegut, and Steiner. The American idiom lynch mob flashed across his mind. Sadly, he had expected this for days.

After barely escaping from Mena House with his life, Dietrich had returned to Ahmed's camp, grateful that the Bedouin had remained faithful to his word despite the chaos in the area. Since the Allies' attention had been focused on Lilith and Malalath, and no one even knew he had been there, he had easily made the rendezvous with Hoecker's U-boat at the initial landing site.

That had been when his return boded ill. Once underway, Hoecker had handed Dietrich a message from Heydrich informing him that a plane would be waiting for him in Venice and ordering him to report to the *Reichsführer*'s train upon his arrival in Europe. Dietrich had typed up his report on the submarine, which had been a good thing because the Junkers had taken off for Poland less than an hour after he made land in Italy. Heydrich had greeted him upon landing in Poland, taking Dietrich's report so the *Reichsführer* could read it and allowing the *obergruppenführer* just enough time to shower and change into his SS uniform before being ushered into his meeting.

He now waited to hear his fate.

After nearly five minutes of reading, Himmler glanced up from the report and removed his *pince-nez*. "You can relax, *Obergruppenführer*. This isn't a formal inquiry."

"That will come later," added Heydrich with a wry grin.

Dietrich could not be sure if he was joking. He did allow himself to stand at ease.

"I'm disappointed about this entire situation, not only the failure of your mission but also the spectacular way in which it failed."

"The only saving grace is that everyone who witnessed this fiasco is dead," added Heydrich.

"If you don't include Churchill and the British occult warriors who already know what's going on," said Vonnegut. "According to MARLENE's last connection with the woman, they were the only ones to make it out alive."

"Yes," Heydrich said with a humorless grin. "The intended target was one of the few who survived the attempt."

Himmler picked up the report and pretended to read a passage from it. "You never stated why you disobeyed my order and accompanied Lilith and Malalath to Cairo."

"That was a spur of the moment decision, *Reichsführer*. I felt having a command presence on the scene would be useful to exploit any opportunities that arose. I never intended to participate in the operation."

"And yet you did. In fact, you nearly got yourself killed."

"Was it your decision to raise the dead and have them attack Mena House?" Heydrich asked.

Dietrich shook his head. "Lilith did that without consulting me."

Steiner sat forward in his chair. "In fairness to *Herr* Dietrich, that is probably the truth. Lilith has always been the most grandiose and independently-spirited of my master's wives.

Commanding an army of mummies is not something I would put past her."

"How does your master feel about losing all four of his wives?" Himmler asked.

"He's furious, but not at you or Hitler. You used their services the way they were intended. He wants the British and Russians to pay dearly for what they did to his succubi."

Vonnegut sighed. "We underestimated the British on this one."

"And the Russians," Heydrich added.

"Next time will be different," said Himmler.

"Will there be a next time?" Vonnegut asked.

"Of course," said Himmler. "We're not going to let one setback stop us from forming a Thousand-Year *Reich*."

"And my master has told me to inform you he will provide whatever support you need to achieve your goals," added Steiner.

"Excellent. Please thank him on behalf of myself and the *Führer*." Himmler focused his gaze on Dietrich. "That leaves only one final matter to contend with."

Dietrich tried not to show fear.

"You disobeyed me by going to Cairo when I told you not to. However, you didn't precipitate this disaster, and if wasn't for you we might never know what actually happened."

"Thank you, *Reichsführer*."

"On the other hand, you did a poor job in handling Lilith and Malalath. I know they were not technically under your command, and you had little or no influence over them, but in the future, you're going to have to do better in working with our netherworld associates."

For a moment, Dietrich was confused. "In the future?"

Himmler allowed himself a grin. "Do you really think I'd remove you from command over one mistake? You and Vonnegut are the most knowledgeable occult soldiers I have. I need you to continue this war against the British. I only trust you've learned from your mistakes and will never let an incident like this happen again."

"You can count on that, *Reichsführer*."

"I thought I could." Himmler paused as he studied Dietrich. "When was the last time you slept in a real bed?"

"Ten days ago."

"I want you and Steiner to fly back to Wewelsburg this afternoon. Get a good night's sleep and tomorrow the two of you can plan our future strategy. Also, have MARLENE maintain her link with the British woman in case we can get intelligence out of her."

Dietrich snapped to attention. "Yes, *Reichsführer*."

Himmler slid his *pince-nez* back onto his nose and resumed working, a signal that the meeting had concluded. Steiner and Vonnegut got up and exited the train car. Dietrich fell in behind them.

Dietrich could not believe how fortunate he had been. He had fully expected to be shot or sent to a concentration camp for what had happened in Cairo or, at the very least, be stripped of his command and shipped off to Russia. Instead, Himmler gave him a second chance, one he would not squander. Dietrich promised himself that next time he would be in better charge of whatever demons Steiner supplied, and he would not underestimate the enemy again. He would help ensure the creation of a Thousand-Year *Reich* and, on the day that occurred, he would take his place alongside Himmler and Heydrich as one of the leaders of the new millennium.

CHAPTER FORTY-SEVEN

SOE Headquarters, London, England
10 July 1941

As HAD BECOME routine, Cody dropped by Curtis' office basement for an end-of-the-day cigar and twenty-year-old scotch. He greeted the two British soldiers guarding the door and was crossing over to Curtis' office when Agrat called to him from her cage.

"Human, come here." Her tone did not contain the usual arrogance or taunting but seemed sad.

Cody stopped walking but did not approach her cage. "Why?"

Agrat slithered from the shadows over to the end of the cage closest to Cody. "Is it true that two of my sisters were killed in Cairo?"

"Why do you want to know?"

"They're my sisters." Agrat paused, and then asked sympathetically, "Please?"

"They attacked us in Cairo. We killed them both."

Cody braced himself for the inevitable tirade from the creature. Instead of a verbal onslaught, she whispered, "Can you kill me, too?"

"Excuse me?"

"Please put me out of my misery. Kill me so I can join my sisters."

Cody had no idea how to respond. "I can't do that."

"You can, but will you?" When Cody did not answer, Agrat sighed. "I don't blame you. If I were in your position, I'd want you to suffer.”

As Agrat slunk back into the shadows, Cody heard her whisper, “I’m alone now.”

He crossed the basement and entered Curtis’ office. The doctor sat behind his desk with the cigars clipped and ready to be lit and the scotch already poured. Cody motioned toward the cage. “What’s that all about?”

“You mean Agrat acting human?”

“Yeah.”

“That started right after you killed her sisters in Cairo. She raged for a couple of hours. At one point we thought she might even break free. Then she quieted down and has been morose ever since.” Curtis placed the cigar in his mouth and held a lit match to it, puffing until the tip glowed red. He exhaled a cloud of smoke into the air. “Who would have thought those things had feelings.”

“Positive feelings, at least.” Cody prepared his cigar. “We already knew they’re consumed by hatred and anger.”

“True.” An awkward silence passed. “By the way, excellent briefing this morning on what happened in Cairo.”

“Thanks.”

“I wish I had been there in Cairo.”

“No, you don’t.” Cody tried to push the memories from his mind. “But you’ll get your chance. The succubi attack on Mena House means the Germans know more about our operation than we originally thought. I doubt Himmler is going to back down after the way we humiliated him. This occult war is going to escalate big time.”

Curtis sighed. “And there are only a few of us in the trenches to fight them.”

“There are even fewer now,” Bellingham said from the door leading into the office. His shoulders sagged and worry-lines creased his face.

“What do you mean?” Cody asked.

Bellingham stepped inside. “Lee left my office about an hour ago. She’s resigned from the SOE.”

"What?" Cody blurted.

"Did she say why?" Curtis asked.

"No. The only thing I could get out of her was that it had nothing to do with us or what happened in Egypt. She says she's a liability to the team."

"How so?" Curtis asked.

"She refused to say." Bellingham walked over to Cody and handed him an envelope. "Before she left, she asked me to pass this to you."

Cody opened the envelope and removed the letter from inside.

Dearest Cody,

I'm sorry for saying goodbye in a letter. I know it's impersonal and cowardly, but I have my reasons. They have <u>nothing</u> to do with you. For reasons I can't go into right now, if I stay, I'm a threat to you and everyone else. I could not live with myself if anything happened, especially to you.

Don't bother coming by my place to convince me to change my mind. I've given up the apartment. Once I leave here, I'm leaving London. Please don't try and find me. If you do, you'll only put yourself in danger, and I don't want that.

Please know that I love you, and I always will. Once this war is over – if we both make it through – I'll track you down and explain everything. Hopefully by then, you'll still want me.

Always yours,

Lee

Cody stared at the letter without saying a word. Lee had left him with barely a goodbye or an explanation why she had run out, both on him and the team. To top it off, she had dropped the bombshell that she loved him, which made the rest of the letter that much more confusing and frustrating. He wished Lee had given him the chance to tell her that he loved her, too.

"Did she say why she left?" asked Bellingham.

"Just that her presence poses a danger to all of us, and she couldn't live with herself if anything happened to us." Cody glanced over at Bellingham. "Did she tell you anything more?"

"That's pretty much the story she gave me. I tried convincing her with the King and country speech, but she was adamant. Nothing I could say could convince her to stay." Bellingham placed a hand on Cody's shoulder. "I'm sorry."

"Thanks, but don't feel sorry for me." Cody's frustration morphed into anger. "Lee screwed the entire team by walking out."

"Try not to be angry with her," said Bellingham.

"I am angry, but not for the reasons you think. I didn't want to be here, but you guys dragged me into this occult war. And now the only one of us with any psychic ability hides her tail and runs. Without her, it's like fighting the Germans blindfolded."

"I know," Bellingham emphasized. "I have MI5 and Scotland Yard looking through their files for anyone with similar capabilities."

"We don't have time to recruit and train someone new. After what happened in Cairo, the Germans are going to hit us back hard, sooner rather than later."

"What do we do now?" Curtis asked.

Cody grinned. "I'm sure the group captain has something special up his sleeve for the Germans."

Bellingham nodded. "I've got several proposals for bringing the occult war back to Jerry that I plan to run by the prime minister later this week. After Cairo, I have a feeling he'll approve most of them."

"What about you?" Curtis asked Cody.

"I'm going to track down Lee and bring her back." Cody took a drag on his cigar, followed by a swig of scotch. "Without her psychic skills, we don't stand a chance in Hell of winning this thing."

CHAPTER FORTY-EIGHT

The Oval Office, Washington D.C.
11 July 1941

WILLIAM DONOVAN SAT in front of President Franklin Delano Roosevelt's desk inside the Oval Office. His purpose for being here today was twofold. First, Donovan had been asked to brief the President on Major Williams' time with the SOE's Project Samail and the details about the incident at Mena House. The second was to witness the signing of a bill that would set up the intelligence agency Donovan had been advocating for months. After listening to his briefing, FDR sat facing out the window looking over the Rose Garden and contemplating his next move.

After several minutes of silence, he spun his wheelchair around to face Donovan.

"I want your honest opinion, Bill. Do you think England can win this war?"

"England may be able to hold out for several more years. Now that Hitler has invaded Russia, Germany's attention will be directed to the east. At some point, the British people may get tired of the constant fighting and replace Churchill with someone who will negotiate a peace agreement with Berlin. As for winning the war, there is no way England can defeat Germany without help from us."

"I agree," said FDR, the frustration evident in his voice. "Unfortunately, there is no way I'll be able to convince Congress to declare war on Hitler. I was nearly impeached over Lend Lease and the destroyer deal."

"Time is working in our favor in that regard," said Donovan. "Sooner or later, Hitler is going to give us the provocation you need to enter this war, or he'll attack us outright."

"When we do fight Germany, do you think they'll wage an occult war against us?"

"Based on what we know about the psychology of Hitler and Himmler, they're going to strike back on a large scale to make up for their defeat in Cairo. To be honest, we're way behind the curve on this one. The English are ahead of us, but not by much. The longer we delay in acting, the more difficult it will be for us to defeat Germany when we finally do get into this war."

"I agree." FDR pulled the sheet of paper toward him. "You read this proposal?"

"I've gone over it several times, yes." And every time Donovan did, it made him cringe. He would be consigned to establish America's first overseas intelligence agency, setting up intelligence gathering and analysis as well as covert action capabilities from scratch, and all without the knowledge or approval of Congress. If that was not bad enough, he would have to fight constant turf battles between Herbert Hoover's FBI and each of the military's intelligence services, and would more than likely have little support from an administration that maintained its influence over the bureaucracy by playing one party off another. Yet this agency had to be formed if America hoped to survive the coming war. Donovan wondered what it said about himself that he was so desperate to lead it.

"You'll be in charge of this agency with the title Coordinator of Information."

"Thank you, Mr. President."

"I assume you saw the portion where you are tasked with carrying out 'supplementary activities'?"

"I assume that is in reference to what Major Williams is currently involved in."

FDR nodded. "You can imagine what would happen if the press or the Republicans in Congress got wind of the fact we're engaged in an occult war. The press coverage could easily bring down this administration. More than anything, I need complete discretion on this."

"You'll get it. You have my word."

"Put Major Williams in charge of occult warfare. He has the most experience and has proven himself more than capable of handling the task."

"That was going to be my recommendation, Mr. President."

FDR removed a pen from its holder and flipped the document to its last page.

"If the agency itself is going to be known as COI," said Donovan, "do you have any recommendations for the name of Williams' unit?"

"Since it's so small, we should probably refer to it as an office," replied FDR as he signed the order. "Let's call it the Office of Supernatural Services."

Thank you for reading *OSS: Office of Supernatural Services*. I hope you enjoyed reading this novel as much as I did writing it. And yes, there will be more books in the series.

If you liked the novel, please go to this link (www.amazon.com/dp/B0D9PZX3XR) or use the QR code below to leave a review on Amazon. The more reviews a writer receives, the more exposure his/her book gets on Amazon, which means the more readers who can experience the adventure. It means a lot to us.

Thank you.

Historical Acknowledgements

OSS: Office of Supernatural Services is a labor of love. I have been a student of Nazi and Soviet history all my adult life and have wanted to write a historical horror drama like this for years. Many of the characters who appeared in this novel existed in real life, and many of events in this book did occur, although my interpretation of why the characters' motivations and the reason events happened the way they did has been altered to fit the plot. I have attempted to make this book read as historically accurate as possible. The below is for those readers who want to know more about the historical reality.

After the initial British success of Operation BREVITY, General Wavell did order a withdrawal back to Halfaya Pass, but not because of any glamouring by a succubus.

The Extermination Order is one of the most controversial topics in the history of the Final Solution. Historians have not been able to find any single documentation that initiated the genocide of twelve million people. In his testimony at the Nuremburg Trails, SS *Gruppenführer* Otto Ohlenburg, commander of *Einsatzgruppen* D, claims the order to initiate the Final Solution was verbally issued to him by Himmler in May 1941 and again in September. SS *Hauptsturmführer* Dieter Wisliceny, who oversaw the liquidation of many Jewish ghettoes, claims to have seen the order and states it was dated April 1942. Diary entries by Goebbels and Himmler written in December 1941 following meetings with Hitler allude to discussions about the extermination of the Jews. While the existence of the *Einsatzgruppen* and the atrocities they committed during the opening months of Operation BARBAROSSA are fact, some historians assess the decision to engage in full-scale industrialized genocide occurred in September 1941 when the decision was made to transport Europe's Jewish populations to the east. This will remain one of the unsolved mysteries of World War II. For the purposes of this book, I chose May 1941 as the issuance date because of the plot's timeline.

Those who follow the history of Wewelsburg Castle will cringe at my having the *Obergruppenführersaal* and the Realm of the Dead in use in June 1941. The actual construction that razed the North Tower and rebuilt it to include the hall and vault depicted in this novel took place during the winter of 1941/1942 and was not completed until late 1942. However, for dramatic effect, I opted to have them both available in June 1941. I had the good fortune to visit Wewelsburg in 2015 and stand in the *Obergruppenführersaal*. Photos of my visit are available here.

scottmbakerauthor.blogspot.com/2013/12/pictures-from-our-honeymoon-in-germany.html

There is no text of or notes on the speech given by Himmler to the SS *obergruppenführers* at Wewelsburg on 12 June; the only indication of what transpired came from one of the attendants, von dem Bach-Zelewski, who at the International Military Tribunal in Nuremburg in 1945 claimed that the focus of Himmler's speech was the "decimation of the Slavic race by thirty million." I extrapolated from there.

ACKNOWLEDGMENTS

I spent months contemplating whether or not to write this novel considering the subject matter, eventually deciding that the story of the Holocaust needed to be told since the nightmare is rapidly being forgotten. In light of the recent rise of anti-Semitism over the past several months, I'm glad I did. The story of the suffering of those who were exterminated merely for being Jewish needs to be told.

Many thanks go out to my beta readers, Doc Fried and Dungeon Dan Uebel, who have been with me for years. They point out grammatical/spelling errors and inconsistencies and offer their opinion on whether they like the story. In this case, they provided insights that helped me to make this novel more accurate and compelling. I would be lost without them. Like all my others, this book is a much better read because of them.

Uwe Jarling created the cover for *OSS: Office of Supernatural Services*. He is a phenomenal cover artist who enjoys creating demons for my books. As with my *Shattered World* series, I gave him my description of the succubi and let him go from there. This is by far the best cover he has created for me, for which I'm grateful.

I recently started a full-time job as a teacher at a charter academy in Manchester, which severely restraints my time to write. It also means that when I get home, my pets are so happy to see me they want to dominate my time. Fred, AKA Turd Burglar, my stubborn Beagle-Bassett mix, is always with me when I write, and sometimes I spend more time keeping him out of trouble than I do at my computer. My cat Archer has discovered that my plugged-in laptop makes the perfect heating pad, so getting him to move is next to impossible. At night, while editing and managing social media, my other cat, Michonne, stands in front of my desktop computer, demanding attention. They make the writing process difficult, but it doesn't matter. I love them all.

The biggest thanks go to my readers, especially those who have been with me from the beginning. Writing is the fun part of my job. I appreciate all of you who read my books and patiently wait for the next one. I have a lot of stories floating around inside my head, and I am looking forward to sharing them with you.

ABOUT THE AUTHOR

Scott M. Baker was born and raised in Everett, Massachusetts, and spent twenty-three years in northern Virginia working for the Central Intelligence Agency. He has traveled extensively through Europe, Asia, and the Middle East, incorporating many of the locations and cultures in his stories. Scott is now retired and lives outside Salem, New Hampshire, with his dog Fred and two cats who treat him as their human servant.

Scott is currently writing *The Chronicles of Paul* saga, his latest zombie apocalypse series and his soon-to-be-released *A World Gone Dark* novel that will tell the story of a handful of survivors of a massive solar event and how they deal with a world deprived of electricity. Previous works include the *Nurse Alissa vs. the Zombies* series, his most popular zombie saga; his Tatyana paranormal series, which is also extremely popular; *Operation Majestic*, his first science fiction novel described as *Raiders of the Lost Ark* meets *Back to the Future* – with aliens; *Frozen World*, his first non-zombie post-apocalypse novel; the *Shattered World* series, his five-book young adult post-apocalypse thriller; *The Vampire Hunters* trilogy, about humans fighting the undead in Washington D.C.; as well as several zombie-themed novellas and anthologies.

Facebook:
facebook.com/groups/397749347486177

Twitter:
twitter.com/vampire_hunters

Instagram:
instagram.com/scottmbakerwriter

TikTok:
tiktok.com/@scottmbakerwriter

Blog:
scottmbakerauthor.blogspot.com

YouTube:
youtube.com/channel/UC5AyCVrEAncr2E0N5XoyUdg/feat
ured

Wyrd Realities Homepage:
www.wyrdrealities.net

You can also sign up for Scott's newsletter, which will be released on the 1st and 15th of every month. He promises not to share your email with anyone or spam the recipients. The newsletter contains advance notices of upcoming releases/events and short stories from the Alissa universe that will not be available to the public. You can sign up by clicking the link below.

Newsletter:
mailchi.mp/0b1401f1ddb2/scott-m-baker-writer